IN VINO VERITAS

Peter Turnbull

This Severn House edition published 2015
in Great Britain and 2016 in the USA by
SEVERN HOUSE PUBLISHERS LTD
19 Cedar Road, Sutton, Surrey, England, SM2 5DA.

Trade paperback edition first published
in Great Britain and the USA 2016 by
SEVERN HOUSE PUBLISHERS LTD.

Copyright © 2015 by Peter Turnbull.

All rights reserved. The right of Peter Turnbull to be identified as the author of this work has been asserted in accordance with Sections 77 and 78 of the Copyright, Designs and Patents Act 1988.

British Library Cataloguing in Publication Data

Turnbull, Peter, 1950- author.
  In vino veritas. – (The Harry Vicary series)
  1. Vicary, Harry (Fictitious character)–Fiction.
  2. Police–England–London–Fiction. 3. Murder–
  Investigation–Fiction. 4. Murder for hire–Fiction.
  5. Detective and mystery stories.
  I. Title II. Series
  823.9'2-dc23

ISBN-13: 978-0-7278-8572-2 (cased)
ISBN-13: 978-1-84751-680-0 (trade paper)
ISBN-13: 978-1-78010-734-9 (e-book)

This is a work of fiction. Names, characters, places and incidents
are either the product of the author's imagination or are used fictitiously.
Except where actual historical events and characters are being described
for the storyline of this novel, all situations in this publication are
fictitious and any resemblance to actual persons, living or dead,
business establishments, events or locales is purely coincidental.

All Severn House titles are printed on acid-free paper.

Severn House Publishers support the Forest Stewardship Council™ [FSC™],
the leading international forest certification organisation.
All our titles that are printed on FSC certified paper carry the FSC logo.

MIX
Paper from
responsible sources
FSC® C013056

Typeset by Palimpsest Book Production Ltd.,
Falkirk, Stirlingshire, Scotland.
Printed and bound in Great Britain by
TJ International, Padstow, Cornwall.

ONE

The young man leaned sullenly against the window frame and just within the doorway of the vacant shop unit. He looked out across the narrow street in a casual, uninterested manner, noting the passing motor vehicles and the foot passengers, observing the world as it went by in front of him but equally not particularly concerned by it. That was the impression he hoped to give: a lazy, unemployed person who had nothing better to do with his time than watch the occupants of the street as they continued about their business before him, either on foot or in a car or commercial vehicle. In fact, the young man was particularly interested in a specific building which stood diagonally across the street from his vantage point. The ground floor of the building in question was given over for use as a grocer's shop which was run by two evidently energetic and enthusiastic Asian youths, so the young man noted. The two storeys above the grocer's shop were reportedly used as residential accommodation and had grey net curtains hanging over each window; curtains which never seemed, to the young man, to move – not in the slightest. The young man shrank further into the doorway in which he stood; a passer-by would probably glance at him once and then forget him. The passing pedestrian would notice the man's worn and torn sports shoes; he would notice the man's pale and threadbare denim jeans, torn at both knees; he would notice the man's baggy and shapeless green T-shirt; he would notice the man's lean face with its three days of beard growth upon it, and he would notice the man's uncombed hair. The passer-by would then dismiss him as a chronically unemployed petty criminal and would walk on. The young man in the shop doorway glanced further up Cornwall Crescent towards Ladbroke Grove, again noting the new-build flats behind the trees which lined the road, then returned his attention to the residential accommodation above the grocer's shop as the world walked or drove past him, each person glancing at him once, if at all, and labelling him as yet another down-and-out, yet another piece of human detritus which rubs shoulders with the rich and famous in the Royal Borough of Kensington and Chelsea, London, W11.

It was, as the man would later recall, sometimes with anger, and sometimes with good-humoured resignation, at about five o'clock that he was approached. It was about that time, just as the heat of the day was beginning to subside, that a foot passenger did not scornfully glance at him as he walked along the pavement, but rather stopped and talked to the man. The second man was tall, very tall, and very broad-chested. He wore an expensive-looking lightweight, cream-coloured, Italian-cut suit. The man wore rings – manly rings – on each finger of both hands; he wore a Rolex watch and his feet were encased in a pair of crocodile-skin shoes. He smiled at the young man, and in doing so revealed diamond studs in his teeth. He smelled strongly of aftershave, and said, 'It's been nice having you with us,' speaking in the calm, self-assured, received pronunciation of a TV newscaster. He was, thought the young man, in his mid-thirties, 'but,' continued the Afro-Caribbean man, 'nothing is going to happen while you are here, my man, nothing. Nothing, nothing at all.' The man paused. 'You see, the trouble is . . . *your* trouble, that is, not ours . . . that you are just not very good at your job. It's as simple as that, my man; it's as simple as that. We pinned you as soon as you arrived. We clocked you on day one, my man, on day one. You try to look like you're not interested. Yes, you look up and down the street but only when you remember to do so; you can't stop giving pretty well all your attention to our little premises above the grocer's shop, but you are looking, my man, you are looking. You see, drifters, down-and-outs, they just stare into space, and they drift . . . they walk down the street, lost in their own little world, or they walk from rubbish bin to rubbish bin. It's like for them there is always one more corner to turn, one more bin to ferret through . . . but you, my man, you . . . you just stand here in this shop doorway, never moving from this location. My man, let me tell you, you need lessons, my man, you need lessons. Well, as I have said, we've enjoyed your company, we've had a good laugh . . . it helped us get through our days . . . it's been cool, really cool, but it's only fair to tell you that nothing is going to go down, not while you are here, and now that we know that you know about the flats above the grocer's shop, we won't be using them – not any more. We'll be giving up the rental and moving on.' The Afro-Caribbean man paused. 'You can search them if you like, but you won't find anything, you can be sure of that. It's been well and truly sanitized. That's what you saw yesterday. Yesterday you saw three women carrying cleaning materials. They were not smuggling anything in or out. They were a team of contract cleaners and they did a very good job; all that bleach, it really made our eyes water. We paid them well, more than the going rate, and they earned their crust. They earned it all right.'

The young man, who was by no means short of stature, continued to stare up at the Afro-Caribbean man, whose white teeth glinted with diamond studs, but he spoke not a word in reply.

'So.' The Afro-Caribbean man glanced casually at his watch. 'Look, my man, it's a nice time to knock off, a civilized time – it's the end of the working day for most honest folk.' He continued to speak in a calm, self-assured manner. 'So why don't you do the sensible thing and go for a pint, or two, or three, and then tomorrow you can tell your boss that he's been wasting your time. We'll be transferring our operation to some other location, and we'll be keeping a good lookout for you and your kind.' And with that, the Afro-Caribbean man walked away, watched by the young man, until he turned the corner, entered Ladbroke Grove and was lost from sight.

'"Go for a pint."' The young man shrugged his shoulders and repeated the advice, aloud, as if talking to himself. 'Go for a pint, go for a pint . . . you know, I might just do that.' He glanced up at the blue and near-cloudless sky which hung over London town and said, 'Yes, yes, I will. I think I will. I'll do just that.' He left the doorway and walked casually towards Ladbroke Grove. When he reached the corner he turned and walked in the opposite direction he had very recently observed the hugely built Afro-Caribbean man walk in.

The young man viewed the Grove as he walked northwards towards the Westway Flyover. He noticed the pub occupying a corner site on the opposite side of the road. Just like the grocer's shop in Cornwall Crescent, the pub was on the ground floor with two storeys of residential accommodation above. It seemed to the man to be built of stone with the tall window frames picked out in white paint which strongly reflected the late-afternoon sun. The pub was richly maintained, so the man thought, with a highly varnished wooden door and the vaulted windows thoroughly cleaned. Seats and benches and small tables stood outside the pub but did not protrude on to the pavement, as did a row of tall plants in large terracotta pots. An awning was pulled out and downwards in front of the southern window. The pub, the man noticed, was called The Tiger, its name proudly emblazoned in large gold lettering on a black background above the windows of the building. Curiously, the man pondered, the pub's name was not followed by an image of the animal in question but of a sailing ship. Inside he found it to be pleasantly cool and shady but not at all gloomy. The name of the pub was, he saw, instantly explained by many images of ships of earlier eras, and he stood briefly and read a short explanation mounted on the wall by the door which advised that Britain had had fifteen warships called The Tiger, the first being launched in 1546 and the last (to date) being launched in 1945. The man saw that there were, at that time, just a few patrons in The Tiger: some standing at the bar, others sitting alone, some standing in twos and threes and others sitting in twos or threes, but the pub was closer to empty than crowded, as if enjoying a lull before the evening crush. The barman, the young man noted, was a heavily built man who seemed to be in his mid-fifties. He was bristlingly clean with neatly cut hair, and wore a neatly ironed light blue shirt which encased a barrel-like chest. The barman eyed the young man coldly, bordering on distaste, as the latter approached the heavily and highly polished wooden bar. The young man stood at the bar for a full thirty seconds before the barman, who was clearly not engaged in any task, growled, 'Yes. Can I help you?'

The young man asked for a pint of IPA and looked about him as his beer was being grudgingly poured. The Tiger, he saw, was very well appointed, with dark-stained furniture, a maroon-coloured deep pile carpet, heavy velvet maroon curtains and a high ceiling crossed with heavy black-painted wooden beams, with ornate plasterwork between the beams. The young man realized that he had stumbled into a 'posh' pub and his lowlife, unkempt appearance and shabby clothing made him feel wholly out of place. He instantly understood the coldness of the barman. But the young man had not drunk enough, nor was he rough enough to be refused service. It was a 'slow' time of day and that, plus the fact that the licensed retail trade was weathering an economic recession, meant that the young man was served. Albeit reluctantly.

His drink was placed in front of him with what the young man thought to be an unfairly large head, but he thought the better of complaining and carried his beer to the far end of the bar, where he stood with his right shoulder resting against the expensive embossed wallpaper which had been hung on the walls. He began to drink, gulping his beer rather than sipping it as his father had once advised and taught him: 'Take thy beer to the back of thy tongue in a gob full, push thy tongue "forrard", then swallow.' It had proved to be good advice, and he waited for a few seconds until the aftertaste of the hops rose with exceeding and satisfying pleasantness in his mouth. He drank the pint and, when he managed to catch the barman's eye, ordered a second one, which was served with the same obvious reluctance as had been his first. The young man would later recall that he had drunk half of the second pint when he was approached by another customer who walked up and stood beside him.

'Not seen you in here before.' The stranger put his pint down heavily on the polished surface of the bar. He spoke with a strong London accent.

'That's probably because I haven't been in here before,' the young man replied, avoiding eye contact with the stranger who had approached him, although he noticed tattoos of the type which are self-inflicted in young offender institutions, and he also noticed the classic LOVE tattooed on the fingers of one hand and HATE on the fingers of the other. The man had clearly been in 'the machine', though probably not for many years by his apparent age which, like the barman, appeared to the young man to be mid-fifties. The stranger was, the young man noticed out of the corner of his eye, overweight, with a beer drinker's paunch. He wore brown corduroy trousers, a chequered sports jacket over a grey shirt and very heavy brogues on his feet. He must, thought the young man, be very uncomfortable or just not feel the heat. Body odour rose from the man and did so of a strength which suggested that he was due, if not overdue, for a bath and a change of underwear, and which served to make the young man feel cleaner than hitherto.

'North country?' The stranger, who was, like the Afro-Caribbean man, also exceptionally tall, looked down at the young man. 'I'm good at accents. North of England?'

'Yes.' The young man took another mouthful of his beer. 'Yorkshire.'

'Thought so,' the man grunted. 'Like I said, I'm good at accents. I'm a regular. This is my local. I drink here all the time. "Big Andy", they call me. Andrew "Big Andy" Cragg.'

The man looked at Andrew 'Big Andy' Cragg and could easily see why he had acquired his nickname. He thought Cragg to be at least six and a half feet tall, probably taller. He was also broad-chested, and despite his paunch would, he thought, be a very useful man to have on your side in a skirmish. Very useful indeed.

'I drink here all the time.' 'Big Andy' Cragg continued looking straight ahead as he spoke, holding his pint glass in one meaty paw whilst resting his other equally meaty paw on the surface of the bar. Cragg fell silent, and for a minute the only sound the young man heard was the low hum of conversation and the muted sound from the huge plasma TV screen mounted on the wall of the far side of the pub. The young man began to grow impatient and wish that 'Big Andy' Cragg, the regular, would pick up his beer, walk away and annoy another customer, but Cragg stayed, as if rooted to the floor next to the young man. 'This is a smart old battle cruiser in the evening.' Cragg continued to stare straight ahead as he spoke. 'Like all the boozers around here, it gets posh in the evening, but the likes of you and me, we can get a drink in the daytime when it's quiet, like now. In the evenings though, well, then it's all stockbrokers and those city bankers and the like with their posh accents. They flash their money about like it's going out of fashion . . . well, they don't, they all pay for their printers' ink with plastic cards, but you know what I mean . . . and when they arrive the likes of you and me'll get told we've had enough or we'll be ignored while the staff serve the posh ones. Right now, it's all right – there's time for another drink or two yet – but by half past six there won't be a welcome for the likes of you and me and all the other good boys who drink in here during the day. It's just how it goes.'

'Is that right?' the young man replied. He noticed that 'Big Andy' Cragg's breath smelled strongly of alcohol and he was slurring his words. He also noticed that Cragg was clearly unsteady on his feet. He watched as Cragg swayed and then grabbed the brass rail which ran round the outside edge of the bar and steadied himself. The young man then realized that Andrew Cragg had been drinking all that afternoon and was on the verge of being refused service.

'It's right,' Cragg replied. Then he added, 'Are you in work? Have you got a job?'

'No.' The young man took another mouthful of beer. 'I'm a doley . . . I sponge off the State.'

'Same here.' The drunken 'Big Andy' Cragg swayed again. 'Same here. I shouldn't be drinking this. I can't afford it, it's too pricey, but I need to come in here to get out of my flat and so I drink my food money. You'll be doing the same if you're on the dole,' Cragg swayed yet again, 'but I'm alive and I've known people my age who aren't alive anymore.' Cragg grabbed the brass rail again to stop himself falling backwards.

'I dare say we can all say that,' the young man replied as his thoughts turned to a classmate in primary school, a friend with whom he used to go walking on long summer days. They'd take their dogs and walk in shaded woods and baked, dry fields. A friend who was killed in a car crash a few weeks before his nineteenth birthday. 'I dare say we can all say that,' the young man repeated.

'Yes,' Cragg replied, 'and the older you get, the more you can say it.' Then he paused. Slurring his words, he added, 'You know, I killed someone once.'

The younger man groaned inwardly, assuming that he had met another barstool ex-serviceman, who, if all were telling the truth, would mean that the British Armed Forces would be ten times larger than they actually were. 'Oh, yes?' he replied, expecting the tall, drunken Andrew Cragg to then claim service in the Parachute Regiment or the Royal Marines, his being far too tall to have served in the Special Forces, where the average height of the soldiers is five feet six inches.

'Yes,' Cragg affirmed, still staring fixedly ahead of him.

'Ex-army?' The young man asked wearily, expecting a rapid, proud-sounding reply in the affirmative.

'No,' 'Big Andy' Cragg replied softly after a period of silence. 'No . . . I was never a soldier. It might . . . it would have been easier if I had been but I never served Queen and Country. I never reckoned Queen and Country did anything for me so I never felt I owed them anything in return. It was here . . . I did it here.' Cragg patted the bar with his large palm.

'Here!' The young man gasped. 'Here, in this pub?'

'No . . . no, I don't mean *here*, here.' Andrew Cragg took a deep breath. 'Not here in this boozer, I meant here in the Smoke . . . here in London.'

'Here in Notting Hill?' the young man asked with interest. 'Here in this part of the Smoke?'

'No . . . no . . .' Cragg once again gripped the brass rail attached to the bar. 'It was south of the river. New Cross, to be exact.'

'New Cross?' the young man repeated. He was becoming genuinely interested in 'Big Andy' Cragg.

'Yes, it was down New Cross way. I was part of a team, a heavy team. We shot this young woman. She was too young. She had most of it in front of her – still had her life to lead.' Once again, Cragg steadied himself.

'Shot her?' the young man repeated.

'Yes . . . a proper shooter. He made sure all right.' Cragg
slurred his words again. 'He made well sure. The geezer what
done it made well sure. Two taps to the head. One to the chest.
Three taps all told. She was going nowhere, not after that. She
wasn't going to get up . . . ever again.'

The young man remained silent.

'Never done nothing like that before . . . never done nothing
like that since.' Cragg was by then talking more to himself
than to the young, unshaven man. 'Yes . . . all right. I've done
a few stupid things, I've done things I am not proud of but
I've never done murder. Not until that night – I hadn't done
murder. All right, all right, so I didn't pull the trigger, I didn't
shoot the old shooter, but I was there and that's all it takes.
People tell me that makes me equally guilty. "Joint venture",
I think it's called. Or something like that.'

The young man continued to remain silent. He was by then
content to let Cragg talk freely. Hugely content. He took a
mouthful of his beer and continued to listen closely.

'Forgot it.' Andrew Cragg gripped the bar in front of him.
'I forgot it. For a lot of years I forgot it had happened. I
forgot all about it. It was like someone had wiped my memory
clean. Then it all started to come back, about eighteen months
ago . . . not all at once but a bit at a time. It all came back
over the space of about three or four days . . . And all out of
order – all the bits, I mean – and then it took me some days
after that before I was sure I wasn't remembering a dream.
And I tell you, it all came back because of this stuff.' 'Big
Andy' Cragg tapped the side of his beer glass, and as he did
so the young man noticed that Andrew Cragg's fingernails
were bitten to the quick. 'You know,' Cragg continued, 'they
say that you drink to forget but you don't – you don't forget
anything when you're drunk, it's the other way round. If
you drink you remember things. This stuff . . . your old
printers' ink . . . it makes you remember. The drink makes
you remember things.'

'Yes, I have heard that.' The young man held his glass in
both hands. 'I've been told that is the way of it.'

'We tapped her cold in a lock-up. Somewhere down the
East End, it was. I don't know the East End, I'm from south

of the river, but she was tapped over the East End. That look
in her eyes . . . the fear . . . the pleading . . . the knowing that
she was going to die. She looked at me. I reckon she did
that because the geezer with the shooter, well, he wore a
mask, didn't he . . . like a pig's face on his head, so she
looked at me because I wasn't wearing no mask. She looked
at me like she was asking me to save her, but I couldn't do
nothing . . . That look in her eyes . . .'
   'Yes, I can imagine.' The young man lifted his beer glass
to his lips. 'Can't say I have seen that look you speak of but
I can imagine it all right.'
   'Yes, well, she had that look.' Cragg swayed on his feet.
'You take it from me she had that old look in her eyes and
when I can't sleep at night, I think about her those nights. I'll
never forget that look in her eyes.'
   'But you didn't shoot her.' The young man put his glass
down on the surface of the bar.
   'No . . . I didn't . . . but I was there. I was part of it, all
right. It makes me equally guilty.' Andrew 'Big Andy' Cragg
steadied himself once more. 'Like I said, it's called "joint
venture" or something, but whatever it's called, I'm in dead
lumber. I was just a gofer but that's close enough. It was me
that carried her old corpse to the van. She was so small, no
weight at all. I tell you, it was like carrying a child's doll. So
anyway, I bundled her into the back of the van and we drove
south of the river, down my neck of the woods. I sat in the
back with her body on the floor of the van. There were two
geezers up front . . . my governor and the geezer who had
done the business. We drove to New Cross at about ten at
night because there was still plenty of traffic about for us to
hide in and because the cozzers change shift at ten p.m., so
there's less likely to be filth about on the streets. That's what
my governor said. He knew what he was doing did my old
governor. If there's business to be done, do it when the filth
are changing shifts . . . about six a.m., two p.m. and ten p.m.
So we did that. We waited until about nine thirty p.m. then
drove from the East End to New Cross. I knew it was New
Cross because I grew up in Deptford.'
   'The next-door manor,' the young man commented.

'That's right,' Cragg replied, 'bang next door to each uvver,' he said, his distinct London accent coming to the fore. He paused, 'Me, I went to Grove Street School, right there by the Foreign Cattle Market. It's not there anymore, none of it, the whole area has been redeveloped . . . That's the area norf of the railway line,' he clarified. 'That's the old railway line that goes out to Blackheath and Charlton. So we drove to Malpas Road.'

'Malpas Road,' the young man repeated. 'Malpas Road . . .'

'Do you know it?' Cragg briefly turned to the young man.

'I think I might . . . I think I might well know it.' The young man pursed his lips. 'I live in Lewisham. That's not a million miles away, if I'm thinking of the right street. Malpas Road. It sounds familiar.'

'Yeah . . .' Andrew Cragg looked straight ahead, 'Lewisham isn't far away – a little to the south – but Deptford, New Cross, Lewisham . . . if you know one you know all three manors. So why come up to Notting Hill if you live in Lewisham?'

'I was visiting someone I know. I came in here for a pint before heading back to Lewisham. I reckoned I'd let the rush hour die down a bit. Saw this battle cruiser. It looked kosher so I popped in for a quick printers'.'

'Yes . . . this is a good old boozer and they know how to keep their beer,' Cragg commented. 'Some boozers ruin their beer because they don't know how to keep if proper. Yes, if you come in when it's quiet it's all right for the likes of you and me and few other good boys here but when them from the City arrive, with their loud la-di-dah voices, flashing their cash around or buying posh drinks with plastic cards . . . well, then it's time for the likes of us to move on.'

'Time to go then,' the young man replied.

'You want me to go?' Cragg turned to the young man.

'No . . . no . . .' the young man replied quickly. 'I never said that. I didn't mean it that way.'

'It's all right if you do.' Andrew Cragg returned to staring straight ahead. He was clean-shaven with short grey hair, balding at the temples. 'Most folk, they just want me to leave them with their beer and not bother them. I hardly get to talk to anyone these old days.'

'You're not bothering me, governor.' The young man stroked his unshaven chin. 'Honest . . . don't worry . . . you're OK.'

Andrew 'Big Andy' Cragg nodded and grunted his appreciation. 'So we took her to Malpas Road in New Cross . . . yes, we did, there's an allotment site there . . . we took her at night, like I said. The governor had it all arranged, all worked out in advance. Even got the weather right.'

'The weather?' The young man studied Andy Cragg.

'Raining, wasn't it? Cats and dogs, coming down vertical, bouncing off the street surface; it was either good luck or he was listening to the weather forecast but whatever, rain like that was well handy, kept folks indoors, stopped them wandering round the streets with their dogs. Anyway, like I said, it was all planned. If the weather wasn't planned everything else definitely was.'

'Interesting.' The younger man ran his fingertips over his bewhiskered chin.

'So we took her at night. It was all arranged, like I said. The governor had a key for the padlock on the gate and the grave was already dug. It was me that carried her from the van to the grave . . . I just dropped her in the hole . . . no dignity, nothing. There were another couple of geezers there – they were waiting for us and did the filling in. I've never done nothing like that before and haven't since. I don't mind telling you, don't mind admitting that I got scared after that. That old team was too heavy for me, too much the business. I'm not out for that sort of game.' Andrew Cragg slumped forward and then straightened himself up. 'So I gave up my old drum and I moved to Notting Hill where I'm not known – not by them anyway. I've been here ten years now and I won't be going south of the river again. It's too risky.' Andrew Cragg drew his right forefinger across his throat. 'Know what I mean, governor? Too, too risky. I'm a dead man if I go back to Deptford. I know where a body is buried. It's only one body but it's enough. I'm only a gofer, an errand boy . . . go for this, go for that. What value is a gofer? None. So I stay here in Notting Hill around the Grove and I pass the days as a daytime drinker. It's all I can do.' 'Big Andy' Cragg raised his glass, then drained it and put it down heavily on the bar.

Without another word he turned and walked unsteadily towards the door and the beckoning sunlight.

The young man picked up the beer glass from which Andrew Cragg had been drinking by gripping it carefully using his thumb and forefinger and lifting it by the rim. With his other hand he produced a plastic bag from the back pocket of his jeans and did so with a flourish. He then placed the empty beer glass inside the plastic bag.

'You're not stealing that glass!' The barman marched angrily towards the young man. 'We lose too much glassware as it is thanks to people like you decorating your bedsits with glassware stolen from pubs. Let me have that beer glass or I'll call the police.'

'Sorry, squire.' The young man smiled. 'I can return it but I can't let you have it. Not right now, anyway. I can save you a phone call, though, I can do that. I *am* the Old Bill. I'm a cozzer, a police officer.'

'You don't look like one.' The barman had calmed but he clearly remained suspicious. The young man sensed his hostility.

'Just as well, eh?' The young man smiled as he produced his warrant card with his free hand and held it up for the barman's inspection. 'I mean, otherwise that old geezer wouldn't have sidled up to me and confessed to having committed a very serious offence, would he?'

'Detective Constable Ainsclough,' the barman read the card, 'Murder and Serious Crime Squad, New Scotland Yard. Well, I dare say that's good enough. So he's confessed to a crime serious enough to be of interest to you . . . the murder squad?'

'Yes.' Ainsclough replaced his warrant card in his pocket. 'He witnessed it, was definitely an accessory after the fact and may be guilty of joint venture but only if he knew the murder was going to take place, which, it seems, he did not. But anyway, I'm afraid I need this beer glass to obtain his fingerprints and probably his DNA as well. The DNA in his saliva might be too badly deteriorated by the alcohol but his dabs will be as clear as day. He'll be known to us . . . all those self-inflicted tattoos . . . Even if he's only been in youth custody, that's all we need.'

'Yes, I have noticed those tattoos . . . "LOVE" . . . "HATE".
I mean, you can't get more original than that.' The barman,
by then having fully relaxed, grinned at his own joke.
'What do you know about him?' Tom Ainsclough asked.
'Not a lot if I'm to be honest with you, guv.' The barman
rested his hands on the edge of his side of the bar. 'He's a
daytime regular, so you'll know where to find him if you
don't have his up-to-date address. We let his sort in during
the day but tend to refuse them service in the evenings
because they drive the big-spending customers away. Never
like doing it but this is a business and we have to make a
living. The licensed retail trade is going through a bad time
right now. The smoking ban has hit the trade hard, mainly
in the working-class areas, but our takings have taken
a significant dive and our management has had to lay off a
few staff. 'Him.' The barman pointed to the door out of
which 'Big Andy' Cragg had exited. 'He spends quite freely
– six, seven, eight pints between midday and about this time
of day, Monday to Friday. Seems to avoid the weekends
completely. But anyway, he buys up to forty pints a week
and that's a handy bit of cash we wouldn't otherwise be
putting into the till.'

'Yes, both he and I assumed that to be the case.' Ainsclough
grinned. 'Mind you, I'd do the same if I was in your shoes.
So, tell me about him.'

'"Big Andy"? Andrew Cragg by name. He's been a regular
in here since before I began as bar staff and that was eight
years ago . . . eight years next month, to be precise. Heavens,
the years have flown by, haven't they just? Well, he lives
locally because all the regulars do; all the regulars live close
to their boozer and I see him in the Grove from time to time.
I'm the deputy manager now, but on my first day here he
came in and one of the bar staff said, 'The usual, Andy?' and
poured him a pint of IPA.'

'So a regular for more than eight years, called Andy or
"Big Andy" Cragg?' Tom Ainsclough held up the plastic bag
containing the beer glass from which Cragg had been drinking.
'But we'll find out soon enough whether he is Cragg or aka
by another surname.'

'So, a serious crime,' the deputy manager of the Tiger folded his arms and stood upright. 'I have always figured him for a burnt-out lowlife crook with the sort of stupid convictions acquired by hot-headed youths: car theft, assault . . . but nothing more serious.'

'Well, that might still be the case.' Ainsclough rested his right palm on the bar. 'He might just be a harmless old fantasist but we have to assume he's telling the truth until we know otherwise. Anyway, we'll try to get this beer glass back to you as soon as possible.'

'Don't worry about it.' The deputy manager held up his hand. 'It's on the house. I dare say we can stand the loss. I just didn't like you stealing it on a point of principle . . . and you seemed to be doing it so brazenly.'

'Yes, I can understand what I might have looked like but I would have identified myself and told you why I wanted it.' Ainsclough smiled. 'I wouldn't have just picked it up and walked out with it.'

'Yes, I realize that now,' the deputy manager returned the smile, 'but keep it, it's just a beer glass. I mean, it's hardly worth the bother of returning it.'

'Thank you.' Tom Ainsclough twisted the plastic bag round his wrist. 'Your public spiritedness is appreciated. Look, I'd rather you didn't tell "Big Andy" Cragg or whatever his name is that I am the Old Bill. We'll do that soon enough when we bring him in for a chat.'

'Mum's the word, squire.' The deputy manager held his finger up to his lips. 'Schtum. Total schtum.'

It was Monday, 18.17 hours.

Wednesday, 09.15 hours –12.55 hours

'Developments?' Detective Chief Inspector Meadows glanced round the table at which his assembled team sat. 'Did anything come in since the last weekly meeting?'

'One very significant development, sir.' Brendan Escritt leaned forward holding a handwritten report in both hands. 'The bank notes from the Southampton robbery have begun to surface and they appear to be doing so in a steady stream.'

'How interesting.' Meadows, a tall man with a thin face, sat back in his chair. 'What is happening?'

'The usual pattern, sir,' Escritt explained. 'The high-street banks in central locations are discovering the notes amid cash that has been paid into various accounts, as is the normal method. The accounts are then credited with the money paid in but the actual notes go into a central pool which is held in the vault.'

'Yes.' Meadows clasped his hands together.

'Only then are the serial numbers checked and the notes identified as having been stolen, and then this unit is notified but there is no way of knowing to which accounts the specific notes were paid into, or who paid them in.'

'As is usual, you say,' Meadows replied. 'And, of course, the sequence has been broken up.'

'Of course,' Escritt grimaced. 'It would be foolish to hope it hadn't.'

'Indeed.' Meadows nodded. 'So how much has been recovered?'

'Approaching one hundred thousand pounds, sir,' Escritt informed him.

'From sixty million . . . So the laundering operation is just beginning and that is quite the normal lapse of time since the "robbery".' Meadows paused. 'So, come on, team. Who do we know who can handle sixty million pounds of traceable money and scrub it clean?'

'There's only two that we know of who can handle a sixty-million-pound wash,' Detective Constable Aird offered. 'The Ponsi brothers – good economic crime name, theirs . . . Alberto and Giovanni Ponsi . . . and a second possibility is Leonard McLaverty, although both will have to subcontract if they're going to launder sixty million pounds within reasonable time.'

'Indeed.' Meadows nodded in agreement. 'So who's your money on?' he appealed to the assembled officers.

'McLaverty, sir.' DC Gwen Cousins leaned forward. She was a serious-minded woman in her early thirties. Few officers in the Economic Crime Unit had ever seen her smile. 'If only because we don't know where he is. The Ponsi brothers are both known to be at their respective homes, so we know where they are and they know that we know where they are. They can't go to the corner shop without this unit knowing about it . . . but McLaverty, as we know, has vanished. He could be anywhere. Heavens, we don't even know what he looks like these days. We just have an old photograph of him when he was heavily bearded with long hair. If he walked into this room now, clean-shaven with a crew-cut, we wouldn't recognize him. So my money is on McLaverty.'

'Yes . . . I'm inclined to agree with you, Gwen.' Meadows turned and glanced out of his office window at the buildings on the Surrey Bank of the River Thames. 'All we can do is wait until he surfaces . . . but he's busy, he's active . . . he'll surface. So apart from him and his crew, what else is happening?'

'A fraud, sir,' Escritt advised, 'referred to this unit from the Hounslow police. The same old story really – an elderly lady is reported to have been persuaded by a very charming young man into paying fifty thousand pounds into his privately run hedge fund . . . and then he vanished.' Escritt shrugged.

DC Aird forced a smile. 'I'll flag up our interest in him to all other units.'

DC Cousins glanced despairingly at the ceiling. 'Don't people ever learn?'

'Indeed,' Meadows groaned, 'as you say, the same old story. So, let's have the details . . . please.'

Tom Ainsclough tapped on the doorframe of Harry Vicary's office and walked in. 'Got the results from the fingerprints on the beer glass, boss.' He held up a sheet of paper with an air of triumph. 'He is Andrew "Big Andy" Cragg, no alias. A lot of relatively minor convictions, car theft, of and from . . . He collected three years for grievous bodily harm which he spent in Wormwood Scrubs – that was fifteen years ago. Present age is given as fifty-six. No convictions in the last ten years.'

'A burnt-out recidivist.' Harry Vicary leaned back in his chair. 'So how do you feel about your three days in Notting Hill? Take a seat.' Vicary indicated a vacant chair in front of his desk.

'Annoyed . . . and also a bit amused.' Ainsclough slid into the chair. 'Annoyed at the waste of time . . . amused at being pinned as a copper as soon as I arrived.'

'I like people who have the ability to laugh at themselves.' Vicary smiled warmly. 'It shows emotional maturity and we have learned something useful . . . down-and-outs don't stand still . . . we'll remember that.'

'Yes, sir, but I do want to nail that gang. You should have seen that Afro-Caribbean geezer, diamonds in his teeth, crocodile-skin shoes, Rolex . . . and all derived from importing and selling cocaine.'

'We know them, Tom, the Holmes Gang, and we'll nail them soon enough.'

'Shall I go and pick up Cragg? I've a good idea where he'll be, at least between midday and six p.m.'

'No . . . not yet.' Vicary held up his hand. 'Let's wait until we know whether there is something in the allotments or not. Victor's on that at the moment.'

Detective Sergeant Victor Swannell, a uniformed sergeant, six constables and the volunteer manager of the Malpas Road allotments in New Cross, London, SE4, formed a loose line as they watched a brown-and-white Springer Spaniel eagerly criss-cross the plots. Swannell took his eye off the dog briefly and surveyed the surrounding area. He noted two-storey terraced houses in the main, of late Victorian to mid-twentieth-century style. An adjacent area of parkland provided additional greenery, above which the sky was an expanse of blue with high, wispy clouds. Swannell glanced about him more closely and noted again how everyone was appropriately dressed for the weather, with the sergeant and constables in white short-sleeved shirts and serge trousers, he in his lightweight summer suit and the allotment manager in a white T-shirt and khaki shorts. Eventually the Springer Spaniel stopped its enthusiastic criss-crossing of the allotments and lay down on a plot of land with its tail wagging and tongue hanging out of the left-hand side of its mouth, a very alert look in his eyes.

'Oh . . .' The allotment supervisor turned to his right and looked up at Swannell, who towered head and shoulders above him. 'I saw a TV drama once where a sniffer dog did just that and it meant he had found something. Does that mean the same thing – he's found something?'

'It does,' Swannell replied quietly as the dog handler strode confidently towards the Spaniel, slipped a leash over its head and around its neck, patted the dog then handed him a small rubber ball to chew on as a reward for scenting something of interest. 'He's scented decaying flesh,' Swannell explained. 'Whether human or not remains to be seen.' Swannell turned to the uniformed sergeant. 'Sergeant!'

'Sir!' The sergeant's reply was prompt, instant.

'We'll need you to dig there,' Swannell said. 'You know the procedure.'

'Yes, sir.' The sergeant, a young man for his rank, Swannell thought, clearly a 'young thruster' with an eye for going a long way with the Metropolitan Police, turned to the line of constables. 'Right, boys . . . the ground is baked hard so we'll dig in twos and do so in half-hour shifts. Constables Pearson and Stubbs, you take the first shift, then Constables Watson and Bailey, then Constables Harrison and Blake. So, three two-man teams, half-hour shifts. Carry on, please.'

'Who rents that particular allotment?' Swannell turned to the allotment supervisor as the dog handler led the tail-wagging Spaniel away and the first two constables, spades in hand, advanced on the area to be excavated.

'Geezer called Bennett.' The allotment supervisor was a short, overweight man, in Swannell's view. He was bespectacled with a round, ruddy-complexioned face. 'But he's only just taken the plot over. That particular plot has been unworked for years. It's well fallow now. It will be a good producer that will, a nice little producer.'

'Do you know who the last rentee was?' Swannell brushed a persistent fly from his face.

'Not off-hand, I don't,' the allotment supervisor wiped a bead of sweat from his brow, 'but I have all the records in the office.' He pointed to a wooden hut which stood near the entrance of the allotments. 'Shall we go and consult them?'

'Lead on,' Swannell replied with a generous smile. 'Just lead the way.'

Victor Swannell found the interior of the hut to be pleasantly cool with a cosy feel, though perhaps a little cluttered for his taste. He noted plant pots and gardening tools, many aged and some rusting. He noticed a mechanical rotavator occupying an over-large floor area of the shed in relation to its size, with dried soil caked to the blades. 'Have you been the governor here for a while, Mr . . . I'm sorry; I have forgotten your name, sir.'

'Vere, Tony Vere,' the man replied as he reached for an A4 bound notebook. 'I am the "reeve" of the allotments, to give me my proper title. It's actually a medieval designation which we have rescued from obscurity and which originally meant a sort of manager or overseer of a specific area of farms, a person who kept an overview of the area of land and one who settled localized disputes. We chose the name for these allotments in preference to "manager" or "coordinator" because we liked the antiquity of the word and its strong agricultural link.'

'That's interesting,' Swannell replied. 'In fact, I have a relative of that name . . . a cousin . . . I can tell him the origin of his name next time I see him.'

'Well, I am pleased to have been of some assistance already.' Tony Vere opened the ledger. 'Computers still have to arrive in Britain's allotments, but I dare say it's only a matter of time before the wretched things reach us. We already have to contend with mobile phones interrupting the work. Beats me that many men come here as a form of escape from home life only to leave their mobile phone switched on. Allotments have a certain peace and a tranquillity about them, even in London, and New Cross doesn't have a great deal of green space. I mean, there's the park over there, these allotments, a few small front and back gardens and, well, frankly that's your lot, but even then this land has to be used to grow edible produce, so at certain times of the year the allotment looks like a lot of little ploughed fields all in two neat rows.'

'I see.' Swannell continued to glance round the shed. 'So I couldn't rent an allotment to sow a lawn to sunbathe on?'

'Good heavens, no!' Vere gasped. 'It wouldn't be permitted . . . just edible produce. The nearest you could get to a lawn would be say half-a-dozen apple trees on an otherwise grassed-over area. I dare say that that might be permitted. But a lawn to use to relax on . . . not a chance. Only edible produce, it's law and I mean by Act of Parliament.' Tony Vere ran his short, stubby fingers down the column of names in the ledger. 'You see, the allotments as we know them were established during the First World War, The Great War as it was then known.'

'Or the war to end all wars,' Swannell commented dryly.

'Indeed.' Vere breathed deeply. 'It didn't quite work out like that, but whatever . . . Anyway, Britain was facing severe food shortages due to the effectiveness of the U-boat blockade which sank many ships bringing food from overseas. As a consequence, Lloyd George's government ordered local authorities to give up all unused ground, or "idle" ground, as the term then was, for the use of cultivation of food stuffs by ordinary people growing their own, so as to help feed the populace, and the rule that only edible produce can be grown on the nation's allotments still holds good.'

'That's interesting.' Victor Swannell glanced around the interior of the hut once again, this time noting framed photographs of people proudly showing vegetables which they had, he thought, presumably grown on their allotment, and he also noted people manning tables upon which produce was displayed for sale. 'I have had a history lesson.'

'Yes, indeed.' Vere continued to look closely at the ledger. 'It really is quite a story. Another fact which might be of interest to you is that the creation of the allotments was the first time that land had been given to ordinary people since the common land in parishes up and down the nation was taken from them during the Parliamentary Enclosures during the seventeen hundreds and the early eighteen hundreds. Oh . . .' Tony Vere followed Swannell's gaze, '. . . that photograph is one of our annual sale of produce – they're very popular. We all grow more than we can eat so we sell off the surplus at next-to-nothing prices. It gives us a little financial float and means we avoid the great sin of wasting good food. Our annual sales are very popular, as I said, not just because the produce is inexpensive but also because they actually taste like vegetables and fruit, unlike the tasteless stuff you buy in supermarkets.'

'Yes,' Swannell replied, 'I have heard that said before about allotment produce.' He returned his gaze towards Tony Vere. 'The usage has changed, which is another interesting fact . . .' Tony Vere turned a page of the ledger. 'The allotments started out as a wholly working-class activity but nowadays they have come to be dominated by the professional middle classes. The allotment which you are interested in is in fact rented by the managing director of a small company, for example, and many holders on this site are similarly employed.'

'I confess that seems to be the way of it.' Swannell waited patiently for Tony Vere to search out the information he sought. 'The working class start something and pretty soon the middle class take it over. Male-voice choirs in South Wales, for example, were started by coalminers as a means of self-improvement during the growth of Methodism and other non-conformist religions, but nowadays you don't get a school headship in Wales unless you sing in a choir.'

'Really!' Tony Vere turned to Swannell with a keen alertness in his eyes.

'So I have been informed.' Swannell nodded in reply.

'That's interesting,' Vere returned his attention to the ledger, 'but I ought not to be surprised. You hear many educated voices on the allotments as neighbours will chat whilst digging or taking a break from weeding to talk to each other.'

Swannell remained silent as he pondered how a 'voice' could be educated, although he knew what Tony Vere had meant was 'the cultivated voice of an educated person'.

'Ah ha!' Tony Vere exclaimed with a note of excitement. 'Here we are: plot twenty-three, which is the allotment in question, was last let to a gentleman called Dickinson who gave up the rental five years ago. I remember him, a nice old boy; he always had time for you. Before that it was rented by a geezer called Hill. He was here before I took over as the allotments reeve. I became reeve upon retiring from the civil service. It gets me out of the house, which is what my wife likes. She got used to having the house to herself during the day when I was working. It's a bit selfish of her but she is a selfish woman. I mean, I worked from the day I left school until my sixty-fifth birthday so as to provide for my own and you'd think she'd let me enjoy my home in my retirement, but she doesn't see that way. If it's daytime during the working week then it's "her" home, not "ours". It only becomes "ours" at weekends and the evening.'

'A little selfish, as you say,' Swannell grunted in agreement.

'Mr Hill appears to have rented plot twenty-three for just six months and sometimes that is the way of it. A lot of folk have a romantic view of being an allotment holder, then find out how much hard physical work is involved and give it up after a few months. Others stay for years. Ah . . . now, before Mr Hill it was rented by a man called Carlyon. He appears to have had it for a number of years. Before him . . .'

'I don't need to go any further back.' Swannell cut Tony Vere off in mid-speech. 'Tell me about Mr Hill, who had the allotment for a few months. When was that?'

'About ten years ago . . . according to this,' Vere replied.

'He will interest me if there are human remains in the allotment. Do you have his address?'

'Geoffrey Road.' Tony Vere read the address in the ledger. 'Number three hundred and twenty-three. Whether he is still at that address or not, I can't say.'

'I'll take the chance.' Swannell glanced behind him and out through the open door of the hut. 'Is that near here?'

'Yes, quite close,' Vere explained. 'A ten-minute walk for a fit man such as yourself, sir.'

'I see.' Swannell turned back to Tony Vere. 'Tell me, when a person takes an allotment, do they have to provide proof of identity?'

'Not to the same extent that a person would have to prove his identity when opening a bank account,' Tony Vere explained. 'I have in fact allocated allotments to people I know only by sight. I see them in the streets round here or in the pub. So no, I dare say the answer is no, they don't have to prove their identity.'

'That might be something of an obstacle for us,' Swannell mused, speaking more to himself than to Tony Vere.

'You still don't know whether the dog found human remains or not.' Vere smiled. 'Don't rush your fences, sir. It's a lesson I have learned.'

'Our informant gave a precise location . . . he apparently seemed genuine and the dog has found something at the given location,' Swannell growled. 'There'll be human remains under the surface of that allotment, if only because the hairs on my old wooden leg tell me so.' Swannell paused. 'So, who was the supervisor . . . the reeve, when Mr Hill rented plot twenty-three?'

'That would be my predecessor, Ron Brazier,' Vere replied.

'Where can I find him?' Swannell brushed another fly from his face.

'You can't,' Tony Vere shrugged apologetically. 'Sadly he is no longer with us. He suffered a small stroke and seemed to be making a good recovery, then he suffered a larger, massive stroke just a couple of months later, from which he did not recover. A blessing, really – he would have been little more than a vegetable. His was a very well-attended funeral.'

'I see.' Swannell forced a smile. 'So he won't be able to tell me much about Mr Hill?'

'Nope . . . not much.' Tony Vere returned the smile. 'Mind you, the next allotment, plot twenty-four, is rented by a geezer called Moffatt, who is one of our long-term rentees. I am sure he will remember Mr Hill. I am reluctant to let you have Mr Moffatt's address without his permission.'

'Fair enough, but you may have to,' Swannell growled again, 'depending on what we find in plot twenty-three. Leaving that issue aside for a moment, though, tell me: how secure are the allotments?'

'Well,' Vere pursed his lips, 'frankly there is hardly any security at all and that is because hardly any is needed; a few plots of soil in which potatoes and carrots are growing is hardly the Bank of England. As you may have noticed, the allotments are surrounded by a privet hedge about four feet high, which anyone with any strength can force their way through.'

'What about the gate?' Swannell pressed. 'Is that kept locked at night? Does it have any sort of alarm system attached to it?'

'No alarm system,' Vere advised, 'and yes, it is locked with a padlock although, having said that, all allotment holders are given a key to the padlock and, of course, it would be the easiest thing in the world to have a copy cut. You see, like I said, our little patch of England is hardly The Old Lady of Threadneedle Street.'

'So . . .' Swannell once again glanced behind him through the open door of the hut and saw the sun glinting off the windowpane of a distant block of high-rise flats. He turned back to face Tony Vere and continued, 'Access during the hours of darkness would be an easy thing to achieve?'

'Yes, yes it would. Very easy.' Vere nodded. 'Especially for a key holder, but, as I have said, anyone with any strength could force their way through the privet. It does not conceal any wire or metal fencing.'

'All right . . . so the soil,' Swannell asked, 'is it at all difficult to dig, would you say?'

'Yes,' Vere replied confidently, 'as the constables will no doubt be finding out. I'm a Londoner; I have never lived anywhere else, never wanted to, so I can't compare London soil to other soil but London soil is known to be a heavy soil. London clay, you see,' Vere explained. 'A lot of allotment holders find the soil particularly difficult to work . . . as I do, but I also find it's worth it.'

'Tasty vegetables?' Swannell allowed himself a brief smile.

'Yes, and also the wildlife you see from time to time – you know, badgers, foxes; mind you, I don't like the foxes. Your average fox is a thoroughly evil animal if you ask me, and especially now they've banned fox hunting. The fox is losing its fear of humans – even the urban fox which was never hunted. They walk around quite nonchalantly, and during the day too.' Tony Vere wiped another bead of sweat from his forehead. 'Weasels, stoats and rats, of course – there's always plenty of rats. Once I was chatting to another allotment holder, just passing the time of day, and a bird table was between us. We were about ten feet apart and a blue tit was pecking away at some birdseed a kind-hearted soul had left on the table when suddenly there was a flash from left to right and the blue tit just vanished. Vanished in a flash . . . in the blink of an eye.'

'Raptor?' Swannell guessed.

'Yes, a sparrow hawk, to be precise. We were able to identity it as it flew away and that happened here, in the middle of

New Cross. Nature goes on all around you and it's experiences like that which make heavy London soil worth digging.'

'I take your point,' Swannell replied, 'but back to the soil itself; would you say that it would take a long time to dig a normal six-foot-deep grave?'

'Oh, blimey, yes.' Vere exhaled. 'I wouldn't want to be a gravedigger in London. Mind you, these days it's all done by machines, small mechanical diggers . . . But in the old days, in the days of spade work, well, in those days a gravedigger would have to work for his money.' Vere paused. 'What you are really asking is whether the grave in plot twenty-three, if it is a grave, will be a shallow grave or not? I would say that if human remains are buried there they will be shallowly buried. I'd say a full six-foot-deep grave would take a fit man a full day to dig . . . longer in these dry conditions. Not the sort of thing you could do during the daytime, more of a night-time job . . . the digging . . . the placing of a body, the filling in . . . your boys won't have to dig very far before they find out what the dog scented. It will be a shallow grave.'

'Thank you, that is very useful. I'll go and see how they're getting on.' Swannell turned and walked out of the hut into the heat and glare of the sun. He noticed at once that the constables had stopped digging and were standing in a circle looking downwards. Swannell approached the group and stood next to the sergeant.

'I was just about to send for you, sir.' The sergeant spoke, continuing to look downwards. 'As you see, sir . . .'

Victor Swannell looked into the grave. A skull, a human skull, seemed to be grinning at him. The remains were, as Tony Vere had predicted, buried shallowly; probably, thought Swannell, about three feet below the surface.

It was Wednesday, 12.55 hours.

TWO

Harry Vicary arrived at the Malpas Road allotments to find that the area had been efficiently and securely cordoned off by the police. A police constable in a white shirt and serge trousers stood sentinel at the entrance while other uniformed police officers were to be seen within the allotments, as was a white inflatable tent. Harry Vicary also noticed that the inevitable crowd of curious onlookers had already gathered and stood on the pavement in ones and twos looking into the allotments. Householders also stood on their balconies overlooking the scene and watched the police activity with solemn interest. As Vicary approached the gate the constable half saluted and lifted the blue-and-white police tape which had been suspended across the gateway. Vicary nodded his thanks to the constable, bent down and slid beneath the tape. Once within the allotments he walked calmly yet authoritatively towards the white inflatable tent which had been erected a few yards from the gate. Victor Swannell stood with the uniformed officers in the immediate vicinity of the tent and looked respectfully at Vicary as he approached.

'Thank you for coming, sir.' Swannell spoke softly. 'We have one human skeleton, sir, partially exposed. The Home Office pathologist is in the tent at the moment. Two constables are sieving the soil which was removed to expose the skeleton. Nothing of note has thus far been found.'

'Thank you.' Vicary smiled. 'You have everything in hand.'

'So far just two persons to be interviewed, sir.' Swannell continued, 'The allotment manager – the reeve . . .'

'The "reeve"?' Vicary raised an eyebrow.

'Yes, sir.' Swannell grinned. 'That is his chosen designation. The "reeve", a retired gentleman, Tony Vere by name, has provided the name and address of the person who rented the allotment at the time the body was buried, according to our informant.'

'Who is he?'

'A man called Hill, sir.' Swannell took his notebook from his jacket pocket and consulted it. 'We have his address. I have phoned those details to Criminal Records . . . they have not come back to me yet.'

'Fair enough.' Vicary glanced over the allotments. 'The reeve said that he was the rentee for a very short time.'

'So . . . you are suggesting that he rented the allotment with a view to using it to dispose of a corpse, and once that had been achieved he gave up the rental?' Vicary asked. 'That implies a considerable amount of premeditation if you're right but it does seem suspicious, I'll agree with you there.'

'I thought it sounded suspicious, sir.' Swannell continued looking with some annoyance at the onlookers who insisted on peering over the hedge. 'Sergeant!' Swannell turned to the uniformed sergeant.

'Sir!'

'Get a couple of constables to move those people on, will you, please. There's nothing to see.'

'Yes, sir!'

'And post a constable there to keep people moving.'

'Very good, sir.' The sergeant turned away.

'Sorry, sir,' Swannell said apologetically, 'I should have done that earlier.'

'No matter,' Vicary replied. 'You were saying . . .?'

'Yes, sir . . . the reeve, Mr Vere, told me that often people take allotments then rapidly give them up when they realize the amount of work involved, and so Mr Hill keeping the allotment for a short time may not be suspicious, but equally you are not going to bury a body in the allotment of which you are a long-term rentee. That would be akin to burying it in your front garden.'

'Yes.' Vicary nodded gently. 'I take your point. As you say, it would be like burying it in your front garden, and who with any sense would do that?'

'So,' Swannell continued, 'we have Mr Hill's address, and

also a gentleman called Moffatt. Mr Moffatt is the long-term rentee of the adjacent allotment, who the reeve . . .'

'The reeve.' Vicary smiled. 'I do like that title. It sounds ancient.'

'It's medieval, apparently, sir,' Swannell advised. 'Anyway, the reeve believes Mr Moffatt will be able to tell us something about Mr Hill. The reeve never knew Mr Hill. He was reluctant to give us Mr Moffatt's address but eventually agreed.'

'So Mr Moffatt will give information, we hope,' Vicary clarified, 'and Mr Hill is a suspect?'

'That's it, sir.'

'All right, well, you can't go and see Mr Hill alone, that's a two-hander. I am needed here, but you could go and see Mr Moffatt, see what he can tell us.'

'Yes, sir.'

'What is Moffatt's address?'

'Seven hundred and twenty-seven Manor Avenue, sir,' Swannell read from his notebook, 'which is apparently the second street to the east of here.'

'And the reeve – where is he?' Vicary asked.

'He has returned home, sir,' Swannell advised. 'I told him that we needed to take full possession of the whole area, not just one plot. He wasn't very happy. He's obliged to return to an unwelcoming spouse who likes her home to herself during the day. She has, it seems, yet to make an adjustment to her husband's retirement.'

'Poor chap.' Vicary's smile was forced this time. 'So many people don't realize how much strain a retirement can place on a marriage . . . but, to the task in hand. If you could call on Mr Moffatt and see what he can tell us, I'll remain here.'

'Yes, sir.' Swannell turned and walked unhurriedly yet purposefully towards the exit of the allotments.

Harry Vicary entered the inflatable tent then rapidly stepped back outside and took a deep breath. He then re-entered the tent.

'Good afternoon, Detective Chief Inspector.' John Shaftoe looked up at Vicary from where he knelt beside the recently excavated hole which contained the human remains. He smiled warmly at Harry Vicary. Vicary noticed that Shaftoe was perspiring heavily. 'You're right, we could use a fan in these tents, especially during the summer months . . . but we get used to them . . . I dare say it's a question of us having to get used to them.'

'How ignominious,' Vicary commented as he looked at the remains in the hole next to which John Shaftoe was kneeling.

'You think so?' Shaftoe did not take his eyes off the skeletal remains.

'Yes.' Vicary continued to ponder the content of the hole. 'I mean, that is a fairly shallow grave,' he explained. 'You see, it seems to be the case that the deeper the grave, the higher the status of the victim when alive, but this grave . . . what is it . . . two and a half, three feet deep? That is quite shallow. She was not highly regarded in life.'

'Oh . . . you can tell that they are the remains of a female?' Shaftoe stood up and brushed soil from his brown corduroy trousers.

'Well, I have learned a few things over the years.' Vicary continued to take shallow breaths. 'I note a smallish frame . . . I see wide eye orbits, so I assume it is a female.'

'You assume correctly, Mr Vicary,' Shaftoe continued to brush soil from his trousers, 'and you are correct about the size. She would have been quite a short woman in life, probably only about five feet tall. She was either European or Asian; those skeletal types are very difficult to distinguish between, so you can rule out any other racial group.'

'How long?' Vicary's voice faltered as Shaftoe turned and gave him a despairing look.

'Of course . . .' Vicary mumbled his apology. 'Sorry.'

'I can't say and I won't even guess.' Shaftoe turned his head away from Vicary. 'No self-respecting pathologist would attempt to pin down the time of death – that is the stuff of TV crime dramas, and very dangerous they can be too. Our field of expertise is always the "how" but never the "when".'

'Of course,' Vicary replied.

'Of interest though is that some sinews remain; there will be some trace of internal organs because of the remaining sinews and that will place the death within the seventy-year cut-off point, probably quite comfortably so. But having said that, this good old London clay soil will have slowed the rate of decomposition and I can tell how she most likely met her end.'

'Oh?'

'Yes . . .' Shaftoe pointed to the forehead. 'See the small holes?'

'Ah, yes.' Vicary looked closely at the skeleton's head. 'Yes, I can see them.'

'Those are gunshot wounds. Appears to be two shots from a very small calibre weapon – a point twenty-two, and if it was fired close enough to the forehead it would be quite sufficient to be fatal. A point twenty-two is an assassin's weapon of choice.' Shaftoe panted, also taking shallow breaths. 'I'll probably find the remains of the bullets inside her skull and what remains of her brain matter. But it could be that she was shot to make sure that she was dead or to cover up some other form of murder . . . strangulation, drowning, suffocation . . . all are still possibilities.' Shaftoe paused. 'There is no indication of clothing – the material would have deteriorated by now – but wooden toggles, metal zip fasteners, jewellery, all that sort of paraphilia would have remained if she had been clothed when she was buried. I have come across nothing of that sort. I think it is a safe bet the wretched woman was naked when she was buried, which is another assassin's trick – there is less to identify her. And that, I think, concludes all that I can do here. I'll have the skeleton lifted and removed to the Royal London and then remain here until the constables are satisfied that they have reached consolidated soil. When they do we'll know nothing has been buried beneath the skeleton, and once all the soil has been sifted, it can be replaced and the allotments may be given back to the allotment holders so they can continue growing potatoes.' Shaftoe once again brushed himself down. He was a short, portly man with a bald head. 'Will you be attending the post-mortem, Chief Inspector?'

'Most probably,' Vicary replied, 'but only most probably. When will you be conducting it, sir?'

'Tomorrow.' Shaftoe's panting and shallow breathing continued. 'That is, tomorrow in the forenoon. Say about ten a.m. I'll aim for a ten a.m. kick-off. Dykk has the post-mortem theatre booked for the whole of this afternoon; he's tutoring a group of recent graduates, all of whom have opted to take the pathology option, and he'll be taking huge delight in telling them that they are all third-raters so they had better get used to it. But me . . . little old me, I am oh-so-deliriously happy to be a third-rater. So very happy.'

'But how so a third-rater?' Vicary was genuinely curious, having over the years learned to view John Shaftoe with a great deal of respect and feeling fortunate to have him and his expertise and skill as a pathologist to call on and depend on.

'Well . . . how can I explain it? I dare say that it's the snobbery and the pecking order within the medical profession which determine the rates,' Shaftoe explained. 'You see, the surgeons have the most prestige, they are the first-raters and the most highly paid – they save lives with ground-breaking surgical techniques. The second-raters, well, they are your hard-pressed family doctors, the first line of defence, if you like. They prevent as much as cure. They work long hours under a lot of pressure. And then there's us poor pathologists who do not save anyone's life or prevent or cure any illness or injury, and so we are the third-raters. But we do have an easy life, less well paid than the first- and second-raters, but it has its compensations. I mean, no one is going to sue us for negligence. No one is going to lose their life because a pathologist has blundered. Any pressure on us is of a legalistic nature. If we don't get our findings correct then the guilty can walk free, or worse, much, much worse, the innocent can be convicted. The only doctors below us are the foreign doctors who have graduated from suspect third-world universities. They take locum work or work in long-term care hospitals . . . or are doctors at seaports or in large companies, who are not in private practice and neither do they work for the National Health Service.'

'I see.' Harry Vicary turned to leave the tent. 'I confess that I never thought the medical profession had a "pecking order", as you call it. I know the difference in status between doctors and nurses but not among doctors themselves.'

'Oh, believe me, Mr Vicary, there is such a hierarchy.' Shaftoe also turned and followed Harry Vicary out of the tent. 'It's really quite vicious and strictly enforced. In fact, I once worked in a hospital in which all the pathologists had to sit in a designated area of the senior common room which was dubbed "death corner", and we were pretty well ignored by the surgeons and specialists who worked in the hospital, who were permitted to sit anywhere they wished to. It isn't like that in the Royal London but the divisions are there all the same, and Professor Dykk will be preparing his students for that sort of prejudice.' Shaftoe stretched his arms and yawned as the sunlight reached his head and face. 'But it happens in all walks of life. Dustbin men apparently see themselves as a cut above road-sweepers, for example, and I once met a man who taught at a teacher training college which produced sports teachers and he always began his first lecture to each year's intake by saying, "Gym teachers always stand up because if they sit down it makes their brains sore", then explained that they're going to get comments like that throughout their working life so they may as well hear it from him first, and then he would try to mollify them by telling them that because of their superb physiques they would enjoy the best sex life of any group of students.'

'That would go down well.' Vicary took a deep breath, being very pleased to have been able to leave the tent. 'It would certainly mollify me.'

'And me,' Shaftoe replied. 'So the pathology laboratory is presently being used to prepare students for life at or near the bottom of the pecking order, but me . . . I like getting into holes in the ground and looking at bits of human remains. So I'll see your good self or one of your officers at ten a.m. tomorrow?'

'Indeed.' Vicary took another gratifyingly deep breath. 'Indeed you will, sir. Thank you.'

'Yes, I had in fact heard that the police had found something of interest to them in the allotments. I mean, this street is hardly the public bath house but if news has to travel then it will travel and the street is alive with the news.' Edward Moffatt smiled warmly at Victor Swannell as he invited him to take a seat in his living room. 'That sort of activity . . . the white tent, all those constables, does not go unnoticed. So what has been discovered? A dead body or bodies . . . an arms cache belonging to a terrorist group . . . buried treasure . . . a hoard of Roman coins?'

'I am not at liberty to tell you. I'm sorry.' Swannell glanced at the settee and then decided to sit in the vacant armchair. 'Not yet, anyway.' Swannell read Edward Moffatt's living room and found it to be age and social status appropriate. It was neat, he thought – cosy, in a word, smelled richly of furniture polish and thus was exactly what Victor Swannell had anticipated finding, being the home of a late middle-aged man who employs a cleaner to help him keep on top of it. Swannell's eye rested on a framed photograph of a middle-aged woman in a blue summer dress which stood proudly upon the mantelpiece above the empty fire grate.

'Oh . . . that's my Sara.' Edward Moffatt followed Swannell's gaze. 'She has gone before me.'

'I'm sorry to hear that.' Swannell settled back into the armchair.

'I'm not.' Edward Moffatt smiled briefly and Swannell noticed that the man had a genuine look of warmth in his eyes. 'Now, don't please misunderstand me,' Moffatt continued speaking with a soft, homely London accent. 'Sara and I had a lovely marriage and we were very happy, but if I had gone first she would not have coped very well at all. You see, of the two of us, she was the much more dependent. She married from home, you see, and so she always had family around her. She got very depressed when the children left and only recovered her spark when the grandchildren arrived. They're all pretty well grown up now; she was feeling a bit redundant with just her old man to look after. So if I had gone before she would have been down in the dumps each day and every day. She would have felt very isolated and been a very lonely woman. Now me . . . me on the other hand, I left home early in life. I had ten brothers and sisters and our family was so chaotic that one of my sisters told me later that it was three days before I was noticed to be missing. Anyway, I joined the army as a boy soldier. After I was time expired I did a stint in the Merchant Navy, then I worked as a long-distance lorry driver which also kept me away from home, though not as long as the navy or the army had done, so I am well used to being by myself – it doesn't bother me at all. I think it is fitting that Sara went first. She went peacefully as well. She was sitting in that chair, the one you are sitting in, and she seemed to be asleep, so I said, "Are you asleep? Come on if you're feeling tired, we'll go up to bed. We'll not stay up to watch the film like we planned, it'll be shown on TV again", but she didn't reply and I knew she had died. She had just slipped away in her sleep, so peacefully, not distressed or knowing any discomfort, and she died in her home, not in some hospital. She just went with a lovely marriage and three children and seven grandchildren behind her. It was her time and the Good Lord called her unto him. It was how it should be . . . it really could not have been any better at all.'

'That is . . . a very uplifting attitude.' Swannell relaxed quickly in Edward Moffatt's company, having found him to be a calm, philosophical and spiritual man. In fact, all the gardeners he had ever met he had found to have similar qualities, although whether it is the case that gardening fosters such attitudes or men with such attitudes are drawn to gardening, he did not know. 'I am pleased for your good fortune.'

'Thank you.' Edward Moffatt inclined his head to one side. 'I do have wonderful memories. I probably don't have a lot to show for my years in terms of possessions but I do have a head full of lovely memories. I sit here thinking of the things that happened, the things we did as a family . . . and that, let me tell you, is far, far better than being one of those elderly people who sit and wonder what might have been if they had done things differently and not taken that decision, not let that opportunity slip through their fingers. That must be an awful way to have to pass your final days. Really awful.'

'Indeed, it must be.' Victor Swannell felt a chill drive through him as he suddenly feared for his own autumn. 'But if you don't mind, I have a couple of questions for you.'

'Of course.' Edward Moffatt was a short, sinewy man who appeared to Swannell to have a strong and wiry constitution.

'I understand that you rent one of the allotments on Malpas Road? Number twenty-four, to be precise.'

'Yes, I do.' Moffatt nodded. 'It's been my little patch of

London for the last twenty years, probably more. I need the allotment: there are no gardens in these flats. We moved here, me and Sara, once the children had grown up; our previous tenancy was too large for our needs. It seemed it was a good move at first but I missed the smell, the aroma of freshly turned soil. So I took an allotment when one became free.'

'I see . . . that could be quite useful because we are interested in the next plot to yours, allotment number twenty-three,' Swannell advised.

'Yes . . . twenty-three is the next allotment to mine, nearest the gate. That plot has had a few rentees over the years.' Moffatt pondered. 'It's not been a good producer but that might have been the way it has been worked. It ought to be quite rich; it's been left alone for long periods and other allotment holders have placed vegetable matter on it to compost down.'

'We are interested in a man called Hill,' Swannell continued. 'He rented it some years ago. Do you remember him at all? He did not have the plot very long, just a few months really.'

'Hill?' Moffatt glanced up at the ceiling of his living room. 'Yes . . . you know, I think I do remember him. He wasn't up to much as a gardener. I think he was like so many others: he fancied the idea of growing crops but the hard work involved came as an unpleasant surprise. The plot had lain fallow for a few months before he took it and so it needed completely digging over. It would have made a good allotment once it had been turned and all that composted material had been worked into the soil. We hadn't got the mechanical rotavator in those days so it all had to be done by hand. He did dig it but his heart wasn't in it.'

'Really?' Swannell glanced out of the window of Edward Moffatt's third-floor flat and saw the upper floors and rooftops of the large Victorian-era houses which made up the bulk of the housing on Manor Avenue.

'Well, yes,' Moffatt continued, 'so it seemed to me anyway. He turned the bottom half of his allotment but had no desire to turn the rest of the plot.'

'Did he plant crops?' Swannell asked.

'None.' Moffatt smiled briefly. 'None at all. He turned half the plot then gave up and bought his vegetables from the supermarket, I should think. Easier maybe, but expensive and tasteless. The plot was eventually taken over by a man called Dickinson . . . he worked it before he gave it up.'

'What did Mr Dickinson grow?' Swannell asked.

'Potatoes,' Moffatt answered promptly.

'They grow under the surface, don't they?'

'Yes,' Moffatt replied, 'just under.'

'So . . . if something was buried say two or three feet beneath the surface, it wouldn't be found by someone harvesting a crop of potatoes?' Swannell asked.

'No . . . no, it wouldn't.' Moffatt pursed his lips. 'Not at that sort of depth. 'You can dig them up with a garden fork. In fact, plant for plant they are quite an easy crop to lift. Digging for potatoes only becomes backbreaking work if you have to lift a whole field of them.'

'I see,' Swannell mused. 'So what can you recall about Mr Hill? The allotment register gives his name as being Patrick Hill.'

'Patrick . . . yes, I do remember that that was his name. I remember now that you mention it.' Moffatt glanced down at the busy pattern of his carpet. 'He and I didn't speak very much at all but I got the impression that he was not a dedicated or keen allotment holder . . . In fact, I got the impression that he seemed to resent the plot. His attitude seemed to be one of "I'm here because I've got to be here". It was the way he would attack the soil . . . like he resented it.'

'That is quite significant,' Swannell commented. 'Probably quite significant.'

'It certainly seemed unusual to me,' Moffatt continued. 'In my experience, all allotment holders are enthusiastic at the outset. Some remain enthusiastic while others lose their enthusiasm, but all are enthusiastic when they step on their little plot of land for the first time.'

'But not Patrick Hill?' Swannell interrupted.

'No. Not Patrick Hill,' Moffatt confirmed. 'From the outset he seemed to resent being there . . . like he was a pressed man. Never showed any sign of eagerness, not from day one, and so it didn't come as a surprise to me when he gave it up.'

'How long did he rent the allotment for?' Swannell asked, taking his notebook from his jacket pocket.

'Well, Tony Vere, the reeve, he'll be able to give you the start date and finish date, but I think it was a few weeks early in the year . . . March, April.' Moffatt paused. 'There was certainly plenty of rain to soften up the ground and make the digging easier. I remember because I said as much – I said to him that the rain will make the soil heavier because it will all become waterlogged, but that he would find it easier to dig than if it was baked hard like it will be now.'

'All right . . .' Swannell took a ballpoint pen from his jacket pocket.

'I remember him as a very distant sort of individual. He was not keen to talk but he'd reply to you if you spoke to him. He tended to keep himself to himself, which is another strange thing about Hill. I never saw him around here.' Moffatt glanced out of the window of his flat. 'You see, I would often bump into people who also had allotments, in the post office, in the pub, or I'd notice them in the street – not necessarily to speak to, but Hill . . . he'd arrive in a little red car, do something to his allotment . . . weeding, turning a little soil, and then he'd leave as if he lived some distance away, but I believe you have to be living close to your allotments to be able to rent one. So it was a bit strange that I never saw him in the locality.'

'That's also interesting.' Swannell adjusted his position in the chair in which the late Sara Moffatt had slept her final sleep. 'Can you describe Patrick Hill's appearance?'

'Thin . . . but he seemed muscular,' Moffatt began. 'He had short, dark hair, as I recall . . .'

'Eye colour?' Swannell pressed.

'Good heavens, I couldn't tell you that.' Moffatt grinned. 'I never got close enough to him. In any way you can mean.'

'Fair enough.' Swannell returned the smile. 'It was a bit of a long shot. Was he clean-shaven?'

'Yes . . . yes, he was.' Moffatt looked upwards, as if searching his memory. 'I do recall a five o'clock shadow or even a full day's growth, but yes, I'd say that he was mostly clean-shaven.'

'All right.' Swannell wrote in his notebook. 'How did he dress . . . anything distinctive there?'

'Not that I can recall . . . jeans rather than trousers, sports shoes rather than the heavy footwear that gardeners prefer. You can injure yourself with a fork or a spade if you don't have the correct footwear.'

'I can imagine.' Swannell tapped the notebook with his ballpoint pen. He paused for a moment so as not to give Edward Moffatt the impression that he was being interrogated. Then, in a gentle, soft voice, he asked Moffatt how tall Patrick Hill was.

'Five foot seven.' Moffatt grinned.

'You seem confident, sir,' Swannell smiled.

'I am confident. I am that height myself and we could look at each other without one or the other of us having to look up or down. So he was about five foot seven inches tall. Of that I am certain.'

'Good enough.' Swannell wrote the details in his notebook. 'And then he just gave up the plot after digging up the bottom half of the allotment?'

'Yes. He just handed the gate key in to the reeve and drove away, never to return.'

'Did he have any distinguishing features?' Swannell asked.

'Two that I can recall,' Moffatt replied. 'A broken nose – a boxer's nose. He'd been in a fight or fights and he'd stopped some geezer's fist with his nose . . . probably more than once. He had the traditional boxer's nose, which you don't often see these days because they can straighten out flattened and bent noses.'

'Yes,' Swannell grunted.

'He probably thought it made him look tough,' Moffatt commented. 'He probably thought his nose made him look like a hard man, but me . . . I just thought it made him look like of one of life's losers.'

'He probably was proud of his nose,' Swannell agreed. 'I've come across that attitude.'

'The other noticeable feature was a spider,' Moffatt advised.

'A spider?' Swannell glanced at Moffatt.

'A tattoo . . . a black spider on the back of his left hand.' Moffatt tapped the back of his own left hand. 'Just there.'

'That's very useful. Thank you.' Swannell stood. 'It's all very useful.'

Later, after returning to New Scotland Yard and recording the interview with Edward Moffatt in the file of the as-yet-unidentified murder victim whose buried remains had been uncovered in the Malpas Road allotments, Victor Swannell drove home to his house on Warren Road, Neasden, NW2 and parked his car on the area in front of his house which had, by the previous owner, been cemented over to provide off-street parking, as with many other houses in the area. He got out of his car and was met by the endless hum of traffic on the nearby North Circular Road, the noise from which he and his neighbours had learned to live with. He let himself into his house and walked into the lounge where his wife and two daughters were sitting, engrossed in an Australian TV soap opera. As he entered the room all three glanced up at him once and then returned their gaze to the TV set. Victor Swannell turned and went up to the front bedroom he and his wife shared. There he changed into white slacks, a yellow T-shirt and a pair of sandals. He left the house and walked down towards the golf club links so as to take in the early evening peace and calm.

It is often remarked that one of the drawbacks of being a police officer is that it prevents one from feeling sorry for oneself when, as a police officer, one meets the victims of often dreadful crimes, and one also meets the lowlifes who perpetrate them, often motivated by some fearful addiction to heroin or crack cocaine. It was a view shared by Victor Swannell, but occasionally in his capacity as a police officer he met someone who did not make him think in that manner, and, that evening, as he walked through suburbia to an area of closely cropped green sward, he could not but help compare the emptiness and the emotional aridity of his marriage and his home life to the richness of Edward Moffatt's marriage to his beloved Sara, who had gone before him, leaving Edward Moffatt with little to show for a long life in terms of possessions, but with a head full of golden memories.

*   *   *

Once again, the man huddled into the corner of the room in the empty house and, once again, he looked around the room at the faded flower-patterned wallpaper and the bare floorboards upon which he forlornly tried to find comfort. It was a still, quiet evening, at the close of what had been a very warm, dry day, a day devoid of all sounds except for the incessant cries of the herring gulls. Once again he levered himself up and looked out of the window at the small cottage which lay half a mile distant, keeping himself well back from the window as he did so. He did not want to be seen. The man saw no signs of activity around the cottage, no sign of any strangers paying attention to the cottage, and he saw no strange motor vehicles, foreign to the area. The man sank back out of sight. He would stay where he was, periodically looking at the cottage until sunset, then he'd walk over the fields to it. He thought they still did not know where he was. But he also knew that nothing stays a secret forever.

Tom Ainsclough sat in the armchair of his house on Hargwyne Road, Clapham, and watched as the evening slowly gave way to dusk, sipping a cold lager as he did so. He had returned home earlier that day and had entered the front door of the house, then unlocked the door which opened on to the stairs and led to the upper conversion which he shared with his wife. He had arrived just in time to spend thirty minutes in the company of his wife before she had to leave to get to her work as a staff nurse at Lambeth Hospital.

He often thought that passing each other at the door as they did kept their marriage alive and healthy. He thought it kept them intrigued with each other. If there was no such fantasy, he doubted their marriage would survive.

It was Wednesday, 22.15 hours.

THREE

Thursday, 10.10 hours – 12.33 hours

'I freely, freely confess that I hate the man.' John Shaftoe reached up and pulled the anglepoise arm with the microphone attached to the end of it downwards so that it was level with his mouth and also hung directly over the dissecting table. 'I freely own that I hate the ground he stands on.'

'Yes, sir,' Harry Vicary replied for want of something to say. He knew very well what Shaftoe was going to say, having heard it many times over.

'Dykk, the good professor of pathology at this illustrious hospital, the same man that yesterday would, in this very room, have been telling students to prepare for life on the third level of the "pecking order" . . . him . . . he hates me and I hate him . . . him and his super-privileged background, attending the most impressive of private fee-paying schools, father and grandfather both in the medical Profession . . . He believes that only people from that background should enter our profession . . . and also enter the law . . . with their traditions and hallowed halls, but not miner's sons from South Yorkshire . . . It matters not to the great Professor Dykk if you have the qualifications and the application to stay the course of study which will lead to said qualifications . . . Oh, no . . . no . . . if you come from Barnsley and your old man's a miner, then according to Dykk there is only one place for you and that is down the pit with your dad, and the breeding of racing pigeons is your only permitted leisure pursuit. This is one of his little games, pushing the microphone up nearly out of my reach. Petty-minded is just not the expression but I can still reach it, all five foot six inches of me.' Shaftoe paused. 'All right,' he growled, 'rant over . . . no more about Dykk, the supercilious prat that he is. So today, we need a case number and today's date please,

Felicity.' Shaftoe now addressed the microphone, speaking clearly for the benefit of the audio typist who would shortly be word processing his findings as he reported them. 'We have the skeletal remains of a female. The skull is fully knitted, so she was in excess of twenty-five years of age when she died. She had had the soup of the day, she had glimpsed the main course and the dessert, but they have been taken from her.' Shaftoe paused. 'She was short in terms of her statue. Can you pass me the tape measure, please, Billy?'

William 'Billy' Button, who had always seemed to Vicary to be permanently whimpering, nervously handed Shaftoe a yellow metallic retractable tape measure.

'Thank you, Billy.' Shaftoe took the tape measure, extended it and measured the length of the skeleton. 'She was a short woman, as I said, five feet in total, and we can add an extra inch on to that to allow for the flesh on the soles of her feet and also the shrinking of the cartilages, so in life she was probably five feet and one inch tall in old speak and approximately one hundred and fifty-five centimetres in Euro speak. So short, but not a child, thank goodness.'

'Indeed,' Vicary stood at the edge of the room and was dressed head to toe in disposable green coveralls, 'that is a great relief. I confess that when I first saw the skeleton I did fear that we had a murdered teenager on our hands, and a young teenager at that. Child murders are so far and away the worst to deal with.'

'I also feared the same,' Shaftoe spoke softly, 'but as you say, relief is what we feel . . . Murdered children . . . robbed of their life, the distraught parents . . . little could be worse. But we still have a robbed-of-life situation here. She was out of childhood but by not very many years. The initial impression is that all the teeth are present and appear to be in good condition, which is another indication of youth.' Shaftoe paused. 'Racial clarification . . . she appears to be quite finely made, she has a small mandible so she is Asian or North European. She is definitely not Afro-Caribbean or Oriental. She was small but perfectly formed; everything is in proportion.' Shaftoe turned to the pathology laboratory assistant. 'Can you pass me the camera, please, Billy?'

Billy Button made a clumsy lunge for a thirty-five milli-metre digital camera with a flash attachment which stood on the surface of the bench which ran the length of the wall of the laboratory, opposite the wall against which Harry Vicary stood. Once again, Vicary was impressed by the patience which Shaftoe was able to muster when dealing with Button, believing that he could not extend such latitude to the man, who was clearly so unsuited to working with corpses. It was a constant source of wonder to Vicary that the tremulous Button had applied for such a job in the first place, and an even greater source of wonder that he had been appointed to the position.

John Shaftoe adjusted the camera settings and then proceeded to take a series of flash-assisted photographs of the skull of the deceased, which lay face-up on the stainless-steel dissecting table. He turned to Vicary. 'We'll feed the images into a computer and it will produce a likeness of our friend as she was in life. It used to take weeks to build up the skull using plasticine – now it takes a matter of seconds. We still have to guess the eye colour, shape of the nose, hair colour, hair-style . . . but with all the wonders of modern technology we can very rapidly obtain a close, recognizable resemblance of her as she probably was when alive.'

'Indeed, sir,' Vicary replied with forced enthusiasm. He was well aware of the technique to which Shaftoe referred.

'I have photographed her because I want to get into the skull. I want to get into the brain – what remains of it,' Shaftoe explained, 'because there I'll find the bullets which may have killed her.' He handed the camera back to Billy Button and said, 'Saw, please, Billy.'

Button took the camera, placed it back on the counter and picked up a small, circular saw. He switched it on and Vicary saw Button wince at the high-pitched whirring sound which the compact machine made.

'Don't worry, Billy,' Shaftoe grinned, 'she won't feel a thing. I promise you. Not a thing.' He then applied the saw to the side of the skull, at which point Vicary found himself sharing a moment of sympathy with Billy Button as the sound of the saw cutting into the bone echoed in the laboratory, causing a chill to strike through him. He was pleased that he managed to remain composed.

John Shaftoe slowly but purposefully cut round the perimeter of the skull following an imaginary line above where the ears would have been. That completed, he took off the top of the skull, which separated without a sound. 'There is not much left of her brain,' he commented. 'Frankly, I didn't think there would be.' He held up an X-ray image of the skull of the deceased's brain and consulted it. 'I had the skeleton X-rayed when she arrived yesterday. I could do that without Dykk holding me up. There appears to be two bullets in the skull and a third in her chest cavity, so I know where to look. Can you pass me the scalpel, please, Billy? Thank you.' John Shaftoe began to probe the decayed remnants of the brain and then grunted with satisfaction. 'Here it is . . . here's one. Tweezers, please, Billy.'

Billy Button handed Shaftoe a set of surgical tweezers. Using the scalpel as a guide, Shaftoe inserted the tweezers and gripped the small metal object that had shown up on the X-ray. 'One bullet . . . very small calibre . . . appears to be in reasonable condition. You might be able to match it to a specific weapon.' He dropped the bullet into a small, self-sealing cellophane sachet and then returned his attention to the interior of the skull. Moments later he held up, with a triumphant look, a second bullet, which he dropped into a similar sachet. Shaftoe then took the circular saw and sawed down the centre of the ribcage, handed the saw to Button and then forced open the ribs, causing the bones to crack loudly. He consulted a second X-ray then began to poke around in the chest cavity. With a second triumphal expression and the words, 'Got it,' he produced the third bullet, which he held tightly with the surgical tweezers. 'This bullet appears to be in particularly good condition. I'll send all three to the firearms unit.'

'Thank you, sir,' Vicary replied.

'I'll notify them that you are the interested police officer,' Shaftoe added.

'Thank you again, sir.'

'They could have killed her,' Shaftoe remarked. 'Any one

of the three: two to the skull, one to the heart. Somebody was making sure. That is to say any one could have killed her if she had been alive . . . she might have been shot to disguise some other form of murder, as I've said before . . . drowning, asphyxiation. If she drowned there will be diatoms in the marrow of her long bones.'

'Diatoms, sir?' Vicary queried.

'Microscopic beasties,' Shaftoe explained. 'They exist in all forms of water. They are carried into the lungs of drowned persons and from the lungs they migrate to the bone marrow, and there they remain. It is by detecting them that we can show that a skeleton was a victim of drowning.'

'They remain for that length of time?' Vicary was astounded.

'Yes, they do,' Shaftoe replied, 'and so I'll take a sample of her bone marrow and examine it, but if she was suffocated there will not be any trace of that, not after this length of time, and no trace of her being strangled either. So the gunshots killed her, or ensured that she was deceased. As I said, someone was making sure.'

'But she was murdered,' Vicary pressed, 'you believe?'

'Oh . . . yes, I would think so.' Shaftoe grinned broadly. 'Suicides don't need three bullets to kill themselves, and you don't cover up accidental deaths by shooting the person concerned. I'll run a trace for heavy poisonings, just for form's sake, but arsenic and cyanide poisoning went out with the Victorians.' Shaftoe paused and then prised the jaws apart, causing them to give with a loud cracking sound – a noise which made Billy Button jump and put his hand to his mouth in a manner which Vicary thought to be very effeminate. 'Love gobs.' Shaftoe grinned once again. 'I just love a good gob . . . it's all in the gob . . . which I dare say you know is Yorkshire for mouth.'

'Yes . . . I did know that, sir.' Vicary also grinned. 'In fact, it was your good self who told me in this very room.'

'Ah, well . . . good. So long as you know to what I am referring. So many folk south of Watford Gap don't know, but it's all in your old "north and south", as a Londoner would say. The teeth are in excellent condition . . . no extractions . . . some fillings, which means that there will be dental records unless she was murdered more than eleven years ago, after which time dentists are not obliged to keep the patient's records.'

'We think we are still within that timeframe,' Vicary replied, 'just . . . but within it all the same.'

'Good . . . and I note British dentistry, which should help you, and dental records will confirm her identity. They are as unique as fingerprints, although I dare say you know that as well.'

'Yes, sir.' Vicary nodded briefly. 'That is something else I picked up along the way.'

'Yes, well, I'll extract a tooth; that won't prevent her identity being determined,' Shaftoe continued. 'With one tooth I can determine her age at death to within plus or minus one year, but with these teeth I'd say she was in her mid- to late-twenties when she met her end. Still young enough. She had more ahead of her than she had behind her in terms of her life expectancy. Tragic, really.'

'Indeed,' Vicary concurred. 'A tragedy.'

'I mean, every corpse which is laid on one of these tables to be chopped into little pieces is here before their time,' John Shaftoe pondered, 'but it is the case that some are here long, long before their time, and our friend here is one of those. I'll fax my findings to you asap, but it will almost certainly be murder – death by gunshot wounds and three bullets. The two holes in her skull are very close together, which means the gun was held up to her head, fired once then held in more or less the same place and fired a second time. Asian or Northern European female, mid- to late-twenties.'

'Thank you, sir.' Vicary smiled. 'It will be appreciated.'

Harry Vicary strode away from the pathology laboratory, peeling off his green disposable paper hat and coveralls as he did so, feeling pleased to be able to leave the pathos of Billy Button behind him and continuing to wonder at John Shaftoe's charitable disposition towards the man.

Frankie Brunnie settled back in the chair and looked across the table at Andrew Cragg. He thought how dejected the man looked, how sorrowful, how awkward. The man's immense

size seemed somehow, to Brunnie, to contribute to his overall
look of despair.

'A copper.' Cragg sighed. 'A copper . . . a cozzer . . . I was
talking to the Old Bill?'

'Yes.' Brunnie shrugged. 'Sorry, mate, but yes, you were.'
He spoke in a soft, gentle tone of voice.

'But he didn't look like a cozzer; he didn't look like
any cozzer I ever knew . . . he needed a shave, he smelled
like he needed a bath and he was drinking beer. What
cozzer drinks on duty? I didn't think they were allowed to
do that.'

'We are not,' Brunnie replied. 'He was off duty, on his way
home. He was working undercover – that job was finished
and he fancied a beer as a way of letting the rush hour die
down a little before he continued to his home. He wasn't
supposed to look like the Old Bill, so you need not feel so
bad about yourself, Andy.'

'Yes . . . but still,' Andrew Cragg moaned, 'imagine telling
a copper.' He looked at the floor and then up to the ceiling.
'I'll never live it down.'

'Well,' Brunnie leaned forward and rested his hands on
the table top, 'you know, Andy . . . you don't mind if I call
you Andy?'

'No, Mr Brunnie, Andy is all right.'

'Good, thank you, it makes things easier. Perhaps I . . . we
can help you there.'

'You can?' Andrew Cragg looked alert.

'Possibly. You see, Andy, if you play your cards right it
never need go beyond this room . . . well, it need never leave
the police station. We can say that we were acting on information received from an anonymous source. It all depends on
how much you are prepared to help us, Andy.' Brunnie paused.
'You see, there's no getting away from it: you are up to your
neck in it. We checked out your story because we could not
ignore it. We sent a sniffer dog to the allotments which you
had identified and, lo and behold, one corpse was just where
you said it would be, and a female, just like you described.
My boss is at the post-mortem right now, but at the allotments
the Home Office pathologist—'

'What's a pathologist?' Cragg asked, blinking his eyes as he looked at Brunnie.

'A pathologist, Andy?' Brunnie replied gently. 'Well, he's the geezer who cuts up dead bodies to see what made them stop working, and he decides whether they've been a victim of crime or not.'

'Oh, yes,' Andrew Cragg's eyes brightened, 'I've seen those geezers on TV. Clever old boys . . .'

'I imagine you have,' Brunnie replied, continuing to speak softly and warmly, anxious to obtain Cragg's cooperation. It was, he felt, as if a voice in his head was saying, *Easy does it, Frankie, you don't want to scare him . . . you want him on your side . . . reel him in . . . that's it, gently does it . . . give him some slack then a little tug . . . then some more slack, then another little tug.*

'I just didn't know that that was what those geezers were called,' Cragg said apologetically.

'So now you know they're called pathologists.' Brunnie smiled. 'Anyway, he saw the bullet holes in her head at the allotment, and we thought then that it would be the likely cause of death . . . so we are assuming it's not a domestic which got out of hand, not an argument between husband and wife which got messy. It's not the case that some geezer was shooting his old trouble and strife with a legally owned shotgun . . . We think it's gangland . . . the old criminal fraternity.'

'What does fraternity mean?' Cragg asked meekly.

'A brotherhood, Andy,' Brunnie explained, 'like when you're part of a gang . . . I'll watch your back and you'll watch mine . . . don't grass anyone up . . . they're family . . . they are yours and you are theirs.'

'Yes . . . fraternity,' Cragg repeated. 'I never knew it was called that.'

'So you're learning, Andy.' Brunnie once again relaxed back in his chair. 'That's life, it's one endless learning curve.' He paused. He thought it time to give the line a little tug. 'So, come on, Andy, you know about the murder – how much else do you know? How much more do you know? Like, especially, who else was involved? We need names, Andy.'

Andrew Cragg remained silent and looked downcast. It was, thought Brunnie, a silence borne out of fear, of a man being a long way out of his depth, rather than a silence borne out of a 'no comment' stubborn refusal to cooperate.

'Look, Andy,' Brunnie leaned forward and continued, 'this little chat we're having is unofficial, it's just an easy little talk between you and me. This is not being recorded; you have no brief sitting beside you advising you what to say or how to answer. I am not writing anything down for you to sign but you will not be going anywhere when you leave the police station, except Brixton Prison.'

'The pokey?' Andrew Cragg sounded alarmed.

'Can't be anything else but remand, Andrew. You're implicated in a murder. So come on,' Brunnie urged, 'get real. You're looking at life behind bars . . . or a few short years . . . or nothing at all . . . it all depends on the extent of your cooperation.'

Andrew Cragg buried his head in his hands and groaned deeply, as if wishing himself a long way away. 'I didn't know he was the Old Bill. I had been drinking all afternoon.'

'And you like your beer, do you, Andy?' Brunnie asked.

'Yes.' Cragg nodded. 'I like it. I'm fond of a drop, I can't deny it.'

'Me as well, Andy. You and me both, mate. I love it, in fact.' Brunnie leaned back and stretched his arms. 'I couldn't survive without pub culture . . . the banter, the bar billiards, the dominos rattling on the table top, the weekly quiz nights . . .'

Andrew Cragg's face brightened. 'Pub culture – I've never heard it called that before . . . And yes, the old nights in the pub, I remember them, they went down well, like the beer. I only drink during the day now, but I remember the nights in the old battle cruisers.'

'So you might like to think that that is something you won't be getting a lot of in the next ten years,' Brunnie suggested.

'Maybe more.'

Craig looked crestfallen. 'Ten years . . .'

'Possibly fifteen or twenty, Andy.' Brunnie spoke calmly but firmly. 'It all depends on the level of your involvement, and it also all depends upon the extent of your cooperation with the police. It really is time for you to decide whose back you are going to scratch. If you want to help yourself you'll assist the police.'

'I want to help myself,' Cragg whined. 'I can't go to prison for that sort of time.'

'Good man.' Brunnie smiled broadly. 'So tell me what happened?'

'I was on the payroll. I was on a decent wedge each week as a gofer . . . you know, go for this, go for that,' Cragg explained. 'Running errands.'

'Yes.' Brunnie nodded. 'I know what a gofer is.'

'Then I got told to carry a body from a lock-up in the East End to the allotments in New Cross.' Cragg spoke haltingly. 'I mean, not all the way to New Cross. I carried it from the lock-up to the van and from the van to the allotments.'

'All right.' Brunnie nodded slightly.

'So we drive out to the East End, to the lock up . . . it was like a storage depot . . . and there is a woman in there, young, very small . . . no clothes on . . . nothing . . . she was terrified. I mean, that look in her eyes . . . Then this geezer, quite a small geezer, comes out of the dark, walks up to her as calm as you please, puts the gun to her head just here,' Cragg placed his right forefinger to the middle of his forehead, 'and shoots her twice. There was hardly a sound.'

'There wouldn't be,' Frankie Brunnie commented, 'not if the end of the gun barrel was pressed on her flesh. There'd be very little sound. But carry on.'

'Then he shot her in the chest. Again, he put the gun right on to her skin . . . no sound to speak of,' Cragg continued. 'Well, then I am told to pick up the body of the girl and carry it outside and dump it in the back of the van – our van – which had been driven to the lock-up. Then we drove to New Cross and the allotments. At the allotments I carried the body from the van into the allotments where a couple of geezers were waiting for us. They were standing by a hole which had been dug in the ground. I put her in the hole like I was told to do then went back to the van and we drove away, leaving the geezers who were waiting for us to fill the hole up . . . and that's what happened.'

'No one saw you?' Brunnie asked.

'No one. It was a wet, dark night . . . raining vertically.' Cragg drew his finger downwards through the air to the table top. 'No one in the street, no one looking out on a night like that. Anyway, I was bunged a good wedge for that and then I went back home to my little drum and I carried on crookin'. You know the sketch – small stuff, just magistrates' court stuff. It was then that I got to thinking that I'm in deep . . . like deep, deep . . . I'm part of a murder, burying a body . . . and I know where they put her, and they know that I know, and who was I? Just a gofer, I wasn't anything special . . . I wasn't needed . . . I could disappear. I was . . . what's that word?' Cragg appealed to Brunnie.

'Expendable?' Brunnie suggested. 'Is that the word you are thinking of?'

'Sounds like it.' Cragg nodded. 'So I left my drum and I moved north of the Old Father. I vanished before I was made to vanish. No one knows me north of the river.'

'All right . . . this is good. You're doing well, Andy.' Brunnie smiled. It was another little tug on the line . . . *bring him in . . . slowly does it.* 'Keep it up, Andy. So, names, Andy. Give me some names.'

'Names!' Cragg gasped.

'Yes, Andy, names . . . we need names.' Brunnie spoke softly yet forcefully. 'We'll start with the easy ones first. You said "we" drove out to the East End and "we" drove to the allotments. So who is "we"? You and who else?'

After a moment's pause, Cragg said, 'Me and a geezer who hired me sometimes and he hired me for that job. A geezer called "Chinese Geordie Davy". He's like a half-caste guy from Newcastle.'

'Mixed race?'

'Whatever the term is. I'm too old for all this political correctness mumbo jumbo. He's from up Newcastle way. He speaks with a weird accent; at least he did back then. I don't know what he is doing these days. I lost contact with him when I moved north of the river, but to be right, it was me that carried the girl's body in the van and "Chinese Geordie Davy" drove.'

'I see.' Frankie Brunnie nodded. 'But he drove you to the lock-up and he was there when the girl was shot?'

'Yes, boss,' Cragg grunted. 'He was standing next to me.'

'All right.' Brunnie scratched the back of his left hand. 'So who hired you?'

'"Chinese Geordie Davy", like I said,' Cragg replied. 'It was him who offered me the wedge to do some tidying up. Somebody else had hired him and his van but he couldn't do it on his Jack Jones. He needed another pair of hands, but me, when I saw the job I reckoned he could have done it easily on his own. She was such a small woman . . . I mean, I've seen bigger schoolgirls.'

'And "Chinese Geordie Davy" said all he wanted you for was to help with some tidying up?' Brunnie clarified.

'Yes. Exactly what I wasn't told. I knew it would be something iffy, like shifting stolen goods, but I didn't think it would be what it was. Never thought that.'

'So you got to the lock-up and you and Davy found this girl on the floor, then what?'

'Then this geezer just stepped out of the shadows, like I told you, walked right up to her, put the gun to her head and pulled the trigger. Twice. Then once in her chest. Then he walked back into the shadows. I don't know why he waited until we got there before he shot her. He could have done it before just as easily. And he wouldn't have had witnesses to worry about.'

'He probably waited until you and "Chinese Geordie Davy" arrived so as to implicate you,' Brunnie explained. 'That was probably his reasoning. It means you could be charged with conspiracy to murder. That carries a life sentence and that possibility hanging over you . . . well, that buys your silence. If he had shot her before you and Davy arrived, and if you and him got rid of the body, you would only have committed the offence of accessory after the fact . . . up to five years in prison. Like I said, he was buying your silence; your silence and Davy's silence. He was pulling you into his boat. If he goes down for a life-stretch, then you go down with him.'

'So why am I telling you this?' Cragg appealed to Brunnie. 'I'm just working against myself.'

'You're telling me because you spilled the beans to an off-duty copper. The cat's out of the bag and it won't be going back in, and you're telling me because you're doing the sensible thing and working for yourself,' Brunnie explained patiently. 'The more you tell me, the more you are working towards a reduced sentence. You know you could even turn Queen's Evidence, go into witness protection; do that and you'd avoid prison completely.'

'Is that possible?' Cragg's voice trembled. 'I have heard of that, but is it possible?'

'Yes.' Frankie Brunnie's eyes watered in reaction to the industrial-grade disinfectant which had been used to clean the floor of the interview room. 'So, let's press on, see where we get to. Tell me about the gunman. What was his name?'

'That I don't know, honest,' Andrew Cragg replied. 'Davy only told me that we were doing a "tidying-up" job; he didn't say who for.'

'All right, so what did this guy look like?'

'Dunno that either. When he came out of the shadows he was wearing a mask, a pig's face mask. He shot the girl then takes the mask off, hides his face with his forearm then he's back in the shadows. After that I never got a good look at him. All I can tell you is that he was a white geezer and quite short. The girl was short and the geezer who killed her was short, and I confess that I didn't want to see him. When I saw what sort of turn was going down, I thought the less I knew the better, so I didn't want the geezer to know I had clocked his old boat race. He sat in the front of the van with Davy; I sat in the rear with the girl's body. At the allotments I put her in the hole and me and Davy walked back to the van and drove away but the shooter stayed. Davy said the shooter was making sure she was covered up and the other guys would run him back to the East End.'

'Good.' Brunnie smiled. 'You're doing well, Andy.'

'So when we get back to where I live Davy hands me a wedge for two hundred sovs . . . and this is ten years ago . . . not bad for a night's work. Then within a few weeks I realize I am into something heavy and that I need to put the river between me and Davy. So I give up my drum and move to

Notting Hill and I forget what I have done. For years I forget it, then I start to remember it, bit by bit.'

'And you tell an undercover police officer, and now we are here.' Brunnie stood. 'Look, Andy, try to remember anything you can . . . any detail. I perhaps shouldn't be telling you this but you've scratched our back so I'll scratch yours: when you come to give a written statement you must say you didn't know you were going to witness a murder and lift a dead body,' Brunnie advised.

'But that's the truth,' Cragg persisted. 'That is how it was.'

'Say that they threatened to shoot you if you didn't cooperate.' Brunnie pressed the bell beside the door of the interview room. 'That's not true but say it anyway. It will be better for you if you claim you acted under duress. You'll get a much lighter sentence. It's worth a punt,' Brunnie emphasized. 'It's what I'd do.'

'That's a good idea.' Cragg's face brightened up. 'I'll do that; I'll say that . . . Thank you, sir.'

'Turning Queen's Evidence will be even better,' Brunnie smiled, 'but you've made an excellent start. Keep it up.'

The door of the interview room opened and the uniformed officer said, 'All finished, sir?'

'Yes, all finished, thank you,' Brunnie replied cheerfully. He then turned to Cragg. 'You're up before the magistrates in a few minutes, Andy. You'll be remanded. I'll come and see you in prison. So remember what you can. Next time I'll be bringing another officer with me and we'll be taking a statement. So think carefully about what I said.'

Victor Swannell and Tom Ainsclough approached the door and what saddened both men, though neither man commented, was the long concrete ramp with handrails at either side which rose up from the pavement at a gentle angle to the front door. The vertical metal grab poles protruded from the bricks – one at either side of the blue painted door, which had a low keyhole and handle. The threshold of the door was level with the top of the inclined ramp. Eventually Swannell said what both men were thinking. 'Wheelchair,' he growled.

'Yes,' Ainsclough sighed in reply, 'but the murder was ten

years ago; a lot can happen in that sort of time. We're still in with a chance. We might yet get a result.'

'We might,' Swannell began to walk up the ramp, 'but somehow I doubt it.'

'I doubt it too,' Ainsclough walked behind Swannell, 'but we'll see what we see and find what we find.'

Swannell reached the top of the ramp, extended his hand and pressed the doorbell, which action caused the sound of the Westminster chimes to echo inside the hallway of the flat.

The door, when it was opened, was done so by a middle-aged man who occupied a wheelchair. The man smiled warmly at his unexpected visitors, as if hungry for company. 'Yes?' he asked of Swannell and Ainsclough.

'Police.' Swannell showed his ID. 'I am Detective Sergeant Swannell and my colleague here is Detective Constable Ainsclough. We're from the Murder and Serious Crime Squad of New Scotland Yard.'

'Oh, really. How can I help you?' He glanced at Swannell's ID and nodded.

Swannell replaced his ID in his jacket pocket. 'You are Mr Hill? Mr Patrick Hill?' he asked.

'Yes . . . yes, I am he.' Hill looked puzzled.

'Well . . .' Swannell began, 'I'm sorry if this is a bit indelicate, but can we ask you if you rented an allotment in the Malpas Road allotments about eight or ten years ago?'

'Oh . . . that's hardly the sort of thing I can do.' Hill tapped the wheels of his wheelchair and forced a smile. 'I came into this world fifty-four years ago this coming November. I was told it was a particularly cold and windy day . . . and seventeen years later I came off my motorbike at great speed. I've been in a wheelchair ever since.'

'I'm sorry,' Swannell offered. 'We noticed the ramp and knew what it implied, but as my colleague said, a lot can happen in ten years . . . so we rang your doorbell anyway.'

'No . . . no need to be sorry, squire.' Hill clasped his hands together in front of him. 'It was hardly your fault. You were probably not even alive then, thirty-seven years ago, and if you were alive, you wouldn't have reached adulthood and I have made the adjustment. You go through all the anger and the reproach and self-reproach and the sense of unfairness and injustice, in my case because the accident wasn't my fault, and then you accept there are things you can do and things you can't do and digging an allotment is on the "can't do" list.'

'Were you living here, at this address, about ten years ago, sir?'

'Yes . . . good heavens, yes, this little one-bedroom flat adapted for the needs of the physically challenged – low toilet, hoist over the bed and bath – this little palace has been my home since I was twenty-two years of age. It's been my little private space for the last thirty-two years. I thought, "life's a bitch, then you die", then I thought I'm going to be in the clay soon enough anyway and we're all a long time dead, so I may as well keep walking the dog. So I put the plastic bag away.'

Swannell smiled. 'That's a good attitude. Good for you.'

'It's the only attitude.' Hill was thin of face, had grey straggly hair and wore a baggy yellow T-shirt and faded denims. His feet were encased in a pair of white running shoes. 'I've filled my life by taking an interest in current affairs, reading and watching films and drama and documentaries on TV. I live in a little quarter square mile of London. I have a post office, a library and a wheelchair-friendly supermarket, but I have never turned a wheel on the Malpas Road allotments. That's why I assume you are here . . . the body that was found there or found to have been buried there the other day?'

'You know about that?' Swannell raised his left eyebrow.

'Yes, it's the talk of the post office and the library,' Hill explained. 'It's caused quite a bit of local interest.'

'Well, yes.' Swannell nodded. 'We are here about that but we can't tell you what we found.'

'Fair enough,' Hill replied in a contented tone of voice. 'So why knock on my door?'

'Because the person who rented the allotment at the time we are interested in, about ten years ago, rented it under the name of Patrick Hill and gave this house – your flat – as being his address.'

'Ha!' Patrick Hill scoffed. 'That is quite clever: find a guy who lives locally who is not going to want to rent an allotment, follow him home, obtain his name from the electoral roll in the public library . . . very clever.'

'Yes,' Swannell glanced to his left, 'it's fairly obvious that that was what happened – that's how it was done. We are sorry to have been of bother.'

'No bother at all.' Patrick Hill smiled. 'Hardly anyone knocks on my door and I appreciate all the company I can get. I get cabin fever within my little four walls, what with the days blending and merging as they do.'

'Well.' Swannell turned to go, as did Ainsclough. 'Thanks anyway.'

'Take care,' Ainsclough added.

'So all we know about the geezer who rented the allotment was that he was in his forties at the time. He had a boxer's bashed-in nose and a tattoo of a spider on his left hand.' Vicary reclined in his chair.

'Yes, sir,' Swannell replied. 'We'll trace him if we can using that description – age, distinguishing features . . . we might get a result. I'll do that directly.'

'Thank you, Victor.' Vicary pyramided his hands in front of his face. 'We do know the name of the felon who hired Andrew Cragg. What was his name?'

'"Chinese Geordie Davy",' Brunnie advised.

'Ah, yes.' Vicary smiled. 'He will be a real-live felon; a name like that springs from a culture. You couldn't invent a name like that. If I was a betting man I'd wager large sums of money that there was once a felon in this fair city called the Artful Dodger who Charles Dickens would have met. Dickens grew up in poverty and later in life he was a prison visitor. I am quite happy that Dickens invented the name Gradgrind for a schoolteacher. I think we can all recall Mr or Miss Gradgrinds from our school days. Usually they taught maths. But the Artful Dodger existed all right and his name has become immortalized, and in the same way, "Chinese Geordie Davy" exists . . . so let's find him. All right, can you and Frankie team up on that please?'

'Yes, boss,' Swannell replied for him and Frankie Brunnie. 'So . . . Penny, I think you've got a possible result for us?' Vicary looked at Penny Yewdall. 'Yes, sir.' Penny Yewdall sat forward and consulted a computer printout which she held in her hands. 'It's feedback from the missing persons database. We have a possible identity of the person whose remains we found at the allotment. She is one Victoria Keynes, spelled with an "e" but pronounced "Kaynes".

She was twenty-six years of age when she was reported missing by her parents – right age, right height, just five feet one inch tall, reported missing ten years ago, last March. Another girl was reported missing at the same time but she had an address in Croydon, and although not a million miles away from Victoria Keynes's home she was nearly six feet tall with the ironic surname of "Short". So I think that Victoria Keynes is our girl.'

'All right, Penny, you and Tom team up – find out what you can about Victoria Keynes. The investigation into the Cornwall Crescent Gang now takes second place. The importation of cocaine is a serious crime, but it's trumped by murder.'

It was Thursday, 12.33 hours.

FOUR

Thursday, 13.40 hours – 22.40 hours

Tom Ainsclough and Penny Yewdall stood side by side in front of the outside door of a bungalow on Devonshire Way, Addington, south-east London. Ainsclough tapped loudly but also reverently on the door using the time-honoured police officers' knock . . . *tap*, *tap* . . . *tap*. As the two officers waited for a response from within the house they looked curiously around them. The house itself, they noted, was a bungalow and occupied a corner plot. It was of modest size with a garden which the officers both thought was close to the state of being fairly described as 'overgrown'. A long-past-its-prime wooden shed stood in the corner of the front lawn. Further away, the garden of the neighbouring houses provided a plethora of rich foliage. The air was filled with birdsong.

The door was opened, slowly and silently, by a tall, middle-aged woman with angular facial features, which suggested to Tom Ainsclough a woman, who, when in her prime, would most likely have been considered something of a beauty. She wore her hair close cut and was dressed in a white blouse with a calf-length green skirt. She wore black shoes with a modest, sensible heel. She had a brooch at the collar of the blouse, a watch on her left wrist and a wedding ring and engagement ring but no other jewellery. She wore no make-up that neither Yewdall nor Ainsclough could detect, except for a trace of very pale lipstick. 'Yes?' she said in a haughty manner as she looked down at the officers from the elevated position of her doorstep.

'Police, ma'am.' Yewdall produced her ID from her handbag. Ainsclough took his from his jacket pocket.

'Oh . . .' The woman gasped.

'Mrs Keynes?' Yewdall asked.

'Yes . . . that is I.' Mrs Keynes's haughty tone was replaced with a note of fear.

'Are you the mother of one Victoria Keynes?' Yewdall asked.

'Oh . . .' Mrs Keynes put her hand to her mouth. The officers noted she had an artist's hands, narrow and with particularly long fingers. 'Yes, yes, I am . . .' Mrs Keynes's voice cracked. 'Is there news of her?'

'Possibly,' Yewdall replied softly. 'Do you think we might come in, please? It would be better than doing this on the doorstep.'

'Yes . . . yes, of course . . . I am sorry.' Mrs Keynes stepped backwards and stood on one side as Yewdall and Ainsclough entered the front hallway of the bungalow. It was, they noted, a cleanly kept home which smelled of air freshener and wood polish. There was no sound from within the house, no radio or daytime TV. A man approached the officers, walking down the hallway from the direction of what the officers saw, by reason of the open door, to be the living room. The man was noticeably shorter than the woman and wore a lightweight blue woollen pullover despite the summer heat.

'It's the police, Eric,' the woman explained to the man. 'They have called on us about Victoria.'

'Oh . . .' The man's jaw sagged and he put his hand up to his chest. 'Please . . .' he addressed the officers, 'come through here.' He led Yewdall and Ainsclough down the hallway and back to the living room from whence he came.

'Excuse me,' Mrs Keynes said in a hushed tone, causing the officers to stop before entering the living room, 'my husband has a heart condition and wears a pacemaker,' she explained. 'He must avoid exertion and shock.'

'I see.' Tom Ainsclough nodded. 'We'll be as diplomatic as we can be.'

'I'd appreciate that.' Mrs Keynes smiled. 'We both would. There is a definite skill in breaking bad news. I hope and trust that you are both possessed of it.'

'You think we have come bearing bad news?' Yewdall held eye contact with Mrs Keynes.

'Yes, frankly I do. What else can it be if it's about Victoria after this length of time?' Mrs Keynes returned to the front door of the bungalow and shut it gently. She then re-joined the officers. 'After ten years I doubt that you are going to tell us that she is alive and well and married with a growing family. So, please, if you'd go into the living room? Just follow Eric, my husband.'

'Please take a seat.' Eric Keynes swept an extended hand from left to right as the officers entered the room, indicating the settee and two armchairs. Yewdall and Ainsclough sat side by side on the settee while Mr and Mrs Keynes each sat in an armchair, gravitating, quite naturally, to one or the other as if, thought Yewdall, they had been designated 'his' and 'hers' status, and had acquired such a status over the years of the Keynes's marriage.

After a moment's pause, Yewdall spoke in a soft manner. 'We are sorry to inform you that some remains . . . some human remains have been discovered. We believe they may, and I emphasise *may* be the remains of your daughter Victoria, whom you reported missing some ten years ago. A positive match has still to be made but we know when the remains were placed where they were found, and that is about the same time that you reported Victoria missing, and we have determined her height to be similar to Victoria's height.'

'Were they, the remains you mention, were they found yesterday?' Mrs Keynes asked. 'Sometime in the early afternoon?'

'Yes.' Yewdall nodded gently. 'I believe that they were.'

Mrs Keynes's head sank forward and then she looked up at her husband. 'I told you . . . I told you so.' Mrs Keynes then addressed Yewdall and Ainsclough. 'Someone walked over my grave yesterday in the early afternoon . . . just after lunchtime. I have never experienced the like before, but I was out shopping and I was walking alongside the supermarket car park when I felt myself being consumed by something and I felt a distinct chill go through me. The sensation remained for a few seconds and in certain circumstances a second can be quite a long time. It remained long enough to be significant and distinctive. It was real and it was tangible. I returned home and told Eric that someone had walked over my grave. That must have been the precise moment our daughter's remains were discovered. Her soul was released and she visited me on her way to the hereafter. We were always very close, she and I. We had more than a mother and daughter bond – we had a special connection.'

'There is still no evidence . . .' Yewdall began.

'It will be Victoria.' Mrs Keynes spoke emphatically. 'Do not dismiss the paranormal. I am not a psychic but I have learned not to dismiss the paranormal. I have seen ghosts where other people cannot see anything and I have had contact with the dead and I know, I just *know*, that Victoria came to visit me yesterday in the early afternoon.'

'We'll see what Timmy does,' Eric Keynes added. 'We'll probably know before you do if the remains of which you speak are those of our daughter. If they are those of our daughter he will be very helpful today and tomorrow.'

'Timmy?' Tom Ainsclough queried.

'Timmy . . . yes . . . he's the poltergeist who lives in this house,' Eric Keynes explained in a calm, matter-of-fact manner. 'He's about ten years old and plays pranks from time to time but he also does helpful things for us.'

'He puts milk in the fridge to stop it going sour and he switches off the oven to prevent our meal being ruined,' Mrs Keynes added, equally calmly.

'The first we knew that there was a presence in this house was shortly after we moved in – that was when Victoria was about three years old, during the summer months, about this time of year, in fact, and then later that year, in the autumn, we returned home one Saturday when there was about twenty minutes of daylight left and that path out there . . .' Eric Keynes pointed over his shoulder to the garden at the rear of the bungalow, '. . . that path out there was covered in a blanket of leaves and I turned to Gillian and said, "Well, that's a job for me tomorrow. I'll have to sweep all those leaves up".'

'That's what he said.' Gillian Keynes smiled at Yewdall, but there was a faraway look in her eyes.

'So I got up the next morning,' Eric Keynes continued, 'after a calm, windless night, and knock me down with a feather but there wasn't a single leaf on the pathway. Not one.'

'That's true.' Gillian Keynes clasped her hands together and rested them on her lap. She still possessed a distant look in her eyes. 'We knew then that we had a fourth person in the house. But as well as helping us, he plays pranks. He hides things and we find them weeks later in the most unlikely places, like the framed photograph of the three of us, me, Eric and Victoria, taken for us by another holidaymaker when we went to the Gower Peninsula in Wales one summer. We kept it on the mantelpiece and suddenly it wasn't there, it had just gone missing. Months went by and then one day Eric found it in the garden shed standing on top of an upturned plant pot.'

'Weird,' Yewdall commented. 'I couldn't live like that.'

'There is no sense of fear . . . not with Timmy,' Eric Keynes explained. 'We contacted a spiritualist who visited us and was able to contact him, and who told us that his name was Jonathan and he was very happy when he lived here. But when there have been difficulties, Timmy . . . we still call him Timmy . . . becomes particularly helpful. When Victoria disappeared a lot of things were done for us. We'd get up in the morning to find the kettle had been boiled for us to make our morning tea, and once we returned home to find all the washing up, which had accumulated in the sink, had been done for us.'

'How interesting,' Yewdall sighed, 'but I still couldn't live like that.'

'The point is,' Eric Keynes explained, 'that if the remains are those of Victoria we can expect Timmy to become particularly helpful. It'll be his way of being supportive of us through our time of need, which is why I believe that we will know before you know that our daughter's remains have been found.'

'I always thought poltergeists were harmful and violent,' Ainsclough commented.

'They have that reputation,' Eric Keynes glanced down at the carpet, 'but they are not all like that. Fortunately.'

'Unfortunately we can't rely on the supernatural to confirm the identity of the remains as being those of Victoria – we need to be more scientific.' Tom Ainsclough held eye contact with Eric Keynes, and as he did so he detected a coldness in them. 'We'll come to that in a moment, but what can you tell us about Victoria at the time she disappeared, assuming the remains are hers?'

'Assuming . . .' Eric Keynes repeated. 'You wouldn't be assuming that if you were not certain in yourself that they are the remains of our daughter, but as you say, everything points to them being our daughter's bones . . .'

'Is that Victoria?' Penny Yewdall spoke suddenly, indicating a framed photograph on the mantelpiece.

'Yes,' Gillian Keynes looked longingly at the photograph, 'that is Victoria. She was our only child. She was very warm spirited, a very pleasant young woman . . . we loved her deeply. She worked in a bank, just a lowly position. She was quite short and was a little self-conscious about it.'

'She took after me,' Eric Keynes shrugged, 'me, her little old dad. It isn't the case that sons take after their fathers and daughters take after their mothers . . . that might be a rule of thumb but it doesn't always apply and it didn't apply in the case of our little nuclear family, otherwise Vicky would have been as tall as her mother, a lanky five feet ten inches . . . instead she was a half pint, like her old man. I'm five foot two inches tall.'

'Then she got married.' Mrs Keynes looked down and to one side.

'You sound as though you did not approve of the match,' Yewdall observed.

'We didn't care for him at all,' Eric Keynes growled. 'Not at all, not one little bit, and neither did our dogs.'

'The dogs?' Yewdall queried.

'We had two mongrels, about the size of a Springer Spaniel. They looked like scaled-down Labradors and both had calm, very placid natures,' Gillian Keynes explained. 'Sooty and Sweep, we called them – hardly original, but that was what we called them and when he first came into the house, instead of barking at him as they would normally react to a stranger coming into their domain, they both turned away from him and sat in the corner of the room, just staring at him.'

'That says a lot,' Yewdall observed.

'It says everything.' Eric Keynes continued to growl. 'Dogs and children don't lie, and they have an intuition which adult humans lack, but he had all the superficial charm of the classic psychopath. He was tall and handsome and wealthy, with his

black Porsche and its tinted windows. He was a city trader
and much older than her but Victoria . . . Vicky, she was
awestruck. She believed that she had fallen on her feet, but
we, well, we shared the dogs' opinion of him . . . We didn't
like him at all and that wasn't the worst of it . . . the full worst
of it was that it was me who introduced them.'

'Really?' Yewdall raised her eyebrows.

'Yes. Try living with that.' Eric Keynes sighed. 'I went to
visit my brother Zolton over in Pinner and Vicky came with
me . . . on a Sunday . . . just for the ride out, and he was
there. He had some business dealings with him.'

'Zolton?' Tom Ainsclough queried.

'My brother . . . our father is Polish and our mother's
English. They had two sons; the eldest was named after his
Polish grandfather and the youngest after his English grandfather, so we became Zolton and Eric Keynes. Our father
anglicized his name before he married,' Keynes explained,
'but that's how they met . . . when I suggested she come with
me to visit Zolton.'

'She was very reluctant,' Gillian Keynes added, 'but I
persuaded her to go. I said her uncle Zolton would love to see
her . . . and that was Victoria, so very compliant. She went
and because she went she met her husband . . . we're both to
blame . . . and they married with indecent haste.' Gillian
Keynes sighed. 'It was all so fast . . . all too fast.'

'And he would be?' Yewdall held her pen poised over her
notepad.

'He would be one Elliot Woodhuyse,' Eric Keynes informed.
'His name is spelled H-U-Y-S-E but pronounced "house" . . .
Woodhuyse.'

'I see.' Penny Yewdall wrote the name on her notepad.
'Interesting name,' she commented, and then looked up at
Gillian Keynes and said, 'but Victoria was reported to be a
missing person under her maiden name. We have her in our
files as Victoria Keynes with her parents as her next of kin.'

'Yes . . . that,' Gillian Keynes explained, 'is because the
marriage was not a resounding success. It lasted all of eighteen
months. She left him and returned to live under her maiden
name.'

'I see,' Yewdall said again and tapped her notepad thoughtfully. 'We also have an alternative address for her as being . . . where is it?' She turned to the pages of her notepad. 'Ah, yes, here it is . . . c/o Parker, in Samos Road, Anerley.'

'Yes, Dorothy Parker. She and Victoria were friends from the time she worked in the bank and they kept in touch with each other. Victoria moved in with her when she walked out on her husband – it was only later that she returned to live here and only for a very brief period before she disappeared. She had not even removed all her possessions from Dorothy's house, but she often went out and visited Dorothy Parker,' Gillian Keynes said. 'The two girls were very close.'

'We'll have to call on her,' Ainsclough stated.

'I'd advise it,' Eric Keynes once again growled.

'She'll be able to tell you more about Victoria than we could, I am sure she will.' Gillian Keynes sat back in the armchair she occupied. 'As is the way of it . . . friends know things which parents are not privy to.'

'Do you know if any suspicion fell on Elliot Woodhuyse in respect of your daughter's disappearance?' Yewdall asked.

'Yes it did, but not for long,' Eric Keynes advised. 'He had a cast-iron alibi for the time of Vicky's disappearance. As I recall, he was north of the border, up in Scotland on a business trip, and the police told us they don't investigate the disappearance of adults unless there is clear evidence of foul play.'

'Yes,' Yewdall confirmed, 'that is indeed the policy.'

'So there was no body and therefore no investigation.' Eric Keynes sighed. 'Her case went cold and her file gathered dust.'

'It is often the manner of it,' Yewdall replied apologetically. She then asked, 'Was it in keeping with Victoria's personality that she would disappear for extended periods?'

'No.' Eric Keynes shook his head. 'Definitely not – she wasn't at all like that. She would always let us know where she was and what time she intended to return home. She was always very good like that.'

'And your suspicion, off the record?' Yewdall asked.

'Off the record? Her husband did her in or paid for someone

to do her in while he was up in bonnie Scotland fixing his cast-iron alibi.' Eric Keynes spoke slowly then fell silent, setting his jaw firm.

'So what do you think his motivation was?' Yewdall asked.

'Money.' Gillian Keynes made the motion of rubbing her thumb and forefinger together. 'Ye olde filthy lucre. We never had much – we were both schoolteachers. Teaching never did pay well. In a sense it is vastly more important than teaching any other age range . . . without that foundation, no person can learn anything . . . but we were able to afford to buy this little house . . . Woodhuyse was dripping with the stuff, though, and so Victoria was confident of a good settlement.'

'So she was proceeding with a divorce?' Yewdall clarified.

'Oh, yes, and she was doing so with a lawyer who was attacking the case like a hungry wolf. She began to demonstrate a ruthlessness about her which we had not seen. Victoria was the wronged party and her lawyer was determined to take Woodhuyse to the cleaners on her behalf.' Gillian Keynes glanced towards the fireplace. 'I wonder if it was worth it? A young woman's life . . . for money? It is as my old grandmother used to say: "There's no pockets in a shroud".'

'Well,' Tom Ainsclough glanced at Penny Yewdall, who nodded in agreement and closed her notebook. 'Thank you, this has been very useful. We still have to confirm the identity of the remains. We can do that by taking a sample of your DNA or we can compare the teeth in the remains to your daughter's dental records. Do you have a preference?'

'Her dental records, if you don't mind,' Eric Keynes replied quickly. 'I'm sorry but I care not for the idea of my mouth being swabbed so as to confirm my daughter's death.'

'Fair enough.' Ainsclough smiled briefly. 'I'd probably feel the same. Who was her dentist?'

'Mr Graham,' Eric Keynes advised. 'He's been our family dentist for ever and Vicky never changed to another one.'

'Mr Graham,' Yewdall repeated. 'I can remember that.'

'Percival Graham by the nameplate on his surgery door. His surgery is a converted semi-detached house further down the road . . . in that direction.' Eric Keynes pointed to his left. 'You can't miss it.'

'Thank you. We'll call on him with a warrant to oblige him to release Victoria's dental records to our forensic pathologists' team.' Tom Ainsclough stood. 'Thank you again for your information, but I am afraid you must prepare yourself for some bad news.'

'No,' Eric Keynes also stood, 'it will be good news. After this length of time it will be good news. It will be Vicky and we can now bring closure to it all. We'll have a funeral . . . and then we'll have a grave to visit, and that is a lot, lot better than not knowing. I'll see you to the door.'

Victor Swannell approached a blue-painted door for the second time that day. On the second occasion he did it in the company of Frankie Brunnie. The second of the two blue-painted doors was of a lighter shade of blue, much faded and indeed even peeling in some places. The door was the front door of a house in Raul Road in Peckham, SE15. Solid Victorian houses stood at either end of the short road, with low-rise post-Second World War flats occupying both sides of the road in the middle section.

'A bomb fell here,' Victor Swannell remarked as he glanced up and down the length of the road.

'You think?' Brunnie replied with a smile.

'I know . . .' Swannell returned the smile, 'in the Hitler war. You see how the line of the original Victorian houses is interrupted by a small pocket of post-war, more recent developments?'

'Yes.' Frankie Brunnie ran his eye along the length of the road. 'Yes, I see that.'

'Well, it's always a sign that a bomb fell and destroyed a number of original houses. This is pretty classic; it's a very good example of that having happened.' Swannell knocked on the door. 'In fact, it's probably as good an example as you'll find anywhere.'

The door was opened slowly. A man peered out of the gloom of his house, blinking against the bright sunlight. 'You're the Old Bill.' The man, who stood on the threshold, was short, had oily-coloured skin, narrow eyes and long black hair which did not, in the opinion of both officers, suit a man of his years, being, they guessed, late middle-aged.

'Are you asking or telling?' Brunnie replied.

'Neither.' The man scowled. 'I'm guessing.'

'Well, you guess correctly.' Swannell showed his ID. 'We are the Old Bill . . . Murder and Serious Crime Squad, New Scotland Yard, to be exact.'

'Scotland Yard!' The man gasped. 'That's premier league.'

'Well, we'd like to think so.' Frankie Brunnie also showed his ID. 'We're looking for a geezer called "Chinese Geordie Davy" . . . also known as David Danby. He's known to us and this is his given address.'

'That's me.' The man peered at Brunnie's ID card. 'What can I do for you?'

'We'd like a chat, Davy,' Swannell replied.

'But I never did no murder . . . never done no serious crime.' Danby became agitated.

'Nothing to worry about then, have you, Davy?' Swannell replaced his ID card in his jacket pocket. 'So, let's have a chat. We can do it inside, or here on the step, or down the Yard.'

'Don't know how I can help you.' Danby spoke in a strong Newcastle accent. 'I told you I never done no murder.'

'So, like I said, nothing to worry about, have you?' Swannell replied. 'Do you like putting on street theatre for your neighbours or can we come inside?'

Danby mumbled something unintelligible to both officers, turned and walked into the gloom of the hallway of the Victorian-era house in which he lived. Swannell and Brunnie followed him, shutting the door gently behind them.

'Not much to show for a life of crime, is it?' Danby shrugged his shoulders. 'They always said that crime doesn't pay, but would I listen? Mind you, I got to stay in bed all morning . . . all day if I wanted to, no running for the bus for me . . . so there is that. I have had a laid-back life . . . sometimes I had money, sometimes I was hungry. If I needed money I'd go crookin'; sometimes I'd go crookin' to get remanded. If you did it on a Friday you'd get your cot and three until the following Monday morning . . . and if you boxed clever and did it just before the old Easter weekend you'd get clean sheets and hot food from Thursday until Tuesday morning.'

'Got it all worked out, haven't you, Davy?' Frankie Brunnie glanced round him. It was true, he thought, 'Chinese Geordie Davy' did not have a lot to show for a life of crime. He saw a small, untidy, very cramped living room, an old TV set and clothing strewn hither and thither. The room smelled musty and damp.

'Well, that was the advice given to me by the old lags when I was a young street turk, building up my street cred. Now I'm an old lag and I hand the same advice down to today's street turks. So . . . you'll not be calling on me social, like . . . what's it about?'

'Nope.' Swannell also read the room and felt grateful that he and Brunnie would not be staying long. 'You're right, this isn't a social call, Davy. It's a little bit more serious.'

'Well, I haven't been a wrong 'un for a while,' David Danby protested. 'Not for a good few weeks.'

'That's "a while" for you, is it, Davy?' Brunnie sighed. 'A few weeks?'

'Yes, for me that's a while. I had a bit of money. I've still got about thirty sovs left. I won a hundred and fifty sovs on the horses so I haven't had to go out crookin'. Mind you, if you set that against the bundle I gambled and lost over the years, well, all told, I've lost big time.'

'Well . . .' Brunnie smiled briefly, 'that's the old way of it, Davy. That's why the bookmakers stay in business. If everybody saw it like that the bookies would go out of business.'

'I dare say that's the old truth.' Danby sighed. 'I mean, you get Gamblers Anonymous but you don't get Bookies Anonymous. But I'll be back at the bookies when the money gets low, chasing that big win – that'll be me – or out thieving what I can . . . food to eat or stuff to sell.'

'Only you can stop yourself, Davy,' Swannell growled, 'but let's cut to the chase . . . ten years ago . . .'

'Ten years!' Danby scoffed. 'Look, I can't remember what I did yesterday. How do you expect me to remember what I did ten years ago?'

'Few of us can, Davy,' Brunnie pressed, 'but we all remember incidents. So, ten years ago . . . one dark, rainy night . . . we have good information that about ten years ago you were involved in a murder.'

'Murder!' Danby held up both hands, palms outwards. 'Now just hold on. I may never have been made the blackboard monitor but I never done no murder. I told you . . . never done no murder. That's gospel, squire. I swear . . . I never stopped no one's ticker. Never.'

'Wait on, Davy,' Swannell spoke calmly, 'we didn't say you actually did the deed, but we have information that you helped clean up the mess.'

David Danby fell silent.

'A young woman,' Swannell continued, 'a small, petite girl barely five feet tall. You arrived at a lock-up and found her as naked as the day she was born . . . sitting on the floor, terrified, and you stood there while some other geezer with a pig's face mask on shot her in the head . . . twice . . . then once in the heart.'

'As soon as he shot her he took the mask off,' Brunnie continued. 'Why did he do that? Why wasn't he bothered about you seeing him, you and the other geezer? Yet he didn't want the girl to see him, even though two seconds later she'd be dead.'

'That puzzles us,' Swannell spoke softly, 'but I dare say we'll get to the bottom of it. Then you drove her from the East End to the allotments in New Cross, you and the gunman in the front, and another geezer in the back with the girl's dead body. The other guy carried her from the van into the allotments and dumped her into a hole in one of the allotments. Then you and the other guy drove away and the shooter and two other men stayed behind to cover up the body.'

'Remember now, Davy?' Brunnie pressed. 'Is it all coming back?'

David Danby sank into one of the armchairs in his dimly lit flat. 'So who grassed me up?' he whined. 'Who do I have to thank for this?'

'Can't say,' Brunnie replied, 'and we won't say . . . but do you remember now? Does it all flood back as clear as daylight?'

'Has to be Cragg.' Danby lowered his head. 'It has to be. It could only be Cragg. I never did trust that big geezer. Never did. He had a reputation for having a loose tongue . . . always running off at the mouth.'

'It didn't have to be him; it didn't have to be anyone, Davy,' Brunnie towered over Danby, 'but let's just say for a minute it was Cragg . . . let's just say you're right and then let's say he's doing the right thing . . .'

'Giving information to save his neck,' Danby sneered. 'He'd do that, all right . . . that's not the right thing . . . Cragg . . . he'd shop his own mother.'

'It might fly in the face of your code of ethics, Davy, but it is the sensible thing to do.' Swannell stood beside Frankie Brunnie. 'It's what I'd do if I was in his shoes.'

'And me,' Brunnie added, 'without hesitation, it's what I'd do. Help yourself or work against yourself. I'm sure some cozzer has given you that bit of advice before.'

'Many times,' Danby exhaled, 'like about as many times as I have had a hot curry.'

'So it's time to decide what you're going to do, Davy,' Swannell pressed. 'Work for yourself or work against yourself. We'll be seeing the other geezer later today.'

'Cragg!' Danby spat the name.

'Whoever . . . but the first one to give information helps himself the most,' Swannell reiterated.

'I reckon I'll deny it all.' Danby sat back in the chair, developing a smug expression as he did so. 'I'll do that, I suppose.'

'You can't very well deny it, Davy.' Brunnie grinned.

'Perhaps, but you're not recording this and I haven't signed anything.' Danby spoke sourly.

'It's still a bit late, Davy,' Swannell advised. 'Now that we know you are the man, all we need to do is find some way of linking you to the crime . . . just one more witness will do . . . like the geezers who dug the grave. If we can find them and if they'll testify that you drove the van that night, that will clinch it very nicely indeed.'

'So what can I do?' Danby rested his head in his hands.

'We keep telling you, Davy . . . it's time to start working

for yourself,' Brunnie urged. 'Look, Davy, you're in a real mess and you can either dig yourself in deeper . . . or you can begin to dig yourself out. So which is it going to be?' 'I want to climb out,' Danby replied wearily. 'I'm too old for the pokey.'

'No one's ever too old for the pokey,' Swannell snarled. 'We have put geezers away for the first time who are in their seventies. There are geezers in the slammer who are serving whole life sentences and they'll die in there. So right now, you appear to be an accessory after the fact . . . that could still get you five years . . . even ten.'

'Ten years . . .' Danby moaned.

'Yes . . . think of it . . . the next time you walk into a pub or a betting shop you'll be in your mid-sixties,' Swannell continued. 'No more beer or lucky wins on the horses for you for the next few years, but plenty of free food.'

'You know, when I woke up this morning I had a notion it was going to be a bad day.' Danby shook his head slowly. 'I just did not think that it was going to be quite this bad. It's like the bottom has fallen out of my life.'

'That's how it is sometimes, Davy,' Brunnie commented. 'The past has a way of catching up with us all. You know, we can see you are just a gofer . . . just a small cog in a huge machine. No big-time crook lives like this. You'll have seen how the big-time crooks live: big house, flash cars, trophy wives and girlfriends . . .'

'Yes, yes . . . I've seen all that.' Danby ran his stubby fingers through his greasy hair.

'Well, they are the geezers we really want to nail,' Swannell added. 'The big-time Joe's . . . not the small Joe's like you. You know we can even help you avoid prison altogether. We'll drop all charges in return for a testimony . . . you know . . . witness protection . . . we can offer that.'

'No.' Danby held up his hand. 'I don't feel bad about anything I've done . . . not ever . . . all down the years, but I haven't eaten well for a few days now and the money I won on that horse is practically all gone. Prison food isn't good but it's better than nothing . . . and I haven't changed my bed linen for six months. I haven't had a bath in the same length of time . . . just a strip wash in front of the kitchen sink each day. I keep my clothes clean, though, I do that. I always seem to manage to have enough coins for the laundrette.'

'I confess, Davy,' Brunnie observed, 'you are a lot cleaner than we thought you'd be. You're a lot cleaner than your old drum, so there is some self-respect there. It seems to us like you're a man who'd want to do himself a favour or two. OK, Davy, on your feet, you're coming back with us. We want to know who hired you and your van for a night's work. You hired "Big Andy" Cragg to help you, but who hired you? Who bought your time?'

'Enjoy the ride to Scotland Yard, Davy.' Swannell took hold of Danby's left forearm as he stayed quiet. 'Look out of the car window during the drive . . . look at the streets, the houses, the people . . . look at the young women in their summer clothes and remember . . . just think that when you see the like again will all be down to you and the level of cooperation you offer.'

'A detective inspector? I am honoured.' Philip Standish inclined his head to one side. 'Usually I get detective constables . . . once in a while a detective sergeant, but a DI . . .'

'All my team are committed,' Vicary explained, holding eye contact with Standish yet noticing the flattened boxer's nose and the spider tattoo on the back of the man's left hand. 'So you've got me.'

'I won't complain.' Standish sat in a large, high-backed armchair in the TV room of the Salvation Army Shelter. 'So how did you find me?'

'We have this as your last address, Philip,' Vicary explained. 'It was the obvious place to call.' Vicary glanced around him; the TV high out of reach, the yellow and black floor tiles, men sitting in chairs, not talking to each other, staring into space, comfortably out of earshot of Harry Vicary and Philip Standish. 'So, ten years ago you took an allotment in New Cross . . .'

'I was told to,' Standish replied.

'By whom?'

'Just a geezer . . . never knew his name. I think he was working for another geezer,' Standish replied in a strong

London accent. 'I was offered two hundred sovs . . . that was ten years ago. Even today I wouldn't sniff at two hundred sovs for digging an allotment.'

'What did you have to do?' Vicary asked.

'I had to take an allotment in the name of Hill . . . Patrick Hill of an address I can't remember but I had it written down.'

'OK.' Vicary nodded. 'Then what?'

'I had to dig it; I had to work the soil over. Go there two or three times a week and turn the soil over – just the bottom half of the plot,' Standish explained. 'Not plant nothing, just turn the soil and keep it turned . . . a hundred in advance, the second hundred when I was told to leave it.'

'How long were you doing that for?' Vicary asked.

'A few weeks . . . winter and spring time. It was hard old work. I never was a fit man.'

'Not even as a boxer?' Vicary smiled.

Standish touched his nose. 'No . . . I got my nose smashed when someone tried to flatten my face with a spade. This was a lot of years ago when I was still a teenager. They could have rebuilt it today . . . those days . . . well, they just said "get on and live with it and think yourself lucky you're not brain-dead or even dead". If the flat of the spade had struck my forehead instead of my face I would have been either brain-dead or outright dead. He got six months' youth custody and I got this life sentence.' He pointed to his nose. 'It's made me a marked man all my days, like, "Can you describe the man who snatched your handbag?" and then I'm huckled. Bet that's how you traced me.'

'You had no luck,' Vicary commented. 'Anyway, did you do anything other than turn the soil?'

'No . . . nothing else,' Standish replied, 'nothing else at all. Once in a while the geezer who hired me came to check I was working, just glanced at me from the other side of the privet, nodded to me and went away.'

'Did you ever notice any other activity at the allotment?' Vicary asked.

'Only possibly once, quite early on,' Standish replied. 'I was still getting to know the plot . . . getting familiar with the soil, but I came one day and I thought "someone else has been here" – the soil was still turned but it looked different somehow.

I was still only a few weeks in when I noticed that. I never noticed anything like it again . . . so I thought that's just me imagining things . . . and carried on digging and kept on digging for the next few weeks, but towards the end I reckon I got to know that little patch of London so well I could say definitely if someone had been at it when I wasn't there.' Standish took a deep breath, struggling as he did so as if suffering from a chronic pulmonary condition. 'Then one day the geezer who hired me came to the allotment and gave me one hundred sovs and said, "Right, that's you paid up." Then I gave up the allotment and never returned.'

'Thanks, Phil.' Vicary took a ten-pound note from his pocket. 'Go and buy yourself a beer. That's been useful.'

'You don't want a statement?' Standish took the note greedily.

'Not unless you can tell me the name of the geezer who hired you?' Vicary stood.

'Sorry . . . I can't do that . . . never knew him from Adam. I was drinking in a battle cruiser where a lot of guys will work for cash-in-hand drink . . . you used to go there to get hired as much as drink beer. The White Cock, it was called, down Whitechapel way. Last time I walked past it, it was a shop run by Asians selling halal meat.'

'This time, it's official, Andrew.' Frankie Brunnie spoke solemnly. 'It's being recorded.' He pointed to the wall of the interview suite. 'See the tapes going round? See the red light? So for the record, and for the benefit of the tape, I am Detective Sergeant Frankie Brunnie of the Murder and Serious Crime Squad at New Scotland Yard. I am now going to ask the other persons present to identify themselves.'

'I am Detective Sergeant Victor Swannell, also of the Murder and Serious Crime Squad at New Scotland Yard.'

'I am Claire Highmore of Highmore, Highmore and Venning, solicitors and notaries public.'

'Andrew Cragg.' Cragg sighed. 'Big-mouth Cragg of no fixed abode.'

'All right, Andrew.' Brunnie leaned forward. 'Let's cut to the chase, shall we? For the record, you told us a body had been buried, and you told us that you played a part in the burial operation. We found the body exactly where you said it would be, so you are at least an accessory after the fact. At the very least.'

'Ah!' Claire Highmore, a bespectacled young woman with close-cut blonde hair, dressed in a plum-coloured suit and black patent leather shoes, raised her pen, which she held poised over her notebook. 'He . . . that is Mr Cragg, my client, may possibly be charged with the crime of accessory after the fact but only a jury can decide whether he is guilty of the crime or not.' Sitting beside Andrew Cragg, she looked over the top of the rim of her spectacles with a piercingly disapproving look directed at Frankie Brunnie. 'Let's keep it correct, shall we?' She added, 'For the benefit of the tape.'

Frankie Brunnie paused and breathed deeply. 'Very well, Miss Highmore, point taken. So, Andrew, you may be charged with being an accessory after the fact, which could carry a sentence of up to five years in prison. If convicted.' Again Brunnie paused. 'You have told us that you were present when the murder was committed, which might make the jury agree that you are guilty of conspiracy to murder.'

'That's a life sentence,' Swannell added.

'I've told you all I know.' Cragg's head sagged forward. 'I agreed to help "Chinese Geordie Davy", but it wasn't until we got to the lock-up that I knew what the job was about. I was set to leave but the other guy had a gun and I knew I wouldn't have made it to the door . . . and "Chinese Geordie Davy", he knew what I was thinking and he said, "Look, Andy, she's past caring now, it's a good wedge and you're in it now anyway." I was in debt to a heavy crew and I was to be paid enough to clear the debt and give me a bit of a float. I reckon that's why I stayed. The heavy crew were going to break my legs if I didn't come up with their money within a few days.'

'Can we be clear on a very important point, please, gentlemen.' Claire Highmore spoke slowly. 'My client informed me . . . he insists that he didn't know that the "job" as he calls it involved the crime of murder until after a man, whom he did not know, emerged from the shadows and shot the victim.

That is no more than accessory after the fact. So what can the police offer?'

'Nothing much yet,' Brunnie replied. 'Just the advice that you probably would give . . . being to go "guilty" and get one third remission for a guilty plea . . . three years . . . but if you know more, Andrew, if you can help put a bigger fish away . . . if you'll climb into the witness box then, perhaps . . . the dropping of all charges and you'll disappear into the witness protection programme. New identity . . . new start.'

'I honestly don't know much,' Cragg appealed to Brunnie. 'I have told you . . . it isn't good to know too much if you're only a gofer. Gofer's who know too much, they vanish in the fog. Never seen again.'

'So what do you know, Andrew?' Swannell persisted. 'You sound as if you know something, more than you're letting on.'

'I know that you should really speak to "Chinese Geordie Davy" – he does favours for some geezer.'

'Favours?'

'He gets rid of bodies.' Cragg sighed. 'OK, he's a refuse collector . . . a "dustman". He sweeps up after the other guy has done the business. When Davy . . .'

'"Chinese Geordie Davy", aka David Danby?' Brunnie confirmed.

'Yes . . . Davy . . . him. When the other guy has done the business he contacts Davy . . . David Danby . . . to make the bodies disappear, and if Davy wants a bit of help, he offers a wedge to someone who might need it.' Andrew Cragg spoke softly.

'Someone like you, Andy?' Swannell pressed. 'So how many bodies are we talking about?'

'A couple?' Cragg sighed.

'So . . . what you mean is what . . . ten . . . fifteen . . .' Brunnie's voice hardened. 'That sort of couple?'

'Don't put words into my client's mouth,' Claire Highmore snapped. 'Confine yourself to simple questions and remember that nothing my client tells you, despite the tape recording, is worth anything until he signs any statement he may care to make. The criminal justice system will not accept tape record-ings, only written and signed statements. Oral admissions or statements are not acceptable, unless given under oath in the witness box.'

'It's all right, miss.' Cragg turned to Claire Highmore. 'I want to get all this off my chest.'

'Very well, but I will be here to advise you.' Claire Highmore spoke clearly and confidently. 'And we will not be signing anything unless we have good and fair offers from the police, in the sense of reduced charges or the dropping of charges.'

'All right . . . so where are they all buried, Andrew?' Swannell asked firmly. 'What on earth is in the allotments all over London?'

'They are not buried.' Andrew Cragg spoke calmly. 'They're in the river . . . you'll never find them. They are cut into little bits and fed to the fishes. He puts them in the river at low tide into the mud at Shadwell Stair or Greenwich Reach, and when the river floods the rising water swallows the bits. It's done at night, just as the flood begins. If over the years a severed leg or an arm is found at the side of the river it might be "Chinese Geordie Davy's" work but it's not likely; the parts he leaves at the water's edge are cut up small, in weighted bags with holes torn in the bags to let the Old Father in.'

'So you have conspired in at least two murders . . .' Swannell ran his fingers through his hair.

'That is still to be determined.' Once again Claire Highmore held up her ballpoint pen. 'Let's not rush our fences . . . and my client seems to be admitting to conspiracy after the fact, not the murder.'

'Very well, fair enough,' Swannell murmured in agreement and then thought, *Softly, softly, that's the ticket.* 'So,' he continued, 'what do you know about the other victims of "Chinese Geordie Davy"?'

'Nothing,' Cragg replied firmly. 'They are not his victims. You see, this is how it works . . . or used to work when I knew Davy. He comes in . . . he used to come in afterwards to tidy up. So who the victims were I don't know, I never knew. All I ever saw him deal with was a pile of body parts. I never wanted to know 'cos I didn't want to end up like that. Davy said that to me once . . . he said, "A lot of geezers end up like this because they know too much . . . so learn to keep yourself in the dark. The less you know, the safer you'll be.'"

'So what you're saying is that the other victims you helped dispose of were members of the underworld? Criminals?' Swannell clarified.

'I believed so . . . I still believe so,' Cragg replied with a shrug. 'I don't think Davy knew who they were. The Big Man . . . he liked it like that.'

'The "Big Man"?' Brunnie echoed. 'Who is that?'

'Or was . . . I mean, I haven't seen "Chinese Geordie Davy" since we buried the girl. I don't know what he's doing now. I don't even know if he's still alive,' Cragg replied meekly.

'He's still alive,' Brunnie growled. 'In fact, he'll likely be joining you in here before too long. So who is the Big Man?'

'The guy that Davy works for . . . or worked for . . . big in terms of power, but if he was the guy who shot the girl then he's quite short.'

'So what you're saying is that the Big Man is some kind of hitman . . . a contract killer?'

'Seems so,' Cragg replied. 'He "offs" them then he cuts them up, then "Chinese Geordie Davy" takes the bits away.'

'So why didn't he cut up the body of Victoria Keynes?' Swannell sat forward. 'Why did he bury her whole?'

'You'll have to ask him that.' Cragg looked to his left. 'I thought it was a bit out of the way to bury a whole body rather than the usual script of dropping small bits of it into the river. But I didn't say anything . . . I never want to know too much. I just took Davy's advice. I kept my old loaf of bread down and my old north and south shut. That way I get to live . . . so I thought.'

'And you don't know the identity of the shooter . . . the Big Man?'

'Nope,' Cragg smiled a thin smile, 'and I don't want to either. I keep telling you.'

'So what's his MO?' Swannell asked. 'How does the Big Man work?'

'I only know what Davy told me,' Cragg protested.

'All right, that'll do for now,' Swannell advised. 'That'll do for a start. What did Davy tell you?'

'He's given a target,' Cragg advised. 'He has heavies who bring the target to his lock-up.'

'He murders for money?' Brunnie clarified.

'Don't know,' Cragg shrugged, 'whether he's an independent operator or whether he's on the payroll of some firm . . . I don't know.' Cragg sat back in his chair. 'He shoots the victims in the head in his lock-up. Then he lets them cure.'

'"Cure"?' Swannell repeated. 'What does that mean?'

'Well . . . I mean, that's just the word Davy used,' Cragg whined. 'Davy told me that the Big Guy, he chills them, then he and the heavies strip the dead men naked, get rid of all their clothing and other possessions . . . then he leaves them for three or four days, during which time he ensures the clothes and other stuff are got well rid of. Anyway, after three or four days when the victims' blood has dried he cuts them up with a woodman's bow saw . . . not a carpenter's saw but a bow saw . . . the sort of saw which is designed to saw tree branches up. It cuts right through the bone, so Davy said.'

'It would,' Brunnie sighed. 'Anyway, carry on, Andrew. This is good – you're doing well.'

'So he saws them up . . . cuts them into little pieces, Davy told me: feet, hands, forearms, upper arms . . . head, thighs, calves . . . They all get put in shopping bags or rucksacks or suitcases which he buys from charity shops – all used gear, can't be traced to him. He adds a weight – a lump of concrete, a brick . . . He picks them up from demolition sites and cuts a hole in the bag so the water can get in, to make sure the bags sinks, or that it at least doesn't rise with the tide because, like I said, the Big Man likes them put at the water's edge at low tide, but I've been with Davy when he drops 'em off a bridge . . . the Big Man doesn't check and Davy, well, sometimes he takes risks . . . at least he did ten years ago.'

'All right . . . keep talking, Andrew, you're doing well,' Swannell encouraged.

'Very well,' Brunnie echoed in agreement.

'Davy said the problem was the stomach gases . . .' Cragg paused and patted his stomach. 'They can't escape and they'll cause a body to float so the Big Man has to puncture the stomach . . .'

'Yes . . .' Brunnie nodded.

'So the Big Man does that at night,' Andrew Cragg informed the officers in a matter-of-fact manner, 'so Davy said. He carries . . . what is it called?' Cragg put his left hand up to his neck and his right hand down to his stomach. 'This bit . . . without head or arms or legs?'

'The torso,' Swannell advised. 'That's your torso.'

'OK . . . this bit,' Cragg continued. 'He carries that out of the lock-up and into the street.'

'The street?' Brunnie gasped. 'The street, did you say?'

'Yes . . . the street . . . at night, so Davy told me once.' Cragg continued to speak in a calm, matter-of-fact manner. 'No people about then . . . all business premises round about. No houses, no pubs, no late-night shops and takeaway eating places . . . just a dark street full of lock-ups. So he carries the . . . what is it . . .?'

'The torso,' Swannell repeated.

'Yeah . . . that bit. Anyway, after three or four days it's getting bloated, so he carries it outside on to the pavement, does a quick shuftie in case there is someone about . . . takes a deep breath, turns his head away and sticks a carving knife into the stomach. The gases escape with a loud hiss, Davy told me. Then the Big Man shreds the stomach, just to make sure, and carries it back to the lock-up, bungs it into a weighted suitcase which has been holed to let water in then leaves the suitcase with the other bags until "Chinese Geordie Davy" collects them and puts them in the river . . . feeds them to the fishes off Shadwell Stair, or if he's feeling lazy, or lucky, he'll drop the bag off Tower Bridge. So I helped him once or twice when I needed the cash.' Cragg took a deep breath. 'Oh . . . and then we burn the cloth.'

'The cloth?' Brunnie queried.

'The cloth,' Cragg repeated. 'Davy says that when the Big Man is letting a body cure he lays it on a cloth, like an old bit of curtain, which he spreads on the concrete floor of the lock-up. He cuts the bodies up on the cloth as well, so once the body is in bits and in bags and suitcases, the cloth is folded up and given to Davy, and once the bags have been fed to the Old Father, Davy douses the cloth with petrol and puts a lighted match to it. Davy always does that in a remote place, well out of the way. So, I have helped myself . . . yes?' Andrew Cragg appealed to Brunnie.

'You haven't harmed yourself, put it like that,' Brunnie replied. 'So how many bodies do you reckon you helped "Chinese Geordie Davy" get rid of, would you say?'

'Over the years . . . about ten,' Cragg replied, 'or fifteen . . . I have lost count.'

'And my client can't be charged with any one of the incidents.' Claire Highmore folded her notepad. 'Not without any corroborative evidence, which leaves you only with the part he played in the murder of Victoria Keynes, where he was but an accessory after the fact. But you will need my client's testimony if you are going to successfully prosecute David Danby and the so called "Big Man", and for that we need the assurance that all charges against my client will be dropped.'

'Well . . . that all depends.' Brunnie stood and pressed the bell on the wall beside the door. 'So, to use your own expression, Miss Highmore, let's not rush our fences . . . either of us. But for now your client will be charged with accessory after the fact in respect of the murder of Victoria Keynes. He'll appear before the magistrates again tomorrow and will almost certainly be remanded back into custody.'

Harry and Kathleen Vicary, she raven-haired and slender, fetching in a calf-length skirt, he tall and neatly but casually dressed, sat quietly, side by side, in a large room containing, perhaps, Vicary estimated, seventy to eighty persons sitting in rows facing the front of the hall. To Vicary's right the curtains over the window had been left open so as to permit the mid-evening sun to stream into the room. The windows themselves, where possible, had also been left open to provide ventilation. The chairman who was sitting facing the audience, and who was well known to the regular attenders, stood and introduced that evening's guest speaker. Upon being introduced, the immaculately dressed speaker stood and said, 'Hello, my name is Steve and I am alcoholic', to which all the persons in the room replied by saying, 'Hello, Steve'. That evening's guest speaker then proceeded to tell the audience of his personal descent into his 'own private hell', via the bottle, and how he reached his 'gutter', losing everything – his job, his marriage – and then he went on to talk about his slow but steady road to full recovery, not, by that evening, having consumed a single drop of alcohol in five years. Upon the completion of his talk he earned what Harry Vicary thought to be a well-deserved round of applause, because Steve, unlike so many previous guest speakers, did not seem to ever exaggerate his consumption. He had admitted to reaching a level of consuming only one bottle of whisky a day, whereas other speakers, often frail and finely made females, would lay claim to consuming three bottles of vodka a day for twenty years – all highly unlikely, Vicary had always privately thought. But Steve's 'hell', the loss of his job and his marriage, and his relatively modest consumption of alcohol, made his story far more believable than the stories of many other speakers, many of whom claimed to have sold their children's toys to buy alcohol. And all of whom, Vicary had always thought, with the cynicism of a long-serving police officer, to be self-pitying attention seekers, but Steve seemed to be genuine and Harry Vicary was pleased to put his hands together for him.

After staying for thirty minutes after Steve's talk to enjoy coffee and a chat with friends, the Vicarys made their farewells and took their leave. From the public meeting rooms the Vicarys walked to The Raven's Nest where they sat in the lounge, both drinking soda water with lime and sharing a bag of dry roasted peanuts. Just because they were both 'dry alcoholics', they argued, was no reason to deny themselves the joy of the English pub. Later they walked home to their house in Hartley Road, via Bushwood Road, so that they might enjoy the breathable dusk air of Wanstead Flats, Leytonstone, London, E11.

Frankie Brunnie and the nurse sat facing each other in the corner seats of the Old Swan Inn in Walthamstow. The short nurse gazed at Frankie Brunnie: he was tall and dark haired, with a striking black beard which he always kept immaculately trimmed. Frankie Brunnie, in turn, gazed at the nurse, enjoying his smooth, aesthetically pleasing features and the sparkle in his eyes. To an observer, the nurse and Brunnie would appear to be good friends – two men who liked each other and who had momentarily exhausted their conversation while out for a few beers. In fact, for Brunnie and the nurse, the silence was a thing of value, of great depth and great beauty, because they were deeply and utterly in love with each other.

It was Thursday, 22.40 hours.

FIVE

Friday, 10.15 hours – 17.35 hours

'Food suit you, Davy? In Brixton Prison?' Swannell took out his notepad and laid it on the table surface in the agent's room. 'You did tell us that you wanted some food and clean linen to sleep in. Is it all to your liking, Davy?'

'I've tasted worse food and I've tasted better.' David Danby shrugged his shoulders. 'But I reckon it's all there . . . the vegetables are boiled to nothing, the meat is always stringy with too much fat, but if the alternative is starving . . . well, then it's all right.'

'You should complain to the management,' Brunnie advised with dry sarcasm. 'You might get a refund.'

David Davy raised his eyebrows in despair at Brunnie's cynicism. 'You know, I read once that Charles Dickens was doing his prison visiting and observed the food served in London's prisons was up to the standard of the food served in the best hotels. Don't know whether that meant the food in the hotels was awful or the grub in the prisons was good, but he wouldn't be saying that today. I'll take your advice, Mr Brunnie – I'll complain to the management and I'll ask for a refund. I'll even threaten to take my custom elsewhere – that'll make the kitchen staff shake-up its ideas. I also don't like the view I've got from my room. I'll ask for a room with a sea view.'

'Good idea, Davy.' Brunnie glanced around the agent's room. He saw the carpetless floor, white tiles three-quarters of the way up the wall, cream-painted plaster above that and a cream-painted ceiling above that. A single fluorescent bulb behind a Perspex screen provided the illumination. 'I mean, you might as well get the most out of your stay.' Brunnie paused. 'Anyway, let's get this show on the road. Myself and Mr Swannell here, well, we had a very interesting chat yesterday.'

'Very interesting,' Victor Swannell added.

'Who with? That Cragg geezer?' David Davy sneered. 'I bet it was with big Cragg.'

'We can't tell you.' Swannell smiled firmly. 'That is for us to know and you to assume or guess at . . . but we, Mr Brunnie and I, we've both been doing this job for a long time, haven't we, Frankie?'

'Oh, yes . . .' Brunnie nodded. 'Between the two of us, me and Mr Swannell have got a fair few years in . . . a fair few . . . more than halfway to the pension now.'

'The point is, Davy,' Swannell continued, 'that both of us can tell when a person we are talking to is going to turn Queen's Evidence and request protected person status . . . it's always very obvious.'

'It's as plain as the old nose on your old boat race,' Brunnie added.

'You see, if we are talking about Cragg, then right now he's looking at five years for being an accessory after the fact, but, unlike you, he doesn't relish the thought of prison food each day and clean sheets once a week.' Swannell took his ballpoint pen from his pocket. 'He's not looking forward to it at all. We'll let him have a night or two in prison to help him focus his mind, although it seems that it is already focusing quite nicely, thank you very much.' Swannell paused. 'You'll go down, he'll be a protected person . . . a new name, a new start in life . . . He'll be enjoying liberty while you'll be composing letters of complaint to the governor of whichever prison you're in. Cragg will go to the pub each evening; you'll sit down in front of the TV with forty or fifty other lags watching the programme they want to watch.'

'Or,' Brunnie smiled, 'you could take a leaf out of his left hook.'

'So we know about the murdered girl, the woman you and Cragg drove from a lock-up in the East End to the allotments in New Cross. We also know about the bits of bodies which you removed and put in the river . . . once the geezer you worked for had sawn them off the corpse.'

'Cragg!' Danby exploded angrily. 'I knew it was Cragg. He's grassing me up; he could never keep his north and south shut, the huge toe rag that he is.'

'Whether it's Andrew Cragg or not, Davy,' Swannell explained in a calming manner, 'we are not allowed to confirm or deny either way.'

'It's him.' Danby sighed. 'It's Cragg you've been chatting to. I mean, who else could it be?'

'So, tell us, Davy,' Brunnie pressed, 'about the woman. Why was it that the geezer who you worked for wore a mask when he shot her? Why didn't he want her to see that it was him who was offing her? And why wasn't her old body chopped up like all the others . . . Why did she get special treatment?'

Danby lowered his head. 'I don't know the answer to any of those questions.'

'Implying very neatly and very nicely that Cragg, if it was him we were talking to,' Brunnie continued, 'was being truthful when he told us of all the other murder victims being chopped up . . . so they'll only ever be "missing persons" and no one can be charged with their murder. No body means no murder conviction. It's not wholly true but it's a rule of thumb you can work with.'

'No comment,' Danby sneered.

'That's interesting.' Swannell leaned forward. 'No comment cowboys are always guilty. Otherwise they would not say "no comment" all the time.'

'You think?' Danby sneered once more. 'That's your homespun philosophy, is it?'

'We know it's the case,' Brunnie replied in an icy voice. 'All the experience we have just mentioned – remember, we're more than halfway to the pension.'

'Early retirement with an inflation-proof pension.' Danby once again lowered his head. 'Yes, I remember. Can't be bad.'

'You made your life choices, Davy,' Swannell offered. 'And we – me and Mr Brunnie – we made ours.'

'So let's not beat about the bush, Davy.' Brunnie leaned forward. 'Let's dive straight in. Tell us all you know about the old geezer you worked for from time to time . . . or still work for, but going by the state of your drum, I'll say you haven't worked for him for some time. Your gambling habit can't explain that pigsty you live in. That sort of living is a gambling habit plus no income to speak of.'

'Yes.' Danby nodded. 'That's true, I haven't worked for a long time . . . just cheap crookin' like shoplifting and bag snatching but no proper work. I'm past it . . . But, unlike you, I don't get no pension to see me out.'

'So tell us who you worked for. Who was the geezer that shot the victims who were brought to him, and who chopped them up once their blood had solidified?'

'They were brought to him,' Danby replied quietly, 'I can tell you that. He had a team of four or five heavies: they collected the victims, grabbed them off the street, bundled them into a van and brought them to the lock-up alive and kicking. I don't mind telling you that. They grabbed the girl on the Big Man's orders, I can also tell you that . . . but as to who he is . . . I wouldn't tell you if I knew.'

'So you just got a phone call?' Swannell pressed. 'Come round with your van . . . I've got a mess that needs tidying. Is that how it worked?'

'No comment.' Danby glanced up at the ceiling.

'And sometimes you hired someone to help you . . . big lumps of brain-dead nothings like Andrew Cragg? Andrew-I-may-not-be-very-clever-but-I-can-lift-things-Cragg?'

Brunnie leaned back in his chair. 'You're a refuse man, aren't you, Davy? A refuse collector. I'm right, aren't I? You are a refuse disposal engineer, a garbage man; you clean up after organized crime have done the business. It's you that sets fire to buildings once they're no longer needed as a safe house to destroy any evidence which might have been left there, and you collect bits of chopped-up body parts and drop them off a bridge into the Old Father . . . or leave them at the water's edge at low tide . . .'

'And sometimes . . . sometimes,' Swannell added, 'you dump them whole in shallow graves.'

'No comment.' Danby continued to look up at the cream-painted ceiling and the shimmering florescent light bulb.

'We know the type, Davy.' Brunnie spoke calmly. 'Gangland bosses have their "enforcers" who "encourage" people to cooperate. They have their "minders" to protect them, their "wheelmen" to drive the getaway cars and they have their "dustbin" men, their refuse collectors who ensure dead bodies vanish, never to be seen again, and you, Davy, are a "dustbin" man – you dump bits of body into the river, you burn the cloth the victim's body was laid on to be sawn up. You're in pretty deep, Davy.'

'Help yourself, Davy,' Swannell urged, but he also spoke calmly. 'We need to know who this "Mr Big" is, the "Big Man", the geezer who is hired to snuff out a life . . . in this case the geezer who shot the girl whose body you dropped into a hole in the ground on an allotment in New Cross.'

'What will we find when we turn over your drum, Davy?' Brunnie asked.

A sudden look of fear crossed David Danby's eyes.

'So there is something in that tip you call a home you don't want us to find?' Swannell smiled.

'No comment.' Danby's reply was short and curt.

'So the hitman with the pig's face mask, Davy.' Brunnie picked up the questioning. 'Is he an independent operator or is he on the payroll?'

'No comment.' Danby spat his reply. 'No comment. No comment. No comment. Understand . . .' he snarled, 'no comment. Clear enough?'

'As a bell, Davy.' Swannell leaned back in his chair. 'But it's your funeral. We gave you every chance. You can't say we didn't.'

'It was the shoes.' Gillian Keynes sat in a resigned attitude in the armchair of her living room. 'Just there.' She pointed to the middle of the floor of her living room. 'I knew Timmy would tell us.'

'We've moved them now,' Eric Keynes added. 'We've put them back in the shoe rack by the front door.'

'We got up this morning . . . well, I got up,' Gillian Keynes continued. 'I walked past the front door to get to the kitchen. I didn't notice anything out of the ordinary at first; I suppose I was a bit blurry-eyed. I put the kettle on to boil and while the water was heating up I began to open the house curtains . . . just the normal morning routine . . .'

'It's a bit like that every morning,' Eric Keynes added in a dull monotone, and quite needlessly, thought Tom Ainsclough, who fully understood what 'morning routine' meant. 'I came into this room and found that all the shoes had been removed from the shoe rack, which is by the front door, and brought into here.' Once again Gillian Keynes pointed to the living-room carpet. 'It was Timmy. It's just the sort of thing he'd do.'

'The poltergeist you mentioned?' Penny Yewdall clarified. 'The spirit of the little ten-year-old who was very happy when he lived here?'

'Yes . . . him,' Gillian Keynes replied in an absentminded manner, as if her thoughts were elsewhere, and quite understandably, thought Penny Yewdall. 'Whenever that might have been, but yes, that is who I mean. So this morning I found our shoes had been arranged on the carpet. Eric's shoes were all jumbled up in a pile in the middle of the floor but mine were placed neatly in pairs around Eric's shoes and pointing outwards, so that if I was standing in any pair of my shoes I would be standing with my back towards Eric's shoes. It seemed to me like Timmy was trying to tell us something . . . but anyway, we knew then that he was preparing us for you calling on us to tell us that the remains found were those of Victoria . . . they have been positively identified, but also he was telling us something else, but that something is . . .' Her voice tailed off and she fell silent.

'Yes, as I said, the positive identification was made by using dental records. The results came in overnight and were waiting in my tray this morning.' Penny Yewdall spoke softly. 'Again, I am so very sorry.'

Earlier that morning Penny Yewdall and Tom Ainsclough had tapped reverentially on the front door of the Keynes's bungalow and, when the door was opened by Gillian Keynes, she looked at Yewdall and Ainsclough and nodded. 'Eric and I have been expecting you.' She had then beckoned the officers into the house and led them into the living room where she had slumped, Ainsclough thought, rather than sat, in one of the armchairs, pointed to the floor and said, 'It was the shoes.'

'But at least we know now,' Eric Keynes mumbled. 'We'll

have a funeral and a grave to visit. We'll at least have that, and that is better than not knowing.'

'Yes, there is that,' Gillian Keynes replied abstractly. 'We can have a grave to visit. We'll choose a nice headstone with a sensible inscription . . . she would have liked that.'

'We just called to notify you.' Penny Yewdall stood. Tom Ainsclough did likewise. 'It's not the sort of thing we can tell someone over the phone.'

'No . . . no, of course not.' Gillian Keynes forced a weak smile. 'Thank you, we appreciate the sensitivity, but Timmy forewarned us. It softened the blow.'

'We can arrange for a grief counsellor to call,' Ainsclough offered, 'or ask a neighbour to call and sit with you if you are close to any particular neighbour?'

'No, thank you, to both offers,' Gillian Keynes replied. 'We'll cope . . . we just need each other.'

'Have you made any progress?' Eric Keynes asked.

'A little,' Yewdall told him, and she then also noticed the cold look in the man's eyes. 'But it is still very, very early days yet.'

'We'll be calling on Victoria's friends and we'll visit her husband,' Ainsclough explained. 'It's a slow but sure step-by-step approach, as they say . . . softly, softly, catchee monkey.'

Swannell and Brunnie returned to 'Chinese Geordie Davy' Danby's address in Raul Road, Peckham. They forced the door gingerly and entered the flat, pointedly leaving the door open so as to allow plentiful ingress of breathable air.

'We make our life choices,' Swannell remarked. 'As you said to Danby, he made his.'

'Actually, it was you that said it.' Brunnie grinned as he pulled on a pair of latex gloves.

'Blimey,' Swannell groaned as he also pushed his hands into latex gloves. 'I'm losing it already . . . all my old marbles are going.'

In the event, the thorough search of Danby's living space resulted in the finding of only one item of promising interest in the form of a rental agreement in respect of 'business premises' in Leyton.

'This arouses my interest.' Brunnie tapped the rent book.
'Regular payments, and all up to date . . . and he's been renting
those business premises over in Leyton for fifteen years. So
what does a washed-up old gambling addict who hasn't worked
for years and who lives like this want to keep business premises
for . . . the same premises for that amount of time and pay a
not unhefty rent for said premises?' He handed the book to
Ainsclough, who read the address.

'That,' Ainsclough replied, 'is what we must find out.
Nuffield Road, Leyton.'

'She was very angry, she was a livid woman. Totally livid.'
Dorothy Parker chose to sit cross-legged on the floor of the
front room of her home in Samos Road, Anerley, SE20, but
she invited Tom Ainsclough and Penny Yewdall to sit on the
settee facing her and the fireplace. The floor of the living room
consisted of floorboards covered by a dark shade of varnish,
while dried reeds protruded from a tall jar on the other side
of the fireplace where Dorothy Parker sat. Dorothy Parker
wore a full-length flower-patterned 'hippy girl' dress and her feet
stopped in a pair of faded and much-worn moccasins. She
wore her black hair long and centre parted so it hung either
side of her head and down either side of her shoulders, almost
to her waist. The dress and hairstyle might have looked fetching
on a twenty-year-old, but both Ainsclough and Yewdall felt
that Dorothy Parker, in her mid-to-late thirties, was struggling
to carry off the image of youth to which she was clearly so
desperately clinging. 'She really was the woman scorned,
burning up with resentment and anger. She had been married
for only two years, possibly even less, and he was already
being unfaithful. She had found out that he was seeing someone
else so she walked out on him and started divorce proceedings.
She had promised that she would fleece him, really take him
to the cleaners. I never knew that she could be so embittered.'
She reached for a tobacco tin of green and gold, prised open
the lid and took out a skin of cigarette paper and a pinch of
hand-rolling tobacco and rolled a cigarette with practised and
consummate ease. She lit the cigarette with a blue disposable
lighter and inhaled deeply, exhaling the smoke in two long

plumes through her nostrils. 'Ye olde scorned woman, as I said . . . I mean, imagine her with a machine gun in her hands. It just doesn't bear thinking about.'

'A machine gun,' Tom Ainsclough repeated. 'Did she have one of those things?'

'No . . .' Dorothy Parker flicked ash from the end of her cigarette into the empty fire grate behind and beside her. 'No . . . no . . .' She smiled. 'You see, my husband is fascinated by military history and he once told me that during the Second World War the Yugoslav partisans recruited women as much as they recruited men, but their practise was to keep the young and attractive ones out of harm's way and made them aide-de-camps of the Partisan leaders. The older and less attractive women they issued with machine guns and told them to go and kill Nazis. Imagine that, will you? Scorn a woman because of her looks or age, or both, and then give her a machine gun . . . but this is apparently what they did. That would make for a formidable killing machine, totally without mercy. But that's what Victoria was like in those last days of her life. I tell you, if she had a machine gun the streets of London town would be strewn with male corpses.'

'We understand that she was staying here with you after she left her husband?' Tom Ainsclough asked.

'Yes. Yes, she was. She occupied the small box room above the front door.' Dorothy Parker drew deeply on the cigarette and held the smoke in her lungs before finally exhaling, once again through her nostrils. 'Pretty well all her possessions and all of her valuables she took to her parents' house. All she kept here were a few items of clothing, sufficient for a week and then a weekly wash. That's all she kept here . . . and her wristwatch. She always wore that.'

'So how long was she here before she vanished?' Penny Yewdall glanced through the net curtains of the house at the houses on the opposite side of Samos Road, noting them to be well-maintained, late-Victorian terraced developments on three levels from the ground upwards. The houses did not appear to her to have cellars.

'A few weeks.' Dorothy Parker examined the glowing tip of the cigarette. 'My husband was getting irritated with her even though she was an excellent guest. She kept her head down and herself out of the way, helped a lot around the house, always picked up after herself. Often you would not know that she was there, but my husband started to ask me when she'd be leaving.' She pulled on the cigarette once more. 'But she wasn't allowing herself to get comfortable . . . she was possibly on her way to being, but she had a long way to go before she was settled in. Eventually she moved back to her parents' house, although she kept visiting me and other friends.'

'I understand,' Yewdall replied with a nod of her head. 'So what do you know about her husband?'

'One old smoothie.' Dorothy Parker exhaled through her mouth as she spoke, causing her smoke to be chopped up by her voice. 'He claimed – probably still claims – to be "something in the city", but both my husband and I doubted that. To me he had all the superficial charm of the typical psychopath. He just saw people as being there for his use, to be used to further his own ends, but he did, and probably still does, have a splendid house, so money was coming from somewhere. But what sort of money? I mean, honest or dishonest . . . that remains to be seen.'

'Where is his house?' Tom Ainsclough asked.

'St John's Wood.' Dorothy Parker inclined her head to one side. 'All right for some, eh? But I love this house and we are paying for it. One day it will be ours and bought with moral money.'

'Yes . . . all right for some.' Tom Ainsclough wrote St John's Wood on his notepad. 'But, as you say, moral or immoral money . . . that is the question.'

'Yes, lived in St John's Wood, and when he was still in his forties.' Dorothy Parker forced a smile. 'You can't help but be suspicious.'

'Was her husband any more specific about his source of income?' Penny Yewdall asked. 'Any hint at all could be very useful.'

'No . . . not to me or Nigel, my husband. He just kept saying he was "in the world of finance" . . . "international finance". He talked about "futures" and "commodities"; he talked about "phoning Jo'burg", and "San Fran" and "HK" and places like that.' Dorothy Parker took another deep drag on the cigarette. 'Which could cover a multitude of sins.' Yewdall sighed. 'Nigel used exactly that expression. He said, "It could cover a multitude of sins" – anything from merchant banking and high finance to extortion and racketeering, but probably the latter, Nigel said, because you don't get to own property like that at that age unless you pay hard cash . . . and he wasn't in the world of entertainment where that sort of big money can be had so he was probably, is *still* probably, up to no good. My husband was anxious to leave his home when we had accepted Victoria's invitation to visit and he wouldn't be dragged back. He said he couldn't risk being known to associate with him. If you do visit him and he plays down his wealth, take what he says with a pinch of salt.'

'We'll remember that.' Penny Yewdall smiled.

'Even Victoria didn't know what he was doing and she had some banking experience. She was made to feel wholly out of her depth and eventually she didn't even try to understand his world. I mean, he never had an office phone number; he only ever gave her his mobile phone number. So when he was out at work she never knew where he was. I mean, that's no marriage.' Dorothy Parker took one last drag on the cigarette and tossed the quarter-inch butt that remained into the fire grate. 'But she was totally bowled over by his lifestyle. She grew up in a tiny little bungalow down Croydon way, where her parents still live, and to go from that to being the lady of the house in a property in St John's Wood, more or less overlooking Regent's Park . . . that was quite a step up for her, but she was a very materialistic person. My husband always said that he couldn't understand what I saw in her – she just had no soul, he said, just no soul at all. He said it was all about money for Victoria Keynes. My husband is a banker but he helps with the church youth club and sings in a male voice choir; he is an amateur military historian. There's more in his world than money but he said that Victoria Keynes was all about the old doe, ray, me.'

'Do you know if there was anything unusual . . . out of the
ordinary going on around the time of Victoria's disappearance?'
Ainsclough asked.

'No . . . no . . . I confess I knew of nothing like that.'
Dorothy Parker pursed her lips. 'I can't say I remember
anything out of the ordinary going on. I only remember her
being fixated upon taking her husband for every penny she
could. I thought perhaps she was over-fixated . . . needlessly
angry. If I was in her shoes I doubt that I would have been
so emotional about it. I would have been more calm, more
collected in my determination and I would have been more
inclined to accept a fair settlement, but she was determined
to wring every last penny out of him. I did wonder if she
was being driven by another agenda, as if the anger towards
her husband was possibly a vehicle to express anger at another
issue in her life which was totally unconnected with her
divorce . . . As if her husband's infidelity had released deeply
held emotions about some other matter – something she'd
kept buried. It was as if the future held some form of venge-
ance for her and she was sharpening her knives . . . or her
claws.'

'That might be of interest,' Yewdall replied. 'What was her
day-to-day routine when she vanished?'

'She went out each day – that is, when she was here.'
Dorothy Parker leaned back against the wall. 'I don't know
where she went . . . visiting her parents, visiting her sol-
icitor . . . maybe just sitting in the library, maybe she just
walked about, trying to be a good guest . . . did a little house-
work then kept out of the way. She came back in the evening
and although she stayed in her room it was then that the
house began to feel overcrowded. My husband would make
comments, and he began to go to the pub more often than
he used to go, which I didn't like, and it was then that I
suggested to Victoria that she might want to look for some
alternative accommodation. She promised that she would do
so and returned to her parents.'

'And then she disappeared?' Yewdall suggested.

'Yes . . . one Friday afternoon she didn't call on me as
usual,' Dorothy Parker explained. 'The following day I

phoned her parents to see if she was there because she had left some of her possessions in the box room she had occupied, but no, she wasn't. So we – or rather I – expressed our concern, and her parents reported her to the police as a missing person. The police called here and took a statement, which is apparently all they could do. I believe you do not search for missing adults?'

'No, no, we don't,' Tom Ainsclough confirmed. 'Not unless there is clear evidence of foul play at the time of the disappearance, and we will also search for a person who we have reason to believe might be in grave danger . . . a missing fell walker in bad weather, for example, but in the sort of situation you have described, an adult who did not return home after being out all day with no way of knowing where she spent the day or who she was with . . . then in that case, all we can do is to take a "mis-per" report.'

'Fair enough. I understand most missing persons are found or they return home within twenty-four hours of being reported missing.' Dorothy Parker glanced to her left as her eye was caught by a middle-aged woman walking past her house.

'Yes, that is the case,' Yewdall replied. Then she asked, 'I assume that your husband is at work?'

'Yes, he is a banker, as I said – he's the branch accountant.' She added with a note of pride, 'I worked there too, though I was only a cashier, courtesy of Glenvale School for Girls in Putney. Our "gels" go to university and if a "gel" can't get to university she goes to a teacher training college, and if the "gel" can't get to teacher training college then the "gel" goes to work in a bank. My mother and grandmother both went to Glenvale and when my grandmother was there she and her friend were beaten in front of the whole school for going into Woolworths . . . three of the strap on the palm of each hand. They had stopped doing that by the time I went there but that nose-in-the-air ethos still prevailed and I was a "plonker" who left at sixteen and went to work in a bank. I didn't last very long in banking – it was all too straight-laced and humourless for me, and so I left but not until I had acquired a husband, which is why "gels" go and work in a bank, and not until me and Victoria Keynes had befriended each other.' Dorothy Parker

shrugged her shoulders. 'I dare say we make an odd couple . . .
me and Nigel . . . him so smartly dressed and me sadly clinging
on to my youth, but I don't put flowers in my hair and I can
get dolled up if I have to go with Nigel to a "do" with the
bank staff . . . but it's always uncomfortable.'

'Well that's life for us poor women.' Penny Yewdall grinned.
'As my mother once told me, "If you glam up and you are
not uncomfortable, you're just not glammed up."'

'That's a very succinct way of putting it.' Dorothy Parker
returned the grin. 'But you know, my husband – he *is* in the
world of legitimate finance, and he said that if Victoria's
husband was a legitimate financier then he was a Dutchman . . .
but I didn't think it was my place to interfere or sound alarm
bells. I don't think Victoria's parents were wildly happy with
the union but it was up to them, not me or my husband, to
fire warning shots across their daughter's bows.'

'Fair enough, I dare say.' Penny Yewdall looked briefly
around the room. It was, she thought, definitely a 'her' house,
not a 'his' house. It was the home of an ageing hippy chick, not
an established banker. There would also be, she firmly
believed, a plentiful supply of cannabis in the house kept
somewhere just out of sight, and doubtless to be plundered
as soon as she and Tom Ainsclough had taken their leave.
She then asked, 'What did you feel about Mr Woodhuyse,
Victoria's husband?'

'You mean intuitively?' Dorothy Parker smiled gently as
she and Penny Yewdall held eye contact. 'The old "woman's
intuition foxtrot"? Well, I always felt that Vicky had jumped
too eagerly into the wrong bed. She seemed to marry in haste
and repent at leisure in the hereafter.'

'Repent?' Penny Yewdall repeated. 'Does that imply that
you believe her husband was responsible for her disappearance
and for her murder?'

'Yes, frankly I do,' Dorothy Parker replied with a venomous
tone. 'Yes . . . as I said, it's the old "woman's intuition foxtrot",
but yes, I do think that he was at the bottom of it all. Have you
met him yet?'

'No, not yet,' Penny Yewdall admitted. 'We will, of course,
be calling on him, but we'd like as much information about

him as possible before we do visit. Not only about him, but really the entire situation, you know . . . their lifestyle, friends . . . everything.'

'Friends?' Dorothy Parker raised her eyebrows. 'I think Victoria did have friends whom she met through her husband, but I never met any of them. She would go away during the day as if visiting but I don't know where. Occasionally she would go out at night – that's when she was living here with me and the bold Nigel and so with a sense that she was going somewhere, as if she was addressing a task to be completed. It really was not in Victoria's nature to kill time by riding round and round on the Circle line or sitting in the reference section of the public library, although I suspect she did that so as to keep out of our way as much as she could. I'm sorry; I really don't know who you can ask about her life with her husband.'

'We could get sniffer dogs in here,' Frankie Brunnie glanced round the lock-up, 'but I doubt it would do any good.'

'I'm inclined to agree.' Victor Swannell cleared his throat as the ammonia fumes reached him. 'This place has been well sanitized.'

'Which means,' Brunnie also coughed, 'that it has been very recently used, and used for the sort of purpose to which a sniffer dog would react and used by someone who knows the need to prevent sniffer dogs from detecting what they are trained to detect. No dog would lie down and wag its tail anywhere in here. And with David Danby in custody it means that Mr Big in his pig's face mask and his heavies have got another refuse collector to tidy up after them.'

Brunnie and Swannell had driven to the address in the rental book found in Danby's flat. It was, not wholly to their surprise, unoccupied. The door was poorly secured by a barrel lock which Brunnie forced with his shoulder, and did so quite easily. The interior was wholly empty. Nothing was contained within. All was encased in a concrete floor, unfaced brick walls and a wooden roof. There was no need for elaborate locks when there was nothing to keep safe and secure, and nothing of value to store.

'I reckon they must allow the door to remain open now and again to convince the local felons there is nothing worth stealing,' Brunnie observed, 'and so when a body has to be "cured" over a four-day period, no one will break in.'

'That must be their practice,' Swannell whispered in agreement. 'So why would a burnt-out has-been like David Danby, who lives in squalor, have a rental of a lock-up which is kept empty and spick and span?' Swannell commented. 'I mean, you could eat off this floor, not that I would want to, but if you did you wouldn't get food poisoning.'

'We'd better secure it anyway.' Brunnie turned to go. 'Get the scene-of-crime boys and girls in here. There might be something of interest which is not visible to the naked eye, but somehow I don't think they'll find anything of interest to us.'

'I doubt if they'll find anything at all,' Swannell replied dryly. 'The owner might be able to tell us something. We ought to check with the Land Registry.'

'I confess I was wondering when you'd deign to call on me.' Elliot Woodhuyse stood in the doorway of his home on Springfield Road, St John's Wood, NW8. Penny Yewdall and Tom Ainsclough had parked their car in the nearest available space and had walked the hundred yards to the last known address of the husband of the late Victoria Keynes. The house revealed itself to be a detached property on four levels, one being a basement. The basement level and the elevated ground floor were both painted white, which glared in the sunlight and caused Yewdall and Ainsclough to squint as they viewed the property from the pavement. The upper floors of the house were of unpainted light grey-coloured London brick with only the window frames painted in white paint to match the lower floors of the building. A small paved area stood in front of the house, upon which a black Porsche 911 was parked. Black painted railings separated the paved area from the pavement and from the road beyond the pavement.

'How much money do you think we're calling on?' Yewdall had considered the property. 'Twenty, thirty million?'

'More, I'd say.' Ainsclough had walked from the pavement in front of the Porsche. 'Probably twice as much, but I can see what Dorothy Parker meant: I can't see a man in his forties getting a mortgage to buy this house. A man in his forties who is a rock star or a successful actor might be able to buy this house with honest cash . . . any other forty-something buys it with suspect cash. We'll see what he says.'

Ainsclough and Yewdall had then walked side by side up the flight of steps to the door which was at the side of the house. Yewdall had rung the bell, upon which they'd heard the sound of the Westminster chimes echoing loudly within the house. There had been a few moments' delay and then the white-painted door had opened slowly, and somewhat imperiously, Ainsclough thought, by a tall, clean-shaven man who appeared to be in his late fifties. He wore a white T-shirt, white trousers and white sports shoes. Ainsclough and Yewdall had showed their identity cards and given their reasons for calling before he'd spoken. He stepped to one side and beckoned the officers to enter his house. 'I am Elliot Woodhuyse, her husband.'

'So you're expecting us?' Yewdall replaced her ID in her handbag.

'Of course I was expecting you,' Woodhuyse replied with a strong note of sarcasm. 'I read the papers, I watch the TV news. So she has turned up . . . or rather her body has? I thought she might. I confess I didn't think that it would take the best part of ten years though. Confess that surprised me. But do come in, it's better than chatting on the doorstep.' Woodhuyse stepped further to one side, allowing Yewdall and Ainsclough to enter the house. Yewdall noted that Woodhuyse wore an expensive-looking watch but no other decoration. He wore his black hair neatly cut. It crossed Yewdall's mind that he was of the appearance that would make middle-aged women go weak at the knees if he were wearing a cassock and a clerical collar.

She also sensed that the man was evil.

The officers found that the inside of the house exuded a superficial air of wealth. No books were in evidence, no wall decorations other than a mirror; the walls were painted white like the exterior of the house and the furniture was modern in white upholstery suspended from chrome frames. The floor was of varnished floorboards with white goatskin rugs, six in all, scattered in a haphazard manner. A large plasma TV screen was attached to the wall and expensive-looking hi-fi equipment stood on a low table beneath the screen. A modern-looking dining table stood beside the window on the opposite side of the room to the roadway side, which was surrounded by six very high-backed chairs, also of modern design. The rear window of the house, beyond the dining table, looked out on to a large, neatly kept garden, with a closely mown lawn and with shrubs and trees at the bottom of the garden.

A young, slender, yellow-haired woman wearing a multi-coloured body-length kaftan in lightweight cotton stood by the table looking quizzically at Yewdall and Ainsclough.

'We need privacy.' Woodhuyse addressed the lemon-haired woman who then proceeded to glide silently out of the room, exiting by a second door which Yewdall and Ainsclough could not see from their vantage point. As she left the room the woman gave Yewdall and Ainsclough a smug, self-satisfied 'I-bet-I-live-in-a-better-house-than-you-do' look.

'Do take a seat.' Elliot Woodhuyse indicated the designer furniture. 'I mean, there's no point in standing when you can sit . . . none that I can see anyway.'

Ainsclough and Yewdall sat on a low-slung settee; Elliot Woodhuyse occupied a chair of similar, matching design.

'So we don't have to tell you that your wife's body has been found?' Tom Ainsclough began.

'No . . . no, you don't – you can dispense with that formality,' Woodhuyse replied in a reserved manner, holding his head slightly inclined backwards, looking down his nose at the officers. 'She was found buried in an allotment some-where south of the river – New Cross, I think the newscaster said. Do you know I had to look up what an allotment was – in that sense, I mean. I have heard of an allotment of money for one thing or another, but I never heard of a bit of land being allotted to someone to use to grow potatoes to eat. How charming; how very quaint, don't you think?'

Yewdall did not respond but instead she asked, 'I gather that you and your wife had separated at the time she disappeared . . . pending a divorce.'

'Yes.' Woodhuyse ran the fingers of his left hand through his hair. 'Yes, we were separated, that was the case, and yes, we were getting divorced. It was all very bloody . . . all very messy, there is no point at all in trying to tell you otherwise. Victoria was a gold-digger. She was a young woman with all the makings of a very good serial divorcee: marry a succession of wealthy men and then divorce them after a few very short years and take half their wealth with her. She was a calculating, heartless, mercenary little cow.'

'So it must have been quite convenient for you when she disappeared?' Yewdall prompted. 'It saved you an awful lot of money, I mean.'

'Oh, yes.' Woodhuyse nodded in agreement. 'It was hugely convenient and I will not even attempt to deny it. Someone did me a huge favour there. I had lost all feeling towards her . . . all positive feelings anyway. I had no fondness for her anymore. At the end we even slept in separate rooms. I came to accept that she was angling for a divorce. She was making my life very difficult. I assume that you think that I murdered her to avoid a costly divorce settlement?'

'We are not assuming anything,' Tom Ainsclough replied flatly.

'Or suspect I murdered her.' Woodhuyse gave a very slight smile. 'I mean, otherwise you would not be here, would you?'

'Frankly we would still be here,' Ainsclough insisted, 'trying to acquire as much background information about the deceased. But we do not suspect anyone yet.'

'Yet,' Woodhuyse echoed.

'Yes . . . yet,' Ainsclough repeated. 'As I said, right now we are making ourselves acquainted with all the facts of the case, the lifestyle of the victim, and establishing the identity of principal people in the victim's life at the time of her death. It is just routine that we call on you like this. Suspicion will come later. Right now we are keeping an open mind and exploring all avenues. We are not discounting anything or anyone.'

'It's still open season,' Yewdall offered with a smile. 'It's still very early days. So, can we ask . . . what do you do for a living, Mr Woodhuyse?'

'I'm in the world of finance,' Woodhuyse replied in a matter-of-fact manner. 'I see you are taking notes?'

'Yes, just the normal procedure.' Yewdall laid her ballpoint pen on the surface of her notepad. 'We can't be expected to remember everything.'

'Yes, I can understand that. I think I should tell you that my name is spelled H-U-Y-S-E although pronounced "Woodhouse", as though it was spelled H-O-U-S-E.'

'Ah . . .' Penny Yewdall wrote on her pad. 'Yes, I was forgetting. Thank you.'

'You seem to be doing very well out of your occupation, Mr Woodhuyse, if you don't mind me saying?' Tom Ainsclough observed.

'I don't mind you saying at all.' Woodhuyse inclined his head to one side as if in receipt of a compliment. 'I'm not complaining about how my life has worked out. The contents of the house are all bought and paid for, but the house is still mortgaged and the Porsche outside is leased, so I am not as well off as appearances might dictate. Had Victoria lived to see the divorce proceedings become final she would have been a little disappointed with the outcome . . . more than a little disappointed, in fact. If the house was sold her share of my wealth would barely have covered her legal bills. I am afraid that I gave her the overall impression that I was wealthier than was in fact the case.'

'I see.' Penny Yewdall tapped her notepad with her ballpoint pen.

'I let her assume the house was owned outright,' Woodhuyse continued, 'when in fact it was still heavily mortgaged. It still is mortgaged, but not as heavily as it was when Victoria lived here. I have made some good money in the last ten years. I'm afraid it was all a bit of a con . . .' Woodhuyse paused. 'I let her assume that all the flash cars I drove were owned when in fact they were leased. So she would have been quite deflated by the details of my actual wealth. I say this because I think it is significant. I didn't save as much money by avoiding a divorce as the police might think.'

'That is an interesting point.' Yewdall nodded briefly. 'It would certainly reduce your motivation to murder your wife, but we would have to delve into your finances to confirm that.'

'You'll need to acquire a court order for that,' Woodhuyse insisted, 'but once that has been obtained, then . . .' he added with a smile, 'be my guest, delve all you care to delve.'

'You'll forgive me, Mr Woodhuyse,' Ainsclough adjusted his position in the low-slung settee, 'but I was expecting you to be younger. There must have been quite an age gap between you and your wife?'

'About twenty years.' Woodhuyse smiled. 'I am not quite as old as my father-in-law but I am very close to it. Mind you, I have a friend who is older than his father-in-law and his is the most stable and successful marriage I know. But yes, I am getting on now and I am beginning to feel it . . . Yes, I was nearer to my father-in-law's age than to Victoria's age.'

'So . . . back to your occupation, Mr Woodhuyse,' Ainsclough pressed. 'Can you be more specific about exactly what you mean by being in the world of finance?'

'Oh . . . not easily . . . I have fingers in many pies.' Woodhuyse glanced nonchalantly up at the high ceiling of the living room. 'You know how it is . . .'

'No,' Tom Ainsclough sat forward, sensing that Woodhuyse was being evasive, 'I don't know how it is; it is not the world I move in.'

'I buy and sell stocks and shares . . . I make investments . . . I lend money, but . . .' Woodhuyse held up his hand, '. . . don't misunderstand me, I am not a loan shark. I am not engaged in any form of criminality.'

'I am gratified to hear it,' Ainsclough replied. 'We both are.'

'So,' Penny Yewdall held her pen poised over her notepad, 'we gather that you were away from London when your wife disappeared?'

'Yes, yes, I was.' Woodhuyse nodded. 'I was up in Scotland, to be precise. I have a cast-iron alibi. I was north of the border looking at a timeshare investment opportunity.'

'Buying a timeshare?' Yewdall asked.

'No!' Woodhuyse raised his voice in alarm. 'No, I would never buy a timeshare. I have always thought such purchases were and are very ill-advised. I mean, committed to living in your timeshare for the same two weeks each year . . . how restricting is that? No, I was up there for the purpose of looking into buying into a consortium which was planning to purchase a large nineteenth-century mansion and convert it into self-contained apartments, each of which could be sold off as individual timeshares. The house itself was too remote to sell the apartments off as individual homes, but the consortium believed that that remoteness would make it a very attractive holiday destination. In the event, I pulled out. I thought that the remoteness would be just as much a stumbling block to a successful development. It was a very nice property though. It was in very good condition, no rot, no damp, being sold at a bargain basement price . . . but just so . . . so . . . remote. So, like I said, I pulled out and I am pleased I did so. The consortium went ahead and bought the property and couldn't interest anyone in buying a timeshare. Ten years on now and they are in a real mess . . . and that is an example of me in the "world of finance". I have two noses . . . a nose for a good deal and a nose for a bad deal.' Woodhuyse once again ran his fingers through his hair. 'So that's where I was when Victoria disappeared. I was up there for about ten days.'

'And you can prove that?' Ainsclough asked.

'Well, I could at the time,' Woodhuyse smiled, 'and indeed I did so. I could produce credit card bills, hotel bills, fuel purchase bills . . . I drew money from cash machines and kept my receipts, and each time I drew money my photograph was taken automatically by the cash dispensing machine. My business associates vouched for my presence during the time in question. It was sufficient to satisfy the police at the time. I assume it's been documented and remains in her "mis-per" file. I gathered back then that the police refer to missing persons as "mis-pers".'

'Yes, we do.' Yewdall nodded. 'And we'll check, just for form's sake but, as you say, if the police were satisfied with your alibi ten years ago, I assume it will doubtless satisfy the police now.' She paused and then asked, 'Do you know of or did you know of anyone who would want to harm your wife?'

'No . . . no, I don't.' Woodhuyse held eye contact with Penny Yewdall. 'I don't now and I didn't then. All right, she was awkward . . . ill-tempered . . . she would recoil from me sexually . . . All part of the plan to divorce. She wasn't universally popular . . . she had a few friends, all women, but I never knew of anyone who would want to harm her – not to the point of murdering her.'

'But her death was favourable to you, nonetheless,' Yewdall pressed. 'As you said yourself, someone saved you some money, if only in legal bills.'

'Yes.' Woodhuyse nodded. 'Yes, I won't deny that her disappearance was of some financial advantage.'

'Fair enough.' Tom Ainsclough took a statement form from his jacket pocket. 'I'll write out a brief statement for you to read and sign, if you'll be so good. Really, all I will write is to confirm your alibi and also state that you knew and know of no one who would want to harm your wife.'

'All right.' Woodhuyse smiled a thin smile. 'I am happy to sign that.'

Tom Ainsclough wrote a brief statement and then handed it to Woodhuyse, who read it whilst holding the tip of the ballpoint pen in his lips as he did so. Woodhuyse then signed the statement and handed the form and pen back to Ainsclough.

Yewdall and Ainsclough stood and thanked Woodhuyse for his cooperation. Woodhuyse saw the officers to the door of his house and shut it gently behind them.

'Have you ever seen a whiter building than that?' Yewdall commented as she and Ainsclough stepped on to the pavement and began to walk to the car.

'Not outside a hospital,' Ainsclough replied. 'He clearly has a thing about the colour white.'

'As you say,' Yewdall replied. Then she asked, 'Why did you take a written statement from him? It's a little early in the investigation to be doing that, especially when we're telling people we've no suspects yet.'

'I was curious,' Ainsclough told her. 'I wanted to see if we knew him. I wanted his fingerprints on the statement form and on the pen, and him putting the pen to his lips and sucking on it like he did . . . well, what a stroke of luck that was. Now we have his DNA.'

Yewdall turned and smiled warmly at him.

'All right, so we can't use any information we might learn because he didn't consent and we didn't have a warrant,' Ainsclough continued, 'but the geezer's got a history . . . my copper's intuition tells me so, and if we don't know him as Elliot Woodhuyse we'll know him as somebody else. Those icy eyes, that superficial charm . . . we'll know him all right, we'll definitely know him.' He took an evidence bag from his jacket pocket and put the statement and his pen inside it and sealed it.

The short man walked up to Ainsclough and Yewdall as they approached their car. He was a muscular-looking man despite his lack of stature. He wore a wide-brimmed cricket hat, a yellow shirt and white trousers, although his footwear seemed to the officers to be unusually heavy for midsummer wear. He smiled a wide, genuine-looking smile and he had a keen, eager, alert look in his eyes. He said, '771 WJ?'

'Sorry?' Penny Yewdall looked down at the short man with a warm expression. 'What do you mean? What is it?'

'I can't be seen talking to you,' the short man explained, 'but you be coppers . . . you be the police, I'm thinking?'

'Yes, we're coppers,' Yewdall replied. 'You be thinking correctly. How can we help you?'

'You can't help me. I can help you. I'm Sean Rooney.' The man spoke with a distinct though soft Irish accent. 'I work for Woodhuyse. He's the man you've just called on. Can't say what I do . . . a bit of this . . . a bit of that . . . some simple gardening like mowing the lawn and trimming the hedges, buying things from the shops. If there's an odd job to be done for Woodhuyse, then Sean Rooney from Tralee in County Kerry will do it. So 771 WJ.'

'What is that?' Yewdall asked as she found herself warming more to the alert, eager to please Sean Rooney from Tralee. 'It sounds like a motor vehicle registration number – quite an old one.'

''Tis exactly what it is.' Rooney held up his right index

finger. ''Tis exactly what it is. You'll be doing well to remember it now.'

'We will?' Ainsclough commented.

'Oh, yes, to be sure.' Rooney smiled. 'You will.'

'Why?' Yewdall asked. 'Why is that, Sean?'

'It is a new car. It was a new car but it had an old registration number. You know how folks give their cars old number plates to make an interesting number,' Rooney explained, 'but I wouldn't do it – it's like getting yourself tattooed, it makes you a marked man. But that was it: 771 WJ.'

Penny Yewdall took her notepad and pen from her handbag. She wrote '771 WJ' on a new page. 'So why tell us about the car, Sean?'

'Why tell you about the car?' Sean Rooney parroted. 'I'll tell you why about the car. It was a car which belonged to Mrs Woodhuyse's friend, right at the time she went missing. The owner of that car called round at the house every time Elliot Woodhuyse was out somewhere . . . crooking . . . or whatever he was up to.'

'Crooking?' Ainsclough repeated. 'Woodhuyse is a wrong 'un, is that what you're saying?'

'Yes, I tell you, Woodhuyse is so bent he looks straight,' Rooney informed him. 'You should see some of the heavy-end villains that call round to the house, them and their hard-faced girlfriends. I can't tell you what his game is but I'm on to a winner that it will interest the police. Anyway, I've got to fly before he gets suspicious, but the owner of 771 WJ can tell you things. I'm sure she can – her and Mrs Woodhuyse seemed as close as my two sisters. When they get together you can't get between them.' Sean Rooney neatly skirted round the two officers and jogged down Springfield Road towards Woodhuyse's property making a short, lightly stepping figure of a man.

'771 WJ.' Penny Yewdall turned to Tom Ainsclough. 'You know it looks like your intuition may be correct; the fingerprints and the DNA you collected might indeed yield an interesting result . . . heavy-end villains with hard-faced girlfriends . . . and a friend who would only visit Mrs Woodhuyse when he was out somewhere.'

It was Friday, 17.35 hours.

SIX

'He pays in hard cash, as regular as clockwork.' The man wore an open-necked blue shirt and long khaki shorts which covered his knees. 'Every month, first of the month a man called Danby . . . yes, David Danby. He has been renting the lock-up now for fifteen years. He is one damn good tenant. I wish I had more like him. He never complains about the annual rent increase, he just wants written confirmation of it – possibly for income tax purposes, but the rent increases . . . can't be helped. The competition in this business is fierce and that keeps the rent as low as possible. I tell you, the fuss some people make when the rent goes up even if it is impossible to avoid, but not Mr Danby.'

'What is he like as a person? How do you find him?' Brunnie asked.

'I hardly know him,' the man replied. 'He calls in each month, pays the rent, gets the rent book marked up and then leaves, barely ever says more than a "hello" or a "good morning". I have little need to say anything more than a polite reply because he pays his rent on time and his tenancy never requires repair. He would tell me if it did.'

'You are Mr Kirkwood of Kirkwood Rents?' Swannell confirmed.

'No . . . no.' The man smiled. He was short, balding and had a neatly trimmed moustache. 'No,' he repeated, 'I am Mr Lee Kilroy of Kirkwood Rents. That's Kilroy as in "Kilroy was here". I bought the entire portfolio from a Mr Dew, as in "Dew point", the temperature at which water vapour condenses.'

'Yes, we know,' Brunnie growled. 'We went to school as well as you.'

'Sorry,' Kilroy replied sheepishly, 'and anyway, Mr Dew bought the portfolio from a Mr Kirkwood who had built it up over many years. But it's composed only of commercial lets because he was apparently a Primitive Methodist and could not countenance being party to the eviction of a family for no matter what reason, but he had no qualms about evicting businessmen from their rents for rent arrears or if the rental was being used for criminal or immoral purposes. So the portfolio is of entirely commercial properties, and that suits me for the same reason that it suited Joshua Kirkwood because, although I am not a Primitive Methodist, I would still find it difficult to evict a family . . . but I would have no difficulty in evicting a jobbing painter and decorator who didn't pay his rent. I mean, ladders and pots of paint don't know they're homeless.'

'I can understand that attitude,' Swannell commented.

'So can I.' Brunnie nodded his approval. 'So can I.'

'So,' Kilroy continued, 'I have met him often but each time it was fleeting so I have not really formed an opinion of the gentleman and his property is sound, as I said. He has never complained about broken glass or a leaky roof. It's a small rental, a little larger than a garage next to a house in suburbia.'

'We know,' Brunnie advised. 'We've been there.'

'Ah . . . then you'll know it's a storage facility used by Mr Danby in his capacity as a self-employed plumber. That is what is listed here.'

'It might have been used for that reason at one point but not anymore,' Swannell said.

'No?' Lee Kilroy's jaw sagged. 'What is it being used for? I have to know because I have to approve its use. I must ensure all the rentals are being used for lawful purposes.'

'We don't know what it is being used for,' Brunnie informed Lee Kilroy, 'but we can tell you that it is not being used for the storage of plumbing equipment or anything at all. There is nothing in it . . . nothing. Not only has it no contents, it seems to have been sanitized – scrubbed with bleach.'

'How did you get in?' Kilroy demanded. 'Did Mr Danby give you a key? You . . . the police, would need a court order to force the doors open.'

Brunnie and Swannell remained momentarily silent. Then Brunnie said, 'Yes, that's true, but when we arrived there in pursuance of our inquiries we found the door was lying ajar.'

'It had already been forced.' Swannell confirmed the untruth. 'Some local felon out on the theft found nothing in the building and went on his felonious little way.'

'It's often the way of it,' Brunnie added. 'So we opened the door and had a peek inside. It will have to be secured. There might be nothing to steal but a down-and-out, some skippering tramp will find it and turn it into his drum, then you'll have to evict someone from their house.'

'I see . . . well, I'll get a new lock from the stores and nip over there and replace the old with the new.' Kilroy sighed. 'That'll take the best part of two hours, what with the travelling involved.'

'Not until tomorrow.' Brunnie spoke slowly. 'Do not do that until tomorrow.'

'I don't work on Sundays,' Kilroy protested. 'I need a day off each week.'

'Lucky you,' Brunnie growled. 'We are not supposed to work on Sundays either but we often have to. It's a question of needs must. But at the moment our forensic team are spraying the lock-up with Lumisol.'

'Loomie what?' Kilroy asked.

'Lumisol. It's a spray. If you spray it on a surface it will turn blue if blood has been spilled there, even if the surface appears clean . . . even if it has been washed,' Swannell explained. 'But the surface in the property at Nuffield Road in Leyton, that seems to have been bleached clean. Our forensic boys and girls will be lucky to get anything from it. Just going in there will make your eyes water and your throat itch.'

'Nuff . . .' Kilroy glanced down the ledger. 'I know I should have computerized a long time ago . . . but Nuffield Road, you say?'

'Yes, why?' Brunnie became alert to a possibility. 'Is there another address?'

'Yes,' Kilroy replied. 'Yes, there is – it's on Colville Road in Stratford. I am sorry, I just assumed you were interested in that address . . . It's also rented by Mr Danby – again, he uses it for his plumbing business as he has done for fifteen years. Pays the same . . . hard cash each month as regular as clockwork. Never complains about the property so I never go there.'

'And that's the same David Danby?' Swannell's voice contained a note of urgency.

'Yes. Same man,' Kilroy replied quickly. 'This is my register of rentees: Daltry, Danby then Davidson. I have no other tenant of that name and he gives the same home address in Raul Road, Peckham.'

'He rents just two properties?' Brunnie clarified.

'Yes. Just the two,' Kilroy confirmed. 'Colville Road and Nuffield Road.'

'We'll need to have a look inside the property on Colville Road,' Swannell told Kilroy. 'Urgently. Do you have a key?'

'Yes, yes, I can let you have a key.' Kilroy's voice faltered. 'I'll go and get it for you.' He walked nervously away and then turned to face Swannell and Brunnie. 'I couldn't get into trouble over this, could I?' he asked.

'Possibly,' Brunnie replied. 'Landlords are liable to be prosecuted for any illegal activities or use of their property, especially if it can be shown that said landlord knew or had cause to suspect that the property was being used illegally.'

'But I wouldn't worry too much,' Swannell added with warmth in his voice. 'We didn't know of Danby renting a second property – we only found the rent book for Nuffield Road, and we probably would not have found out about the Colville Road property if you hadn't mentioned it. We'll make that clear in our report and I am sure the Crown Prosecution Service will look kindly on you.'

'I would appreciate that.' Lee Kilroy forced a smile. 'I'll go and get the key. Do you want me to come with you?'

'No,' Brunnie replied abruptly. 'Just let us have the key and a note of the address.'

Tom Ainsclough sat down at his desk opposite Penny Yewdall's desk. He glanced to his right, out across the River Thames at the solid buildings on the Surrey Bank which at that moment were gleaming in the mid-morning sun.

'You . . .' Penny Yewdall leaned back in her chair and wore a broad smile as she looked directly at Tom Ainsclough. 'You,' she said, 'have the distinct look of the cat that got the cream.'

'Have I?' Tom Ainsclough turned to Penny Yewdall. 'Really?'

'Yes . . . really . . . you do,' Yewdall replied. 'There is a distinct smug "I-know-something-that-you-don't-know" look about you.' She inclined her head to her left. 'Try as you might, you can't hide it. Don't go into acting, you wouldn't be any good at it.'

'Well,' Ainsclough also leaned back in his chair and drummed his palms on his desk top, 'that is probably because I am feeling a bit smug, because I do know something which you don't know.'

'Which is?' Yewdall pressed.

'Which is that the Police National Computer came back with a result on the fingerprints and the DNA we acquired from Elliot Woodhuyse, Esquire.'

'Already!' Yewdall gasped. 'That was quick.'

'Yes; I asked them to put a wriggle on and, good for them, they did so.'

'And?' Yewdall asked impatiently. 'Let me taste the cream.'

'And Mr Woodhuyse, who is in the world of finance, is also known as one Leonard "Len" McLaverty, who is also in the world of finance, but not in the city, more in the manner of money laundering . . . and big-time money laundering at that. I have just shown the printout to Harry Vicary and he is very much pleased.'

'So the crafty geezer has been hiding in plain sight,' Yewdall gasped.

'Seems so,' Ainsclough replied. 'In fact, it is probably the best place to hide if you ask me. I mean, what bobby on the beat is going to suspect a man who lives in that house, in that address with a Porsche parked underneath his front window?'

'Not many.' Yewdall laid her ballpoint pen on the report she was writing. 'Not many,' she repeated, 'I'll grant you that. I certainly wouldn't.'

'He's been keeping his head down, keeping off our radar,' Ainsclough exhaled. 'Quietly laundering money, and it seems he is living very well off the proceeds.'

'So how does Harry want to handle this?' Yewdall asked.

'Softly, softly as always. Harry being Harry, he doesn't want Woodhuyse to know that we know he is aka Leonard "Len" McLaverty. We'll continue to let him believe that we know him only as Woodhuyse, the body of whose wife has just been found and he may or may not be implicated in her murder, and if he thinks that that is the be all and end all of our interest then he's not going to go anywhere. If, on the other hand, he knows that we also know him as Leonard McLaverty, then he'll vanish, go down a bolthole like a racing snake, using any of a few fake passports he will have acquired, and live off the money he doubtless has in numbered accounts in banks in Geneva.'

'I see . . . that seems sensible.' Yewdall nodded approvingly. 'As Harry says, Elliot Woodhuyse won't be going anywhere . . . but Leonard McLaverty will vanish in a puff of smoke.'

'And we don't want that, so Harry wants us to close down on McLaverty with stealth. Right now he wants us to close up the lead the odd job man gave us.'

'Sean Rooney from Tralee,' Penny Yewdall replied. 'What was the car registration number? I have it written down . . .' She consulted her notebook. 'Here it is: 771 WJ.'

'It's still in use,' Ainsclough told her. 'According to the DVLA people in Swansea it's registered to a lady called Hubbard, as in Old Mother Hubbard, who lives in Hertfordshire. We are to call on her, you and me, that is, our next little job.' Ainsclough stood. 'So to horse . . . let's do this thing.'

Victor Swannell turned the key in the padlock of the small lock-up on Colville Road, Stratford. Colville Road had revealed itself to be a short road leading at ninety degrees from an arterial road into an area of what Swannell and Brunnie saw was of neatly kept late nineteenth-century terraced housing, very self-respecting upper-working class and lower-middle class, Swannell thought. They were the family homes of men in stable, skilled blue-collar jobs who stood shoulder to shoulder with salaried local authority workers. The lock-up in question was one of a row of similar sized properties which stood either side of a redundant electricity substation.

The officers opened the door of the lock-up and were met with a wall of musty air, although the door hinges were liberally lubricated and the door opened silently and without protest, thus indicating to the officers that the rentee called frequently but never left the door open, as if opening the door a little, sliding between it and the frame and then closing the door rapidly behind him once he was within the interior, never giving the inside of the building a chance to 'breathe'. Swannell and Brunnie stepped back from the mustiness and fully opened the door, thus permitting the egress of stale air and the ingress of fresh, breathable air and sunlight. The daylight which flooded into the dark interior of the building revealed many wooden boxes; each was a dull grey colour and they were placed in a neat row on the concrete floor of the building. Each box was secured with a heavy padlock. Victor Swannell entered the building, knelt down and lifted the lock of one of the boxes. 'We're not going to get in any of those boxes,' he said. 'Not without a key or a jemmy.'

'I've got just what we need in the car.' Brunnie, who had followed Swannell into the lock-up, replied. 'I'll be back in a minute.'

Moments later the two officers stood quietly side by side looking at the contents of the wooden crate. Eventually the silence was broken by Brunnie, who said softly, 'You know, you could equip an entire army with that lot.'

'A slight exaggeration,' Swannell sighed, 'but I know what you mean. So what do you think we're looking at? Terrorism or gun crime?'

'Gun crime.' Brunnie pondered the contents. 'That is, if all the boxes contain similar weapons. Look, you have shotguns, single and double barrel, mostly sawn-offs . . . you have hand guns, revolvers and automatics . . . you have blades . . . this is all too puny for terrorists, they want your Uzis and Glocks, they want high-powered rifles like the ones used by snipers . . . No, what we have here is a gunsmith's stock-in-trade. The shotguns could be any age; the design of a shotgun hasn't changed since Victorian times. The handguns, they're later . . . World War Two vintage, I'd say.'

'They have probably been used in armed robberies in London since . . . since . . .' Swannell's voice faltered.

'Since we don't know when.' Brunnie finished the sentence for him. 'One gunsmith retires and sells his stock to a new kid on the block, who adds to it when they belong to him . . . He also eventually retires and sells the guns on to a new up-and-coming gunsmith and it'll be the same deal. The felons rent the guns. If the job goes smoothly and no one is injured, the guns are returned and the felons get half their money back. If the turn goes sour and someone is killed or injured, the felons lose all their money and get rid of the guns anyway they can, usually by throwing them into the river. That's been the rule of the game practically since firearms were invented, as you know.'

'Neat,' Swannell whispered. 'So the gunsmith keeps only those weapons which cannot be linked to any crime which went pear-shaped. Very clever. Very cautious. And he keeps his head down . . . never on the radar . . . never takes part in any of the turns. Just a man in the shadows.'

'Yes.' Brunnie's voice also fell to a whisper. 'We'd better phone this in.' He reached into his pocket for his mobile phone. 'We'd better get those crates and their contents safely into our custody.'

'I suppose it was all quite erotic.' The woman smiled at Penny Yewdall and Tom Ainsclough. 'Both of us young, well, youthful, anyway . . . at least youthful if not young . . . but slender, both doing our yoga workout whilst naked in her front room with the curtains shut, of course. Her husband was always out addressing his course of business.'

'Sounds pleasingly erotic to me,' Penny Yewdall offered. 'I am sure men would find the spectacle agreeably pleasing.'

'Well, whatever, that's what we used to do. Twice a week on average . . . then we'd sip tonic water with a lemon slice and have a good long girly natter . . . still naked, just the two of us putting the world to rights, then I'd claw my kit on and jump into my old 771 WJ and drive home. The car was a beat-up old Skoda, which was eventually scrapped, but I kept the number plate and I transferred it to the next car . . . and the next . . . and then to the one after that, and now it's on a Mercedes-Benz.'

'Yes.' Tom Ainsclough read the room. He found it to be age and social status appropriate, being exactly the home of an accountant and his wife: a detached, very solid, mid-Victorian building. 'We noticed it in the road.'

'Yes, I dare say it looks sort of smug but it's not as expensive as it looks. My husband looks after the accounts of a garage proprietor – that is a repair garage, not a petrol filling station – and the proprietor, with his contacts in the motor trade, found it for me. It's a high-mileage model so few people wanted it, but the proprietor said he knew the car and there's nothing wrong with it. He said it was in better condition than many similar models with much lower mileage, so he acquired it quite inexpensively and passed it on to my husband, who gave it to me. It's the smallest Mercedes saloon which can be had, it's a "lady's Merc", as my husband says. My husband's Mercedes is a huge six-litre beast of a thing. He's quite a short man and I think he looks perfectly stupid when he's behind the wheel because the size of the car makes him look even smaller than he is . . . but will he be told?'

The woman, Sylvia Hubbard, was tall and very slender and sinewy, Ainsclough thought, with a clear, fresh complexion. Now in her late thirties, she enjoyed the figure of a woman fifteen years her junior, clearly courtesy of devoting her life to the pursuit and practice of yoga, and also having enjoyed the financial assistance of being married to a wealthy man. Neither Ainsclough nor Yewdall could picture Sylvia Hubbard scrubbing floors or washing dishes in a café. Her home on Park Road in Tring, Hertfordshire, was, on the outside, lavishly painted in a sensitive pastel shade of light blue, as her neighbours' houses were, and her front rooms looked out across acres of the lush green pasturage to a stand of trees in the middle distance. Within the living room the carpet was of a deep pile in dark blue and fitted wall to wall. The furniture was old and dark and solid. Oil paintings in heavy ornate frames hung on the walls. The Doberman, once calmed, lay in the corner of the room and never took its eyes off Yewdall and Ainsclough, but rather stared at the officers with a look of deep suspicion. 'That's Toby,' Sylvia Hubbard had said once the barking dog had been gently silenced. 'He's very handy to have around when Reginald, my husband, is at work.' To which Penny Yewdall had replied only with a smile but had thought, *I just bet he is.*

'So, Victoria.' Sylvia Hubbard slid from the chair in which she had seated herself and, once on the floor, assumed the lotus position. She wore a long flowing cotton skirt and blouse which allowed her to move silently and freely. 'I had hoped it wasn't her body that had been found when I read the newspaper reports, but I know she had been reported as a missing person and so often that means a tragedy, or so I have noticed. I understand that most people who are reported missing turn up alive and well soon after being reported, but if a person stays missing and the press and the TV people get hold of the story, then such missing persons tend not to turn up safe and well – rather their bodies get found or they remain missing forever.' Sylvia Hubbard put the tips of her thumbs and middle fingers together and rested her hands on her knees. 'So what can I tell you?'

'Well . . . really, we'd like to hear anything which you think is relevant.' Penny Yewdall stroked her hair back so it was hooked over her right ear. 'We'd particularly like to know about the quality of her marriage, and also whatever you can tell us about her husband, Mr Elliot Woodhuyse.'

'All right,' Sylvia Hubbard began. 'Well, I don't think that I can tell you much about her husband. He was never in the house when I visited – we made sure of that. I did meet him fleetingly once or twice when I called in to say a quick "hello" to Victoria, but during our two-hour-long sessions, one hour of yoga and one hour of chat, he was never there. But he always seemed to me to be a bit of a shadowy figure. He was not at all interested in two young women cavorting naked in his living room. In fact, we had more to worry about from his gardener and handyman, Sean Rooney, or Sean Looney, as we called him. What a regular little voyeur he was. I mean, if there was the slightest chink in the curtains he'd find it and exploit it . . . really glue his eyes to the glass until we saw him and fully closed the curtains. He was a real little mole of a man who seemed to burrow his way to the surface if there was something interesting to watch. But you ask about her husband – he was in the financial world but exactly what, I never knew . . . Yes, the financial world, so Victoria once told me, but as I say, exactly what he did, I never knew, and quite frankly I don't think Victoria was all that clear about what he did either. She was in banking herself, briefly, but she moved in different, more modest circles than her husband did.' Sylvia Hubbard interlinked her fingers and stretched her arms out in front of her, then slowly moved them above her head. 'I did get the impression that Elliot didn't like people asking too many questions about what he did. He seemed to keep his working life and his home life set well apart from each other and didn't mix the two. I did hear that he kept strange hours, but then people who work in the Square Mile have to keep odd hours. I mean, if you want to talk to someone in San Francisco you have to work late to allow for the time difference, or you have to get up at the crack of dawn if you want to talk to someone in Hong Kong.'

'Yes, understood,' Yewdall commented. 'How did you and Victoria meet?'

'At a yoga evening class which was run by a highly skilled yoga teacher,' Sylvia Hubbard explained while still keeping her arms above her head. 'It was for women only and was a bit pricey when compared to the local authority courses held in the town hall or in a church hall. They are cold and draughty places with suspect teachers and they allow men to join, most of whom just want to ogle women in leotards. Anyway, me and Victoria met and we clicked pretty much immediately. We began to go for coffee together and after the course had finished we decided to continue working out together in the living room of her home in St John's Wood. We settled into a twice-a-week routine – sometimes we met thrice a week if we felt enthusiastic. Other times we only managed once a week, but twice a week was about the norm. This was before I married, when all I had was a cramped studio flat, so because of that it all had to be done at her house.'

'What was their marriage like?' Yewdall asked. 'What impression did you get about that aspect of her life?'

'Strained.' Sylvia Hubbard slowly lowered her arms and breathed out as she did so. 'It's all in the breathing,' she explained. 'Yoga is all about breathing. You breathe in as you adopt a position, and you breathe out as you leave it.'

'The Woodhuyse's marriage,' Ainsclough prompted.

'Ah, yes . . . quiet but strained when I first knew Victoria. Then came the separation caused by his infidelity, I believe, although they were sleeping separately by then, but once his affair became known, well, then it was blood on the wall time . . . and I saw a side to Victoria which up to that point I had not known had existed.' Sylvia Hubbard rested her hands on her knees. 'It came as quite a revelation. You think you know someone and then . . .'

'Oh,' Penny Yewdall pressed, 'what was the previously hidden aspect of her personality?'

'It was an anger as cold and as venomous as you are ever likely to meet.' Sylvia Hubbard placed her palms together and extender her arms, bent at the elbow, above her head. 'It was an anger bordering on hatred. She seemed to be really burning up with it, but, you know, I sensed that it was an anger which was not really directed at her husband, but that the divorce and her determination to take her husband for anything and everything she could take him for was in actual fact a vehicle to express her anger about another, hidden, more deeply buried issue in her life. It seemed to me that her husband's unfaithfulness was a kind of trigger which released a whole maelstrom of emotion which she had hitherto kept a lid on, deeply buried. It was as if it just needed a spark . . . and the separation was said spark.'

'That is interesting.' Penny Yewdall quickly glanced round the room. 'Do you know what the buried anger was in respect of?'

'No . . . no idea at all.' Sylvia Hubbard breathed out slowly as she lowered her hands. 'And the speed . . .'

'The speed?' Yewdall queried.

'Yes, the speed at which you assume such a position. You must not snap into it, rather you must move slowly and deliberately and hold the position . . . and then move slowly out of it. Yoga is body position, the correct breathing and the correct speed of movement.'

'Fascinating,' Tom Ainsclough scowled at Sylvia Hubbard, 'but could we please focus on the reason for our visit, if you don't mind?'

'Focus,' Sylvia Hubbard repeated. 'Focus. I like that word. Yes, we can focus. The focus is that there was another issue in Victoria's life, something other than her marriage and the state of same. She had a history; she had a monster in her past which she was having trouble keeping buried, and which was emerging with great fury at about the time her marriage crumbled. But exactly what that issue . . . that ferocious demon might have been, I am afraid *I* cannot tell you.' Sylvia Hubbard placed a very strong emphasis on the word 'I'.

It was an emphasis which did not go unnoticed by Penny Yewdall, who remarked, 'But you might know someone who can? Is that what you are saying? There is someone you can suggest who might know what it was that Victoria Keynes was so very angry about?'

'I might. I might indeed.' Sylvia Hubbard extended her legs in front of her, keeping her ankles together and her knees flat on the carpet. She then reached forward and held the soles of her feet with both hands, and did so with consummate ease. 'But whether the lady I am thinking of can tell you, or will tell you, I cannot say. That will have to be seen. I dare say that all you can do is to ask her.'

'I dare say we can do that,' Tom Ainsclough replied. 'So . . . who do we ask?'

'You ask a venerable lady called Dafne Zipes.' Sylvia Hubbard lowered her head and breathed deeply, then exhaled slowly. 'I kid you not, that is her name, Zipes . . . spelled just as it sounds Z-I-P-E-S. A strange name, you might think. Her first name, her given name on the other hand, is not spelled as you might expect. It is in fact spelled D-A-F-N-E. She is Dafne Zipes.'

'A foreign lady?' Yewdall asked.

'From Continental Europe. I don't know her history, but she does speak with a European accent, although her English is word perfect,' Sylvia Hubbard explained. 'I just wish my French was half as good as her English.'

'Who is she?' Penny Yewdall wrote 'Dafne Zipes' in her notepad.

'I just told you,' Sylvia Hubbard replied with her head resting on her knees. 'She is Dafne Zipes. That is who she is. She is a highly skilled and much experienced psycho-therapist. I was advised to seek her help by a friend of mine, and I contacted her and she offered me a series of sessions.

I had an issue . . . I was unable to forgive my mother for her alcoholism which blighted my childhood and my young adulthood. She was able to help me to achieve forgiveness and that enabled me to move on and develop relationships which eventually led to my marriage, although my real marrying years had by then passed me by and my husband is significantly older than me. We have no children ourselves, but my husband has two sons and two daughters from his first marriage, so I have some young people to take an interest in. I enjoy being a stepmother to my stepdaughters; they are at that age where they seek a mother's advice and guidance. All four are at boarding school, so the house is quite empty at the moment.'

'I'm sorry,' Penny Yewdall offered. 'You must feel childlessness quite deeply.'

'Well . . . it's not a perfect life.' Sylvia Hubbard kept her head down and continued breathing slowly, deeply and steadily. 'All the trappings of wealth you see in this house, and the building itself, might seem impressive but they hide a lot of emotional aridity. But to continue . . . to focus . . . I told Victoria about Dafne Zipes and Victoria made an appointment to see her. After an initial visit I understand she had a series of regular sessions. Dafne Zipes was then, and I hope still is, a real sage of a woman, just brimming with wisdom. I am sure that she will be able to help you . . . if she is still with us. She was in her late middle years when I saw her about twelve or thirteen years ago, and a lot can happen in that time.' Sylvia Hubbard leaned up slowly and gracefully, and once again adopted the lotus position. 'There will be an issue of confidentiality to be addressed and she may have to take advice from whichever governing body she subscribes to but that will also have to be seen.' Sylvia Hubbard stood. 'If you'll excuse me, I'll go and fetch my address book. It contains Dafne's address, or at least what her address was when I knew her, thirteen summers ago as it was erstwhile, when the ancients ruled . . .'

'Are you still getting all the food you need, Davy?' Victor Swannell smiled as he sat down next to Frankie Brunnie and opposite David 'Chinese Geordie Davy' Danby in the agent's room in HM Prison Brixton. 'I mean, you did say that a short spell in the slammer would suit you.'

'It would be good for your health.' Brunnie nodded. 'Improved diet, three meals a day, clean bed linen . . . it must be quite an improvement in your standard of living.'

'Yes.' Danby nodded. 'It's true, I get all that but I'm wondering if I wanted to do a spell in prison because it looks inviting from where I was, like the other man's grass is always greener, because there are things I am already missing . . . little things have become big things, like what I want to watch each evening on TV, deciding when to eat and also getting to decide what to eat, but all in all, if I don't stay too long it has been good for yours truly.'

'Yes.' Victor Swannell tapped his pen on his notepad. 'It's interesting that you say "if I don't stay too long" because the truth of the matter is that you are likely to be here, or in another HM prison a little longer than you might have probably imagined.'

'Oh . . .?' David Danby looked up at Victor Swannell, and a look of worry crossed his eyes. 'What do you mean?'

'Well, we found the other lock-up, Davy,' Frankie Brunnie explained. 'The one in Stratford – the one on Colville Road, Stratford.'

'Oh, yes, I pay rent on that one as well,' Danby muttered. 'I forgot about that rental.'

'How convenient,' Brunnie grunted with a clear note of sarcasm in his voice. 'How very, very convenient.'

'Honest,' Danby pleaded with open palms, 'it slipped my mind, honest it did, Mr Brunnie.'

'Yes . . .' Brunnie replied. 'We have noticed that things often slip from felons minds from time to time.'

'Indeed we have noticed that,' Swannell added coldly, 'especially when the remembering of said fact could make things very difficult for the felon concerned.'

'As in this case,' Brunnie continued, 'because, unlike the first lock-up in Poplar, which contained nothing and had in fact been sanitized, the lock-up in Stratford contained weapons . . . many weapons.'

'Weapons!' Danby gasped. 'I thought it was empty like the lock-up in Poplar.'

'Did you now?' Swannell smiled. He looked round the agent's room: the white tiled walls, the hard floor, both scrubbed clean, the filament bulb attached to the ceiling, the block of opaque glass high in the wall to allow in natural light.

'Yes,' Danby continued to plead his innocence, 'I really did think it was empty. It might be used for something now and again, but was kept empty most of the time.'

'Well, Davy . . .' Brunnie explained, '. . . far from being empty, it contained firearms – an awful lot of firearms, sufficient to equip a large number of men and possibly a few women who might be intent on perpetrating felonious acts.' Brunnie paused. 'It puts you in the frame for more . . . more . . . shall we say, serious charges.'

'I tell you I didn't know about no guns.' Danby's voice became high-pitched. 'Honest I didn't. I just paid the rent on the lock-ups.'

'So how did it work, Davy?' Swannell asked calmly, yet with noticeable authority. 'What's the SP? How was it done?'

'Each month, on the first Monday each month, even if it's a bank holiday, I get a brown paper envelope pushed through my letter box. It contains a wedge. Hard cash,' Danby explained.

'Yes, we know what a "wedge" is,' Brunnie replied icily. 'Felons do not use cheques or credit cards – a wedge is used in non-sequential notes which can't be traced back to the sender. Cheques and credit cards and brand-new notes can be traced back to their point of origin.'

'Yes . . . well . . . the lolly is to pay the rent on the lock-ups, just the two of them, and there's a bit left over which is my drink, for my time and my assistance.' Danby spoke softly. 'It makes it worth my while.'

'So who sends the wedge?' Brunnie asked.

'Dunno . . . honest,' Danby whined. 'I mean, I don't have a lot of dosh coming in and paying the rent on the lock-ups once a month is useful. I get a drink out of it. It helps me get through the first week of each month. I never get tempted to steal the rent money because I have seen what happens to geezers who steal from the Big Man, whoever the Big Man

is, and even skimming is very naughty – fingers get broken for skimming, arms broken for stealing and you have to pay it all back plus interest, if you want to live. So I take the wedge; it keeps me in beer for the first week of each month.'
'How did all this start?' Brunnie asked.
'And for how long has it been going on?' Swannell probed.
David Danby lowered his head and remained still and silent.
'The lock-up containing the guns and ammunition has been cleared out.' Swannell broke the silence. He leaned forward, folded his arms and rested them on the table top. 'We debated whether to keep the lock-up under surveillance, but it did not seem to be used very often. It was very musty inside, the air was very stale, so our boss, Mr Vicary, decided to remove all the contents and bring them into police custody to keep them comfortably out of harm's way. So one little gunsmith is going to be exceedingly unhappy when he finds out that his stock-in-trade has been confiscated and will be destroyed. He will not be best pleased.'
'Not best pleased at all,' Brunnie echoed. 'And you know how safe you are in prison, Davy. If the Big Man wants you iced, then iced you will be . . . even in prison. Prison is no guarantee of safety, but I dare say you know that, Davy.'
'Yes, yes, I know that.' Danby breathed hard.
'And the further down the feeding trough you are,' Brunnie emphasized, 'the more vulnerable you are.'
'All right.' Swannell leaned back in his chair. 'We've got plenty of time, so let's get the easy bit out of the way first, then we'll take names. How long has this been extant?'
'Extant?' Danby looked questioningly at Swannell.
'Alive . . . in existence,' Swannell advised, 'but I mean how long has this arrangement being going on?'
'Fifteen, sixteen years.' Danby sighed. 'Possibly more. The years just fly by.'
'So how did it start?' Swannell pressed. 'You must have been approached by someone who knew that you were a wrong 'un.'
'Yes, I was approached,' Danby replied. 'It was in the Scrubs, the last prison sentence I served . . . coming to the end of my bird, just a couple of weeks to go after a two-stretch and this other lag asked me if I wanted a job as a drop man. I had to

take rental on two lock-ups . . . in my name . . . any I could find, and pay the rent on them each month. Don't ask no questions. Each month the rent will be put through my letter box plus a little extra . . . I get to keep the extra.'

'Nice and simple.' Swannell smiled again. 'But I can see a problem; I can see a flaw in that little story.'

'What's that?' Danby asked in a frightened tone. 'It's the truth. I am not keeping anything back.'

'You're keeping a lot back, Davy,' Swannell replied, 'but for the time being, just tell us what happens when the owner of the lock-ups increases the rent. How do you then tell the geezer who drops the wedge through your letter box that your rent has gone up, which it would do each year?'

'I have a phone number to ring,' Danby sighed, 'or I go to the battle cruiser.'

'Who do you talk to?' Brunnie asked.

'The lag who put me up to the job. The old lag who approached me when I was in Wormwood Scrubs,' Danby explained. 'Him and another geezer.'

'And you tell him about the rent?' Swannell clarified.

'Yes, and I hand him a note on headed paper from the landlord to prove the rent has increased.' Danby wiped sweat from his brow. 'To show I'm on the up and up and that I am not pulling no flanker.' Danby paused. 'It was always all OK. The increased rent was paid and my little drink went up as well.' Danby paused. 'But I never knew what it was being used for, I never knew about no shooters . . . honest.'

'You just hand over the rent on a gunsmith's arsenal and you carry dead bodies, the bodies of murder victims away in the back of your van to a shallow grave . . . or if they're in bits, you feed them to the river.' Swannell spoke slowly and softly. 'That's quite sufficient for you to collect a long stretch, but aiding and abetting the illegal use of firearms . . . that's a bit naughty, Davy, really is a bit naughty. It puts you in line to be charged with accessory to murder. Accessory after the fact is bad enough, but if you do something to enable the murder to take place, that is being an accessory before the fact and that is more serious and invites a stiffer sentence.' Brunnie paused. 'And if we can link any of those guns to any unsolved murder . . . or murders . . . then each successful link is a potential charge against you for accessory before the fact.'

'We're testing the guns now,' Swannell added, 'or at least our firearms unit is. They'll examine the striations on the bullet caused when the gun is fired, and if the bullet or bullets which have been test-fired can be matched conclusively to bullets recorded from unsolved murder cases . . . well . . . we might not be getting the actual shooter but you'll be going down for a long stretch.'

'It's time to get out your dancing shoes, Davy,' Brunnie suggested. 'Give them a polish and put them on and tie them up nice and tight.'

'Dancing shoes? I haven't got any, Mr Brunnie,' Danby whined. 'What do you mean?'

'What I mean, Davy,' Brunnie explained, 'is that it's time for you to do the old-time favourite . . . the work-for-yourself-or-work-against-yourself two-step because you're in deep, Davy, you're in very deep . . . well over your head. We need names. The more you help us now before the reports start coming back from the forensic laboratory then the better it will be for you.'

'You know, Davy,' Swannell added, '"Big Andy" Cragg hasn't got two brain cells to rub together, but even he is sensible enough to know when the game is up. He's turned Queen's Evidence and he's now in a protected persons unit.'

'Protected persons?' Danby appealed.

'Used to be known as witness protection,' Brunnie explained. 'It's the same animal with a new name.'

'It helps give the illusion of progress,' Swannell added. 'The top floor like doing things like that – thinking up new names for old tricks. It gives them something to do. Anyway, "Big Andy" Cragg is going in the witness box to tell the jury all about you . . . and your van . . . and the refuse collection service you provide to felons with shooters. Will the jury sit up and listen? You can bet your life they will. They'll lap up every detail, listening to Cragg and eyeing you in the dock.'

'So what do you want to know?' Danby whispered with a strong note of resignation in his voice.

'Good man.' Frankie Brunnie smiled. 'You're being very sensible. You can start by telling us the name of the old lag who approached you in the Scrubs who offered you a job as a bag man. He'll do for a start.'

'Don't ever grass anybody up.' Danby sighed. 'It's the first lesson you learn. You don't ever grass anybody up; it's the old honour among thieves number . . . It's not just one of the rules . . . it's the first rule.'

'Yes, we know all about the rules, Davy,' Brunnie replied calmly. 'We know them all: don't grass on anyone, only steal from those that can stand the loss, burgle a house as neatly as you can . . . straight in and straight out, don't hang around and wreck the property, that's for chavs. An honourable thief doesn't do vandalism or violence – not against the person anyway. We know the code of honour amongst thieves, but there comes a time – there comes a time, Davy, when you have to look after number one because nobody else will. There comes a time when the code of honour has to go out of the window.'

'And that time,' Swannell added, 'well, for you, that time is now. So talk to us, Davy.'

'All right.' Danby kept his eyes downcast as he replied softly, 'You need to talk to an old geezer called "Milkie". "Milkie" Raysin.'

'How are you spelling that name?' Swannell picked up his pen.

'R-A-Y-S-I-N,' Danby explained, 'and "Milkie", that comes from his first names, Malcolm Christopher . . . and Raysin, his name, rhymes with raisin the dried fruit, so milk chocolate raisin, shortened to "Milkie". It's been "Milkie" for as long as anyone can remember. He doesn't like it but he's only a gofer himself. He's not a big man, but he's known, so he came up to me and offered me the job.'

'But you're also known, Davy.' Swannell tapped his pen on his notepad. 'The very fact that you were in the Scrubs means you have a police record.'

'Yes, as a thief, but not as a bag man, and I wasn't known to the landlord, the guy who owns the lock-ups. I told him I was a plumber, but the geezer in the Scrubs – he was both. He was known as a bag man and also known to the bloke who rents out the lock-ups. So I took the job. It was easy money.

It wasn't much but I had no other irons in the fire.' Danby sat back in his chair. 'You know how it is.'

'Yes, we can guess.' Swannell also leaned back in his chair. 'Look, governor, a geezer has to eat.' Danby opened both palms in a gesture of protest. 'I mean, what do I do . . . starve? You want me to starve?'

'Let's just get on with it.' Brunnie scratched the back of his left hand. 'So where do we find the unfortunately named "Milkie" Raysin?'

'He's around. He's got a record, as you know, but he moves from one drum to another quite often. I reckon he's got a bit of Romany in him has old "Milkie". He doesn't like to stay in one place for too long, but he never leaves old London Town; he never sets foot outside the Smoke.'

'So he'll be in London?' Swannell confirmed.

'Yes.' Danby nodded. 'Anywhere outside the Smoke – well, that might as well be on another planet. "Milkie"'s' never been out of London in his life. Even when he's been tucked up it's always been in a London slammer. He's an East End boy though, so if he's not tucked up right now he'll be in some old drum or battle cruiser down the East End.'

'Good man . . . now we need to get this in the form of a statement for you to sign.' Frankie Brunnie reached into his briefcase and extracted a statement form. 'I'll write it down then you can read it and sign it.'

'I need to think about that.' Danby buried his head in his fleshy hands.

'Well, the beans are spilled now, Davy. You may as well sign the statement.' Swannell leaned forward. 'I mean, we'll be letting "Milkie" know how we found him. We'll tell him that you mentioned his name.'

'You wouldn't . . .' Danby's voice cracked. 'You won't tell him I grassed him up?'

'We might not have to . . . the old East End telegraph being what it is, it'll be common knowledge that you and Andy Cragg have been lifted. It'll be common knowledge that the lock-ups have been searched. We'll lift "Milkie" Raysin and we won't have to tell anyone that you grassed him up and told us about the lock-ups.' Swannell spoke softly.

'And one gunsmith is going to be very angry indeed,' Brunnie added in a menacing tone. 'He'll be looking for blood. Much blood. Plenty of claret.'

'We know how you got recruited,' Swannell continued, 'so do tell us about the annual rent increase. He's another contact we have to talk to.'

David Danby glanced up at the ceiling. 'Oh, this is not happening to me. Tell me it's all a bad dream.'

'No dream, Davy,' Brunnie growled. 'It's all too real. So who do you or Milkie tell about the rent increase? He's always on the outside; he is always where you know you can find him. Name a name . . . name the boozer where you meet.'

'That's more than my life's worth, Mr Brunnie,' Danby whined. 'He'll lead you to the Big Man more quickly than "Milkie" Raysin will.'

'So help yourself,' Swannell insisted, 'it's called the Protected Persons Unit.'

'Dunno . . . dunno . . .' Danby once again buried his head in his hands.

'Look, Davy,' Brunnie pressed, 'like we have just said, the East End telegraph will have let all the villainy in London know that you and "Big Andy" Cragg have been lifted in connection with the murder of Victoria Keynes and the villainy is always worried when a gofer gets lifted because they've got nothing to lose and everything to gain by helping the police.' Swannell paused. 'Gofers are kept in the dark for that very reason. Never let a gofer know too much, but occasionally a gofer gets to know more than he should and if he's a clever one he always keeps what he knows to himself.'

'Especially if he knows that he is not supposed to know whatever it is he knows,' Brunnie added with a wry smile. 'And so it is the case that top villains, the big men, are never sure exactly what each one of the lowly gofers knows. It's always a guessing game.'

'So when a lowly gofer like you gets his old collar felt and is remanded in custody, then the major players, well, they get well worried, really panicky. They get to thinking just what the little old gofer might tell the law to save his old skin.'

'I'm not safe nowhere if "Milkie" finds out I fingered him,' Danby whined. 'There's no place they can't get me . . . I mean no place, no place at all.'

'We know.' Brunnie smiled. 'We know what it's like. You'll get carved up in the showers . . . well sliced up . . . all that crimson flowing down the drain. So we'll lift "Milkie" Raysin and we'll tell him about your public-spirited nature. He'll get word out about you being a grass and the crime lord will get word back in here that "Chinese Geordie Davy" is squealing not unlike a stuck pig . . . and you'll go into the showers with a group of other geezers and they'll come back out but you won't.'

'And then,' Swannell added, 'Bob's your uncle.'

'They might let you live,' Brunnie continued. 'It all depends on what the crime lord orders . . . but you'll live without an eye, or an ear . . . or a tongue. Grasses tend to lose their tongues; it all depends on what the Big Man wants.'

'Or how ruthless he is,' Swannell said. 'The really sensible ones, well, they don't have no "ruth" at all. None whatsoever. They are totally ruthless.'

'What can I do?' Danby once again buried his head in his hands.

'Sign the statement and tell us the name of the geezer you or Milkie notify about the rent increases . . . We need his name. Just the truth, we won't write fiction and get you to sign it so as to get a conviction. We won't do that, and then you step into the witness box and turn Queen's Evidence.'

'Because it isn't true that you're not safe anywhere.' Swannell spoke calmly but firmly. 'You'll be safe as a protected person . . . new name, new identity, new city to live in . . . a whole new fresh start, and if you want to you can visit London from time to time, walk your roots. You can disguise yourself by growing a long beard before you visit London and your old streets, and if you do that, don't look at people because if you do they'll look at you and eventually, you'll be recognized . . . And don't visit too often. Once or twice a year – any more than that and it won't be healthy for you.'

'If I don't . . .' Danby probed. 'If I don't sign the damn statement?'

'We have told you.' Brunnie spoke coldly. 'In a few days' time you'll walk into the showers and not all of you will come out. It will be messy, oh so very messy, very messy indeed.' 'You might even end your life in there.' Swannell pointed at Danby with his index finger. 'It all depends on how lacking in "ruth" the man's man is. I'd sign if I were you.' 'I need to think,' Danby pleaded. 'Well, don't take too long about it.' Swannell stood and pressed the button at the side of the door to summon one of the prison warders. 'Your life's on the line.' Brunnie stood. 'You know where to contact us once you have decided to do the sensible thing.'

The short, broad-chested man took aim amid a small, hushed crowd of onlookers. He then sent the dart thudding neatly into the 'double top' slot. One man said, 'Good enough' and another man said, 'Good arrow', causing the short, broad-chested dart player to grin broadly as he was tapped on the back by his teammates, who proceeded to empty the kitty jar.

'So, drinks all round,' announced the grinning man who had thrown the winning arrow. He looked over at the table opposite to where the dartboard hung, and a woman sitting in front of a schooner of sherry smiled approvingly at him and gave the thumbs up gesture. The man and the woman, both in their middle years, were in the tap room of The World Turned Upside Down on the Old Kent Road in Deptford. An observer would see the couple as exactly what they were, and what they wanted to be seen as: a working-class pair, relaxing with their own kind – the man with his beer, the woman with her sherry. If he was close enough, the observer might hear the man and the woman speak and he would note that their speech set them apart from their friends because they spoke with short, clipped vowel sounds, not the elongated vowel sounds of south-east London. And instead of using expressions like the just heard 'good enough', they would rather use expressions like 'champion, just champion', and they would refer to each other as 'pet' or 'love' rather than 'china' or 'darlin''. The couple were in fact from the north of England, both the issue of coalminers and who had grown up in Thurscoe, pronounced 'Thursku', in South Yorkshire. The couple were in fact John Shaftoe MD, MRCP, FRCPath – forensic pathologist who had earlier that week complained of the attitude of Professor Dykk at the Royal London Hospital towards working-class entrants to the medical profession, and his wife Linda Shaftoe, neé Arkwright. John and Linda Shaftoe lived in prestigious Brookman's Park in Hertfordshire amongst other senior professionals and captains of industry, but once every few weeks they sought to 'touch base' and mix with the people of the working class, have a few laughs, sink a few pints or a couple of schooners of sherry and throw an arrow or two, always keeping their full identity and occupation a secret so as to ensure acceptance.

Penny Yewdall lay in bed, naked under a thin summer duvet, and glanced up at the sight sky through the window of her bedroom in her small terraced house in Tusker Road, Greenwich. As she lay there her thoughts drifted to her home in the Potteries in Staffordshire, and to her parents, now retired and living on the coast, and then her thoughts turned to her work – to the murder of Victoria Keynes, so young when she lost her life, or had it taken from her, a young woman so clearly troubled about something when she was shot twice in the head and once in the chest. Penny Yewdall thought about the revelations to come from Dafne Zipes and whatever they would be when she was interviewed the next working day. But tomorrow, *tomorrow*, she reminded herself, was Sunday, and for once she would not be working on the Lord's Day. She would sleep late, enjoy a leisurely breakfast, take a stroll in the park later on, climb Observatory Hill and enjoy the vista of North London from the vantage point on the south side of the river. Penny Yewdall was not a native Londoner but she wouldn't live anywhere else.

It was Saturday, 23.40 hours.

SEVEN

'Leonard McLaverty . . . well, well, well. Who would have thought it?' Detective Sergeant Brendan Escritt leaned back in the chair and closed two very clean, perfectly manicured, meaty hands behind his head and smiled broadly. 'He has been on our most-wanted list for many years. My boss will be delighted that he has been tracked down at last. Where is he?'

'Not so fast, Sergeant.' Vicary held his palm upwards facing Escritt and returned the smile. 'He's a number one suspect in a murder inquiry, now we know he is living under an alias. He was visited in respect of the murder by two of my team, and he proved himself very willing to talk and provided an alibi. He stuck to the same alibi he gave ten years ago when the victim vanished. Indeed, it does appear to be a very strong alibi, and he may be completely innocent. That is still to be seen, but my officers were more than a little suspicious of his lifestyle. He seems very well-to-do, living in the sort of area we are paid to patrol and protect, rather than search for felons.'

'I see.' Brendan Escritt folded his arms in front of him. He wore a neatly ironed white shirt and a tie with silver stripes on a green background. Vicary thought it a university tie, and he noted that Escritt, young to hold a detective sergeant rank, did indeed have the air of being a graduate entrant to the Metropolitan Police about him, having alert-looking eyes and being softly spoken. 'So he's been hiding in plain sight but in an area we would not look for him. Very clever. That is McLaverty all over.'

'That's about it.' Vicary looked to his left as his eye was caught by a tug towing a laden barge making its way down the River Thames.

'We knew he'd be living the good life somewhere,' Escritt continued. 'You don't make the sort of ill-gotten gains he is making and live in a council flat in East London or up in Luton or somewhere like that. We just didn't know where he was . . . So, do we get to pay him a visit?'

'Nope.' Vicary smiled again. 'Not yet, anyway . . . so not so fast, please. He is still a suspect in a murder enquiry and that takes precedence over anything the Economic Crime Unit might want to talk to him about.'

'Yes.' Escritt inclined his head to one side. 'I have to accept that . . . that is the rule – cannot and must not upset the apple cart. But do tell me how you found him – we can know that.'

'Yes, you can know that.' Vicary nodded. 'It was the case that two of my officers visited him in connection with the murder I mentioned and they felt that his standard of living was suspiciously high. At that stage they knew him only as Elliot Woodhuyse and he gave his occupation as being "something in the city", but it was mid-week and he was lounging about his house instead of shouting down a phone in some brokerage or other. My officers took a statement from him and then asked him to read and sign it, and so obtained his fingerprints, and then he doubly obliged them by putting the top of the pen in his mouth as he read the statement.'

'Thus providing you with his DNA?' Escritt grinned.

'In one.' Vicary joined in the grinning. 'Upon their return to the Yard the officers sent the paper and the pen to the forensic science lab, who checked with Criminal Records and got a result, known as Leonard McLaverty, for a few minor offences, so we broadcast it in case any department was interested.'

'And here I am.' Escritt glanced out of the window of Vicary's office. 'I confess I like the view you have from up here – better than us on the lowly second floor – but we appreciate your team's "nose" for a felon.'

'Yes, my officers were on the ball there – they intuitively thought that he might be aka and so showed no interest in any alias he might have because they feared that he might have a bolthole ready to slither down.'

'He will do.' Escritt breathed deeply and then exhaled slowly.

'He definitely will have an escape route . . . as almost all white-collar criminals do. He'll have numbered accounts in Swiss banks; he'll have offshore accounts. Elliot Woodhuyse won't be his only alias and he'll also have property abroad. So thanks to your officers . . . as you say, they were well on the ball there all right, and especially for being discreet . . . If he got the slightest whiff that he was suspected of being an "also known as", we would have lost him for good. We don't even know what he looks like. He is totally cagey.'

'But he's been in prison,' Vicary protested. 'You'll have his photograph on file.'

'Oh, we do . . . a very clear image . . . long hair, beard and about twenty years old now.'

'Ah.' Vicary nodded. 'Point taken. So you don't know what he looks like now . . .'

'Exactly. He also has no known tattoos or birthmarks, no scars or healed fractures . . . he has no distinct identifying marks of any kind, only his fingerprints and his DNA. Quite frankly, I am surprised he touched the pen and the statement pad.'

'Well, he could not have refused without arousing suspicion,' Vicary explained, 'and putting the pen tip to his lips – that was just a moment's absent-mindedness, a lapse of concentration. So, tell me, why is the Economic Crime Unit interested in him?'

'He is believed to be a money launderer,' Escritt advised, 'and not just any money launderer but a very major player. His name gets mentioned in that capacity from time to time but nobody knows where he lives or where his base of operations is. He charges seventy pence in the pound – it's a high rate – but he comes up with the goods and he can handle big money. Give him a thousand pounds of sequentially traceable money and he'll give you three hundred untraceable in return. But he only works in large, very large sums.'

'How does he do it?' Vicary leaned back in his chair. He felt intrigued.

'Well, that is what we'd like to have "a wee chat with him about" as my Scots grandfather would have said. He was a police officer in Glasgow.'

'Ah . . . I thought I detected a faint Scottish accent,' Vicary observed warmly.

'Yes, it's still there. I grew up in Scotland until I was about twelve, when my parents relocated England. But to continue . . . McLaverty aka Woodhuyse will have his overheads, like any businessman. He'll have an army of gofers . . . probably young women who will be working naked.'

'Naked!' Vicary exclaimed.

'Of course,' Escritt replied. 'All quite normal, all quite usual. In fact, the last laundering operation we raided we found thirty women working in a unit on an industrial estate. The top man rented the unit and installed the girls, all with criminal records, so they knew the rules – no skimming or it's a damn good hiding.'

'Yes.' Vicary nodded slightly. 'I know the sort of hiding you mean – one that will put her in hospital.'

'So all the girls had difficulty in obtaining employment . . . they were girls with habits, girls with children, they were the sort of girls whose only other way of making a living was to sell themselves on the street. So they turned up for work each day, working a normal nine to five, entered the unit, stripped naked and sat down in front of a long table, fifteen down one side and fifteen down the other. Quite a liberal atmosphere, apparently. Music on the radio, chatting away whilst they worked, smoking if they wanted to smoke but only loose cigarettes and lighters were allowed. They were supervised by a couple of "matrons" – no men around at all for the most part.'

'Why naked?' Vicary asked. 'And what were they doing?'

'They were breaking up the sequence of notes stolen in a payroll robbery. Forty million pounds,' Escritt told him. 'You must remember it?'

'Up in Peterborough . . . five years ago,' Vicary replied. 'That job?'

'Yes, but it was seven years ago.'

'Time flies.' Vicary sighed. 'Goes too damn fast.'

'Indeed.' Escritt also sighed. 'And the girls were naked to discourage them from skimming, slipping the odd fifty-pound note into their pockets, and no cigarette packets or boxes of matches for the same reason. And it wasn't just the notion of theft, it was also and mainly because if sequenced notes got into the wrong hands it could blow the whole operation . . . which is in fact what happened. That's how we cracked the case. Each girl was given a large wedge of sequential money, and from that wedge they took one note at a time and put the note on one of twenty piles in front of them, so eventually each girl was sitting in front of twenty piles of non-sequential notes, with many hundreds of pounds in each pile.'

'Neat,' Vicary commented.

'Yes, but all very labour intensive,' Escritt replied.

'I can see that.' Vicary stroked his chin. 'But please . . . carry on.'

'So when each girl was left with twenty piles of non-sequential notes in front of her, one of the "matrons" would go along the line and take one pile from each girl and put them in the same sack or bag which contained one pile in front of each of the girls.'

'So further breaking up the sequence,' Vicary commented.

'Yes, exactly.' Escritt nodded. 'So the "matron" then had thirty sacks or bags, each containing one and a half thousand pounds, in new but non-sequential notes.'

'Yes,' Vicary replied softly. 'I see how it works.'

'So then they'd have a coffee break, and each girl would then be given another wad of sequential money to put into twenty piles of non-sequential money, and so the production line worked like that all day until five p.m. when the fat lady sang. So at the end of the day there would be sixty thousand pounds of non-sequential money in ninety or so bags . . . one and a half K in each bag.'

'Yes,' Vicary replied. 'Then . . .?'

'Well, what happened then is that another set of gofers arrived – males this time – each taking ten bags apiece into their cars, and they would drive round certain pubs in London, usually struggling pubs or small independent betting shops, where each bag would be sold for one thousand used in untraceable notes,' Escritt explained. 'So the publican, or the casino or betting shop manager made a swift five hundred pounds on the transaction and mixed up the stolen money with his legitimate takings and then banked it.'

'So neat.' Vicary cleared his throat. 'So very neat. You've got to hand it to him. Simple and neat.'

'Oh, yes,' Escritt replied. 'That operation was washing thirty-six thousand pounds each day. They didn't work on Sundays . . . no religious reason, it was because they thought it might make the activity in the unit look suspicious if they didn't have at least one day off each week, especially since every other unit was shut down on that day.'

'Understood.' Vicary nodded. 'Again . . . sensible.'

'They also distributed the money further afield, out west to Bristol and north as far as Newcastle and the other large industrial cities in the north. It was a nice, steady operation, cleaning one hundred and forty thousand pounds plus each month . . . one million and six hundred plus a year.'

'But,' Vicary commented, 'that is still just scratching the surface of the forty million they had to launder.'

'Yes, I know, and they also knew that,' Escritt smiled, 'so they did other things as well, but the slowness of the operation was their downfall, that and a girl from the ghetto. As they say, "You can take a kid from the ghetto but you'll never take the ghetto from the kid", and one girl couldn't prevent herself from stealing. Just one note, but it was all that was needed. She was daft or deft depending on how you look at it – probably both. Anyway, she dropped a fifty-pound note on the floor when the "matrons" were distracted, put her foot on it and began to crunch it up with her toes.'

'Deft,' Vicary commented, 'as you say.'

'So at the end of the day she walked with the other girls to where their clothes were, keeping herself in the middle of the pack to disguise the slight limp she had because she had to keep the toes of one foot curled up so as to hold the note, but once she had put her sock on that foot she could then stand and walk normally and did not draw attention to herself. Heavens, she took a risk doing that but she was a lowlife individual and, later that evening, because of that, no pub or shop would accept the fifty-pound note, suspecting it to be moody in one way or another . . . either stolen or forged . . .'

'As they would,' Vicary commented dryly.

'Oh, yes, it's a lot of money for a small businessman to lose,' Escritt replied. 'A day's profit before tax in some cases.'

'Indeed,' Vicary commented.

'So . . . the girl asked her flatmate to take the fifty-pound note to the bank the next day and change it for five tens, offering the flatmate five pounds for her trouble,' Escritt continued. 'A fair ten per cent. The flatmate agreed because she was long-term unemployed and five pounds was two days' food money for her. Anyway, she didn't look to the bank staff like the sort of woman who would get hold of a fifty-pound note legitimately and so they asked her to take a seat, which she did. The bank checked the serial number of the note and found it was bent and called the police. The local bobbies took her to their nick and contacted the Economic Crime Unit. So we talked to the girl and she seemed kosher – just doing a favour for her flatmate while the flatmate was at work, for a small drink. So we gave her back the fifty-pound note and told her to tell her friend that the bank wouldn't change it because the staff seemed suspicious of her. We knew we'd recover the note easily enough.' Escritt added quickly, 'And if we didn't, what's fifty pounds out of forty million?'

'Not a lot, I grant you.' Vicary inclined his head with a smile. 'It's a loss you can cope with.'

'So the next morning we followed the girl, who had stolen the fifty-pound note, and found that she went to a street corner in Tottenham where she and other girls waited for a private hired motor coach. The coach picked the girls up at eight a.m. and drove them out of London, up into Hertfordshire and to an industrial estate near Stevenage. They were picked up again at the end of the day and taken back to the street corner. We had a wee chat with the motor coach operator who also proved himself to be genuine and believed he had a contract to run some workers up to the industrial estate six mornings a week and collect them again each evening, Monday to Saturday inclusive. He was happy with the contract because he was able to use his oldest vehicle for the job, and he gave the drive to his youngest son who had just turned twenty-one, got his public service vehicle operator's licence and needed short runs to get his hand in before being given the long-distance drives. We asked him to carry on with the service and not to say anything to anyone . . . then we spent weeks on surveillance and notified other forces who kept the various "drops" under surveillance.'

'The pubs, et cetera?' Vicary clarified. 'And private betting shops in other cities? Those are the "drops" you mean?'

'Yes.' Escritt nodded. 'Anyway, this was about one year after the wages snatch and their operation had been running smoothly in that time . . . and we raided.' Escritt smiled broadly. 'Oh, boy, did we raid them . . . coordinated raids at two p.m. on the same day across the UK.'

'Middle of the day?' Vicary observed.

'Yes. We needed them all to be at their designated places of employment . . . the women in the counting house in Stevenage, all the pubs, privately owned betting shops and small casinos open for business, and we made lots of lovely arrests. All the gofers we lifted at their homes; all the girls and the two "matrons" we lifted at the industrial estate. They all started singing like canaries and named the lieutenants and the top man. He was a geezer called Dominic Hughes: well-heeled background, fee paying school . . . quite a posh felon.'

'Did you arrest the guy who stole the money?' Vicary asked.

'No . . . sadly,' Escritt grimaced, 'that was the downside of it all; we just got the washerman and the washerwomen. Dominic Hughes claimed ignorance of the actual thieves and we believed him; we bought his story. It was all done by word of mouth . . . as it often is among the criminal fraternity. The word went out that forty million pounds in traceable notes was up for sale and all the bids were put in by the established money launderers . . . and our man . . .'

'Hughes?'

'Yes. Posh, well spoken, classy Dominic Hughes – he put in the winning bid. He was able to offer twelve million pounds in untraceable money.'

'That is seriously big money,' Vicary observed, 'when you bring it down to the scale of the individual human being.'

'Oh, yes.' Escritt nodded in agreement. 'As you say, sir,

when you bring it down to the scale of the man in the street . . .
well, it'll pay your gas bill.'

'I'll say.' Vicary breathed loudly. Then he added, 'You
mentioned other methods of laundering money?'

'Oh, yes, if Hughes was solely dependent upon his thirty
women and the dodgy bookmakers and pubs and small casinos
and his fifteen or so bag men, then it would have taken him
five years to recover his outlay, then another twenty-plus years
on top of that to fully wash the forty million, and the great
pressure comes from the Bank of England which changes the
design of its notes once every few years, and if the design
changes all dirty money in the old design is worthless. So any
laundering operation has to be done as rapidly as possible,'
Escritt explained. 'So other methods are used.'

'Such as?' Vicary asked.

'Well, the easiest and yet also the most costly is to sub-contract
to smaller laundering operations – the guys who can handle
one million pounds at a time. So it was that Hughes bought
the forty million for thirty per cent of its face value, then sold
a million here and there for forty per cent of its face value,
then he made one hundred thousand pounds in a single
transaction. Ten such transactions will net him a million in
untraceable money, and it was when telling us this that Hughes
first mentioned the name Leonard McLaverty, or Elliot
Woodhuyse. So it seems that in the intervening years McLaverty
has grown from a small operator to a large one, and has filled
the vacancy left by Hughes.'

'Neat . . . a neat way of laundering money,' Vicary observed.

'Yes . . . yes, it is, but it is hugely expensive, selling ten
million for one million. It gets rid of the dirty money very
quickly but at a very small return,' Escritt explained. 'So, the
best returns are obtained by minimally disrupting the sequence
and then making cash offers for property in Continental Europe,
or buying high-end big boy's toys like light aircraft and luxury
yachts or big girl's toys like diamond tiaras, with all purchases
done abroad so the money gets laundered in unsuspecting
foreign banks. Then, when the sale has been completed, the
launderer resells his acquisitions.'

'For less than he paid for each?' Vicary clarified.

'Oh, yes, often for significantly less so to achieve a quick sale because the speed of the operation is of the essence, as I said.' Escritt paused. 'Dominic Hughes, our man, became quite chatty once he realized the game was up, and he told us that if he hadn't been rumbled then he anticipated that he would clear about fifteen to twenty million at the end of the operation. From that he had to subtract his outlay of twelve million, leaving him three to eight million of clear profit, and once his gofers and lieutenants had been paid then he would have pocketed anything from two to seven million . . . straight into his numbered account. That's not bad for about a year to eighteen months work – two years at the very outside. It's still a nice little tax-free earner for an individual: two million pounds for two years' work, and that is the lowest estimate and the longest time. If he put his mind to it he could possibly have cleared seven million in about a year.'

'He collected fifteen years, I believe,' Vicary commented, 'if this is the case I am thinking of.'

'Yes, he was sentenced to fifteen years, but . . .' Escritt opened his palms in a gesture of exasperation, '. . . he knew the rules. He knew how to play the game; he knew very well how to manipulate the system. His was a non-violent crime; no one was injured in either the robbery or the laundering of the money. He made a show of remorse, he joined the Christian Union, he volunteered to clean the toilets and he never gave any bother to anyone. He got a rapid transfer to an open prison and was released on licence after just five years. He kept his appointments with his probation officer for a year, as he was required to do, but when the year expired the licence was discharged and he dropped off the radar. He vanished like a thief in the night, which I suppose is what he was . . . and possibly still is. What he's doing now is anybody's guess; he's either gone back to what he's good at doing and is washing dirty money somewhere or, more likely, he's retired to the sun and is living out his life in luxury.'

'Did you recover any of the money?' Vicary asked.

'Only partially. We raided when just less than half of the forty million, about twenty million, was still in his storage facility waiting for rinsing. We put our forensic accountants on to the trail of the washed stuff. My heavens, they are a determined set of weasels – totally single-minded. I wouldn't want one of them on my tail chasing me for undeclared income, but our man Hughes knew how to hide money, turn it into washed cash and then pay it into numbered bank accounts or bank accounts opened under an assumed name both here and abroad, and that is what McLaverty, aka Woodhuyse will be doing; that is why he was found to be at home during the working day yet claiming to be a city stockbroker. He won't be going anywhere near the washroom. That job he'll have delegated to one of his lieutenants.'

'So what do you know about him?' Vicary sat back in his chair.

'Not as much as we would like to know but his name is linked by our informants to being the main man in the laundering operation of the Southampton job . . . another payroll snatch. One of the gang has turned Queen's Evidence and is now a protected person. He has given evidence which, if he repeats in court, will put McLaverty, or Woodhuyse, away for a long spell . . . if we can find him, and now it looks like we have, indeed, found him. The Southampton job was the snatch of a cool sixty million, which is being washed somewhere at the moment. The notes keep turning up here and there but can't be traced back to their source. But sixty mill – that will take time to wash, and McLaverty/Woodhuyse will not be anxious to leave London or the UK until it's been laundered. So while he's here we have a chance to fondle his collar. His name is mentioned by other informants and, as I said, we believe he has grown to fill the void left by Dominic Hughes.'

'I can see why Woodhuyse is on your most-wanted list.' Vicary smiled. 'How was the money exchanged?'

'Our informant says it was done in a disused aircraft hanger.' Escritt cleared his throat. 'Two lorries – one owned by the laundry man and the other owned by the gang who did the job. But the top men were not there, just their seconds . . . their middle management, if you like, and neither gang knew the other. It was all arranged by word of mouth. A team of gofers carried the dirty money out of one lorry and into the other, and carried the untraceable money back to their lorry.

McLaverty paid thirty per cent – eighteen million in untraceable notes . . .'

'They didn't count it?' Vicary gasped.

Escritt gave Vicary a despairing look. 'They hadn't the time nor the manpower to count it,' he explained. 'They were criminals but they trusted each other. They had to – no other way.' Escritt once again glanced to his right at the view from Vicary's office window. 'I dare say if one gang cheated there would be some blood spilled but we have heard nothing to indicate that that happened. The gang that did the dirty on the other gang would be named and shamed and no other gang would do business with them, so that knowledge of the consequences for cheating kept both gangs in line.'

'I see.' Vicary pursed his lips. 'So I'll let you know where he lives but you must agree not to move on him until we give the nod. He's still a suspect in his wife's murder and that takes precedence over anything the Economic Crime Unit wants him for.'

'Agreed.' Escritt nodded. 'Fully understood and agreed.'

'And a small favour,' Vicary asked, 'if it's possible?'

'Just ask.' Escritt smiled. 'In return for finding McLaverty, we'll be only too pleased to help the Murder and Serious Crime Squad in any way we can.'

'The felon you mentioned earlier, the protected person who is going to give evidence against Woodhuyse, aka McLaverty,' Vicary asked. 'I'd like him to be interviewed by myself or my officers. Anything he can tell us about McLaverty/Woodhuyse might be very useful. In fact, it will be most useful.'

'We can arrange that.' Escritt stood. 'I'll get right on it. I'll have him brought down to Scotland Yard as soon as I can.'

'Ideal.' Vicary also stood and he and Escritt shook hands firmly. 'That would be ideal.'

'No . . . no, I assure you it's not a problem. Not a problem at all. I can talk to you and I will do so with pleasure.' Dafne Zipes revealed herself to be a tall, slender woman with warm, kindly grey eyes, so thought Penny Yewdall, who wore her long silver hair tied in a neat bun at the back of her head. Dafne Zipes had a soft, mellifluous voice with a distinct

European accent and a gentle smile, causing Yewdall to further think that the woman could fairly be described as 'motherly'. Dafne Zipes lived in a cluttered but also neatly kept semi-detached house in Ribbleside Avenue in Northolt. She kept the curtains of her living room partially closed, creating a dimly lit, near mystical atmosphere in her home, so Ainsclough found as he sat next to Penny Yewdall on the settee. An atmosphere that was deepened by the heavy, dark stained furniture, the dark carpet and a large aspidistra plant which grew in a large brass pot and which stood sentinel-like in the corner of the room opposite the door. Dafne Zipes was barefoot and wore a long dress in dark blue which further enhanced the mystical atmosphere of her room, yet both officers had to concede that said mysticism was not at all threatening and had a rather profound sense of peace and tranquillity and safety about it. It had a certain controlled depth, and neither Yewdall nor Ainsclough found the room depressing or overbearing. The interior of the house had come as a great surprise, if not a shock to the officers, because Ribbleside Avenue was, they had discovered, a new-build development of detached and semi-detached properties, and also of short terraces, but all houses were built with a light-coloured brick, with 'postage stamp' front gardens and with short driveways leading to small garages designed for equally small cars. It was as if, both officers thought, Dafne Zipes's room was in the wrong house. It should, they both felt, be a room in a large, ivy-covered house built in Victorian times, which stood on the edge of a remote village where strangers are viewed with suspicion and hostility. 'I work independently and don't have to consult anymore,' she explained. 'But even if I worked for the National Health Service I would still be more than happy to talk to you if the person in question is deceased, and if I can be of assistance to the police with their inquiries.' She paused. 'So, yes, yes, I do remember Victoria Keynes; in fact, I remember her very well indeed. Some clients you remember more than you remember others, and Victoria was one of the well-remembered ones. She was, as I recall, a deeply troubled young woman.'

'What can you tell us about her?' Penny Yewdall asked as she saw Tom Ainsclough reach for his notebook.

'Well . . . I suppose that I had better start at the beginning.' Dafne Zipes paused again as if collecting her thoughts. 'I remember that Victoria contacted me on the advice of a friend of hers who I was also seeing, one Sylvia Hubbard, who I believe you have already met?'

'Yes,' Yewdall replied, 'we have met her. It was she who suggested we contact you.'

'So she told me when she made the courtesy call that I might be contacted by the police on her suggestion. She then told me what it was about and I then heard the sad news about Victoria. I was very saddened. Murdered and her body hidden for ten years. That is not good, not good at all.' Again Dafne Zipes paused before continuing. 'So it was the case that Victoria self-referred and after the initial chat I decided to offer her ten sessions when I had space available. There was, I recall, something like a six-month time gap between the initial self-referral and the beginning of our weekly sessions. These things take time, you see.'

'So we are given to understand.' Yewdall inclined her head to one side.

'Yes, a psychologist's wheels are like the wheels of God. They grind slow but they grind exceeding small.' Dafne Zipes smiled. 'But I dare say it's less time than you'd have to wait for a hip replacement operation, or an operation to remove cataracts,' she added defensively. 'Often the condition is chronic, not acute; the damage wasn't done overnight and it won't be repaired overnight, and so clients can afford to wait for that amount of time before starting the therapy sessions. And the reason why we offer a limited number of sessions is that it forces the client to focus and work on the issue in question. If the client thinks the sessions are endless they will feel that they are not under time pressure and they won't discuss anything. I often find that it's at about the third or fourth session that the patient discloses a whole minefield of issues.'

'I see,' Yewdall replied. 'How interesting.'

'So,' Dafne Zipes continued, 'Victoria arrived for her first appointment. I remember she was neatly and conservatively dressed. She arrived on time, which was impressive because it was quite a trek from her house in St John's Wood out here to Northolt. She travelled by Tube – just one change at Oxford Street, but it's still a long journey – seventeen stations all told, but most of the journey was above ground so she had something to look at other than her fellow passengers. So we sat down in the consulting room, which is the room above this room, intended as a bedroom but it has two armchairs, a table by the client's chair which has tissues on it because often clients get distressed . . . painted in light coloured, pastel shades. We sat down and it was clear that she wanted to work hard. She had referred herself because her marriage was under great strain and she felt that it was failing. She and her husband had not been married very long and she told me that the union was already in trouble, and that she was blaming herself for the trouble because she could not bear to let her husband touch her. She described herself as having everything any woman could want, particularly any young woman. She had a beautiful home and a wealthy and successful husband who worked in the City of London. She told me that he worked in the world of finance but did not elaborate. She had a little experience of working in a bank before she married but her husband's wheelings and dealings in the world of international finance were beyond her, and so she could not share in his world of work. But the real problem, she told me, was that she would freeze each time her husband tried to touch her. I also felt that it was very significant that she referred herself under her maiden name of Keynes, rather than her married name of Woodhuyse. It was as if she was not accepting her marriage, as if she was not committed to it, although I did not comment about it to her.'

'Really?' Yewdall commented. 'That is quite interesting. A recently married woman using her maiden name – that does not sound healthy.'

'It struck me as being very unhealthy,' Dafne Zipes replied. 'But the freezing when her husband touches her . . . that is a classic symptom,' Dafne Zipes continued. 'And because of that attitude she was sending, she was driving her husband away from her and into the arms of other women. So . . . I began to probe and she told me that she had vivid recollections of her childhood up to the age of puberty, and then there was a huge time gap when she recalls only a few isolated incidents. In her early teen years . . . say early to mid-teens, and mostly at school, with some other none-home memories but nothing of her home life. Victoria seemed to have kept her head above water at school, but she told me that she had not done as well as her potential suggested she might. She told me that her teachers had told her parents that she could "go right to the top, but for some reason she was not willing to work". And being a chronic underachiever at school was another symptom, as was the fact that she was a chronic truant . . . not engaging and running away.'

'Oh . . .' Penny Yewdall groaned. 'You know, Miss Zipes, I think I know where you are going with this.'

'Yes.' Dafne Zipes smiled. 'I thought you might – I can see a certain look in your eyes. Have you worked in some aspect of the child protection service?'

'Yes.' Penny Yewdall nodded slightly. 'I did two or three years in the Female and Child Abuse Unit before I transferred to the Murder and Serious Crime Unit.'

'So,' Tom Ainsclough asked, 'where is it that you are going?'

'She was sexually abused by her father,' Penny Yewdall suggested. 'Is that where we are going?'

'Yes,' Dafne Zipes replied solemnly, 'by her father or by some other significant adult in her life who betrayed her trust in him . . . but yes, that is indeed where we are going. It was, it seemed, so Victoria disclosed, the classic "Lolita Syndrome". Whereas paedophiles are attracted to very young pre-pubescent children, those men with the "Lolita Syndrome" are attracted to immediate post-pubescent girls of, shall we say, twelve to sixteen years. Such men find girls of that age nearly impossible to resist. They are powerfully drawn to such girls. That disclosure of Victoria's came about after a few sessions of gentle enquiring, and I used a technique which I usually only use with children when I work with the police and the social services which is to use my animals . . . by which I mean my farmyard.'

'Your farmyard?' Yewdall smiled.

'Yes.' Dafne Zipes also smiled as she replied, 'I have

a collection of toy animals, a few pigs, a few horses, a few cows . . . four sheep, all largish animals . . . no ducks or chickens or geese . . . and we sit down on the floor and play with them, just helping the cow across the field to get a drink from the stream, to get the children familiar with the animals, and then I sit back and watch them play. This is with children, remember.'

'Yes. Understood.' Tom Ainsclough nodded.

'So it is often, very often the case that if children are being sexually abused, they will tend to manipulate the animals into performing overtly sexual acts, mating with each other, not as animals would and which the child might have witnessed, but face-to-face mating as humans would, in the missionary position, and which the child would not have seen. The sessions are discreetly filmed and if that happens, if the children do that, we have some idea about what is happening in the home and we have evidence on film which the police can use in any subsequent court proceedings.'

'I see.' Penny Yewdall spoke softly. 'How interesting. Do you ever use hypnosis on your clients?'

'No. Never,' Dafne Zipes responded adamantly. 'Some psychologists do but I don't. Hypnosis can be dangerous; it can be very damaging and leave people worse off than they were before they started therapy. You can probe for repressed memories; people describe it as being like remembering a dream. Initially they do not think that they are recovering a memory of an actual event, but the memory is recovered in small, isolated episodes, and not in the correct chronological sequence. I once had a male client, a man in his mid- or even late-forties who told me that he had once recovered a memory of being made to fight for his life in a pub in a foreign country where they would not break up fights or call the police as they would in the UK. He told me that he was permitted to choose his opponent but the fight had to go to the death.'

'Blimey,' Ainsclough gasped, 'that is heavy. Which country was that?'

'Brazil, I think my client said. Definitely a Latin American country,' Dafne Zipes replied. 'But the loser's body was to be bundled into a car and driven out of the built-up area to a bridge which spanned a ravine in the jungle and tipped into the ravine. If he had lost the fight my client's body would never have been found and his family would be left fretting and wondering what had happened to him.'

'That experience will be difficult to live with,' Yewdall commented.

'Yes . . . it was . . . I dare say it still is. My client said he couldn't believe how naïve he was, walking into a bar as though he was walking into an English pub for a quiet drink one evening and suddenly finding himself surrounded by desperados who referred to him as a "Blanco" and made him choose one of them to fight to the death. He said it felt like being a sheep amid a pack of hungry wolves. I don't know the details of the fight . . . how the death was occasioned or whether weapons were used – my client didn't say. All he did say was "like the battle of Waterloo, it was a damn close run thing".' Dafne Zipes raised her eyebrows. 'But I mention this because my client repressed the memory. For fifteen full years he had no memory of it; it was his coping mechanism, which is quite normal, and then it emerged piecemeal, helped with alcohol. It took him four or five days to recover the full memory and to put the episodes in the correct chronological order, and a few more days to accept it had happened and that he was not remembering a dream he had once had. The memory will haunt him for the rest of his life and could possibly remain with him throughout the hereafter.'

'The hereafter?' Yewdall allowed a note of surprise to enter her voice.

'Well, who knows?' Dafne Zipes replied. 'I personally believe in the continuation of consciousness after mortal death, and if memories and regret and guilt are part of your conscious-ness, who is to say that we will not be spending eternity beating ourselves up for the stupid things we did and said during this lifetime, particularly in our youth?'

'I confess I have never thought of it like that.' Yewdall sighed. 'Now I am worried.'

'Me as well,' Ainsclough added. 'That thought has put a damper on my day.'

'Well, it is something I ponder from time to time.' Dafne

Zipes seemed to the officers to blend more deeply into the gloom of her room. 'So, to continue with the story of Victoria Keynes . . . I experimented with the farm animals and I said, "Look, you be the girl and I'll be your mummy and we'll play together." She was hesitant at first but then slipped into the role of the young girl quite easily and we played for a while and then she picked up two of the cows and moved them in a manner which simulated the usual human face-to-face sex act. Then she dropped the two animals and said, "Why did I do that?"' Dafne Zipes paused. 'So then I asked her to tell me . . . one woman to another, about the first man she slept with. She said she could not remember.'

'But we all remember our first time,' Yewdall protested. 'It's one of life's milestones.'

'That is in fact not the case,' Dafne Zipes insisted. 'You take it from me; it's not the case at all. If a young girl's first sexual experience was surrounded by trauma she may bury all memory of it. It is a well-documented phenomenon. Victoria went on to tell me she had memories of being sexually active from her early twenties onwards, although she knew she had had sexual experiences before then. She knew that men or a man had "known" her in the biblical sense, but not who or when or for how often and for what time period.'

'How awful,' Yewdall gasped.

'Yes . . . not a pleasant experience, but then I suggested something very controversial, remembering my client who had unlocked the memory of being made to fight for his life in a Latin American bar by his drinking of alcohol. I suggested that Victoria might make use of alcohol.'

'Controversial, as you say,' Ainsclough sighed disapprovingly.

'Oh, I know, I know the issues . . . and Victoria didn't drink. She was teetotal. She had drunk in the past so I was not introducing her to alcohol so much as re-introducing it into her life. She had already developed a resistance to it. Introducing her to alcohol after a lifelong abstinence could have turned her into an alcoholic, and I was aware of that.'

'Yes . . .' Ainsclough sighed once again.

'So,' Zipes continued, 'I was careful to ascertain that she

had taken alcohol before and then I suggested that she buy a bottle of wine and drink it one evening when she was by herself in the house, just one glass at a time. I knew it was a gamble.'

'A gamble, as you say,' Yewdall said softly.

'Yes, as I have just said to you, I was wholly aware of the issues,' Dafne Zipes continued. 'But you see, alcohol is a disinhibitor. As we grow and are socialized we develop checks and balances which control our behaviour. We learn what is and what is not socially acceptable conduct and said checks and balances are known as inhibitors – they are a little like reins on a horse. Alcohol will relax those inhibitors, hence the disorderly behaviour in drunks.'

'Yes,' Ainsclough replied, 'so I believe.'

'Which goes a long way to explaining why serial killers are invariably teetotal,' Dafne Zipes explained. 'They are afraid of the concept of "in vino veritas".'

'"In wine there is truth",' Yewdall offered.

'Yes,' Dafne Zipes replied gently. 'Yes, precisely. They are frightened that alcohol will make them run off at the mouth and they'll let a terrible secret slip out.'

Penny Yewdall and Tom Ainsclough turned to each other and smiled.

'I see you smile,' Dafne Zipes observed. 'Have I said something that has caused you some amusement?'

'No.' Tom Ainsclough turned to Dafne Zipes. 'No, no, you haven't, but you did say something that is a little relevant. You see, this whole investigation started last week, a week ago on Monday, in fact, when I was standing in a pub in Notting Hill and I was working as an undercover officer . . . wearing old, worn-out clothes with three days' growth on my chin and looking very unlike a police officer, when a man who was well in his cups ambled up to me and confessed to once having been part of a murder, and even told me where the body was buried. He was tortured by guilt and the drink made him want to confess to the crime, or his part in it. The drink made him want to talk to a stranger, you see.'

'He must have been tortured,' Dafne Zipes observed.

'We investigated because he told us where the body had been buried and said body transpired to be that of Victoria Keynes.'

'Well, well, well.' Dafne Zipes's mouth fell open. 'An amazing story.'

'Yes, so not funny, but relevant,' Yewdall added. 'And so we are here, all because a drunken man talked to a stranger.'

'I see why you smiled now,' Dafne Zipes commented. 'So, I suggested that Victoria might try to drink a bottle of wine when alone so she might think and not be distracted by company, so that the alcohol might release the inhibitors that were causing her to black out her teenage years. She took the advice and when she came to see me for her next session she just blurted out that she thinks her father did "some things" as she said, to her. And I said, "Yes, I too think he did some things to you." She asked what she should so. She asked if she should keep drinking alcohol, to which I said "no". I told her that the wine has done its job. I told her that her memory box has been unlocked and the whole story would start to seep out a little at a time. I also told her that she should let it come out and that she was not to push it back into the box. I advised her to tell me what she remembered when she remembered it. By then I knew where to lay the focus and so I asked her to tell me about her family, just to get a little background, you see.'

'Yes.' Yewdall ran her fingers through her hair. 'Quite interesting, I would have thought.'

'Oh . . . it was.' Dafne Zipes nodded. 'It was and still is, really. The really interesting thing was that her father took her mother's name when they married. It is only convention, not law, which makes the woman take the man's surname upon marriage. Her father's surname was Lis. But she didn't know why he did not want to keep his own surname. I said that I might be able to shed light there because I have a Polish background, like her father, and told her that his Lis in Polish can mean "sly" or "fox-like" being of "low cunning". It would be like being called Mr Sly in the English speaking world.'

'That is interesting.' Yewdall wrote 'Lis' on her notepad. 'There won't be many Lis's in the London telephone directory.'

'He was also remembered by Victoria as being something of a "house husband". Initially he was a teacher like Victoria's mother, but then was at home all day looking after the house while her mother went to work and brought home the bacon.

Her mother taught at a school some distance from the home, left very early and returned mid-evening. Victoria's school, on the other hand, was quite close by and so there was a significant time at the beginning and the end of the school day when Victoria and her father were alone together and he also insisted that she return home for her lunch every day, further increasing the time he was able to take advantage of her. She reported in later sessions that he had some strange hold over her which she was unable to resist, and which is often the case. Some people have a very manipulative nature. It is very common amongst psychopaths. She recovered the memory of inappropriate touching and fondling but not of full penetrative sex – that was most probably still blocked out, I thought, rather than because it did not happen. I asked her if she wanted to report her father to the police. I volunteered to go with her to offer some emotional support, but she was reluctant . . . she was reluctant to "plough up the past", as she put it, and she also said that the revelation of what her father had done would destroy her mother, for whom she had a strong sense of loyalty. I told her that "digging up the past" would be the only way she would bring closure to it all, the only way she would ever feel comfortable to let men touch her and that, I regret to say, was the last I saw of her.'

'She stopped attending?' Yewdall asked.

'Yes,' Dafne Zipes replied calmly. 'I offered her a course of ten sessions and she attended for eight . . . I think it was eight . . . I can go over my records, but it was all left hanging in the air and so I never knew if she reported her father to the police or not. It seems now that she did not report him.' Dafne Zipes paused. 'You know, Victoria told me that she recalled her father teaching at a school . . . St Aiden's, yes, that was it . . . The name registered because I have a friend of that name. It is, or it at least was, close to their home. The staff there might be worth chatting to.'

'St Aiden's.' Yewdall wrote on her pad. 'Yes . . .' She glanced at Tom Ainsclough, who nodded. 'Yes, we'll pay them a visit.'

'You know I wrote up the case for the *National Journal of Psychotherapy*, making particular reference to my suggestion

that the patient use alcohol to unlock the memory. The article
generated a lot of correspondence which the journal published
over the next few months, with about half condemning my
approach and half subscribing to the notion that you can't
make an omelette without breaking a few eggs. Some harm
has to be risked, even done, to achieve a greater good. The
end justified the means, in a nutshell. Anyway, the inescapable
truth was that it worked.'

Driving away from Dafne Zipes's home, Penny Yewdall
commented, 'There won't be a lot of Lis's in the London
telephone directory; there won't be many in our database either.'

Tom Ainsclough reached for his mobile phone. 'That's what
I was also thinking.' When his call was answered he said, 'I'd
like to do a criminal records check, please.'

St Aiden's School in Selhurst revealed itself to be a slab-sided,
flat-roofed, brick-built 1950s' building. Yewdall and Ainsclough
parked their car outside the main entrance, climbed the short
flight of wide concrete steps and entered the foyer where they
found two boys about twelve years of age sitting side by side
and both looking very worried. Ainsclough asked them directions to the headmaster's office, upon which one of the boys
raised an arm and indicated a corridor which led away from
the foyer. Ainsclough and Yewdall followed the directions,
walked down the corridor and came to a door marked
'Headmaster'.

'Before my time.' The headmaster, a large, serious-minded
man who appeared to be in his sixties, had instantly invited
Yewdall and Ainsclough into his office upon them tapping on
his door, and had then invited them to sit down rather than
employing an imperious waiting time. 'But it was a name I
heard often. I arrived shortly after Keynes left the school amid
mysterious circumstances and rumours were rife. But you
know you should ask Margaret Debenham about Mr Keynes.
She knew him though there was no love lost between them.
She is recently retired after giving her working life to this
school, and she has clearly bonded with it because of what it
meant . . . and still means to her on an emotional level, and
so she has chosen to retire locally. Me, I have no such plans.

I have enjoyed my career and I am looking forward to my
retirement, but my wife and I will be living in Norfolk in our
declining years . . . up in Hunstanton on the Wash. We both
started out there and we'll both finish it all there. But anyway,
Margaret Debenham . . . I have her address here . . . it's very
close. I'll phone her and let her know you'll be calling on her.'

'Please do,' Yewdall replied as she and Tom Ainsclough
stood. 'Please emphasize we are seeking to pick her brains
and nothing more. People tend to get agitated if they know
the police are going to call on them. We don't want her having
a heart attack.'

'It'll take more than the police calling to give Margaret
Debenham a heart attack.' The headmaster grinned. 'She might
give you one though.'

Margaret Debenham's house on Edith Road was a
late-nineteenth century semi-detached house painted white and
built of pale London brick. The small area in front of the
house, originally grassed, had been concreted over as if to
provide off-street parking, although no car or evidence of one
was to be seen. Margaret Debenham was a short, finely built
lady whose grey hair was close cropped. She wore a pale green
dress and sensible black shoes. She instantly demonstrated to
Yewdall and Ainsclough that she had a strong, almost fearless
personality, and Yewdall had no difficulty imagining Miss
Debenham silencing an entire class with a raised eyebrow or
crushing a misbehaving pupil with a glare.

'There was always something weird about Keynes,'
Margaret Debenham told the officers as the three of them sat
in her living room which held furniture from an earlier era.
'I never did like him. He had a controlling way about him.
Even young teachers found themselves doing things for him
which they knew were wrong, like standing in for him so he
could nip out of school for an hour or so . . . and if he could
make adults do that then a child would have no chance at all,
and there he was with a whole building full of them. I kept
well out of his way, and he sensed hostility from me and
kept out of my way. Anyway, to cut a long story short, I
caught him red-handed . . . him and a fourteen-year-old pupil

together in a stock room. He had her stripped to the waist. I reported it, of course, but the headmaster at the time was a spineless cretin called Martin "I run a tight ship, Margaret" Skidmore. He always called me by my given name even though he knew I preferred to be addressed as "Miss Debenham". He said, "The girl wasn't harmed and no damage was done." All right, she would have been a virgin on her wedding night, which would please the staunchly Roman Catholic family she belonged to and the staunchly Roman Catholic family which she no doubt married into . . . but what about the damage in here?' Margaret Debenham jabbed her finger at the side of her head. 'What about the emotional scarring? What about the confusion, the sense of being used? What about that? Today they would have made more of an issue of it but in those days things tended to be played down. So the upshot was that he was handed the pearl-handled revolver in the form of being allowed to resign for "personal reasons". He collected his personal possessions from his shelves in the staff room and walked out of the building that same day. Me, I would have stood him in front of a firing squad in the form of notifying the police. I never knew where he went and I didn't care. But I do know he had a daughter. I seem to remember her name was Victoria. I confess I found myself fretting for her welfare when she reached her teenage years.'

As Yewdall and Ainsclough drove away from Margaret Debenham's house, Ainsclough's mobile phone vibrated. He listened for a moment and then said, 'I see. Thank you.' He pocketed the phone and turned to Penny Yewdall. 'That was Criminal Records; they have no trace of any felon called Lis.'

'Well, it was worth a try,' Yewdall replied as she slowed at the junction with the main road. 'Those stones have to be turned over. But we'll record it as being a name of interest. We'll flag it up.'

It was Monday, 14.40 hours.

EIGHT

Tuesday, 10.10 hours – 12.25 hours to Wednesday,
11.46 hours – 16.50 hours

'Well, it really was quite a stroke of luck, Milkie.'
Swannell relaxed in the chair in the interview
room. 'You don't mind us calling you Milkie?'
'No, I'm used to it.' Raysin turned his head away. 'I used
to mind but not any more.'

'We thought that we'd have to search every tap room in
every pub in the East End of London.'

'That's a lot of tap rooms,' Brunnie added. 'It could have
taken us years.'

'But what do you do, Milkie?' Swannell grinned. 'What do
you do but walk right into our front parlour?'

'Milkie' Raysin showed himself to be a short, round man
with a red face who breathed with difficulty, as if living with
a serious chest condition. A man Brunnie had once met and
who suffered with emphysema had presented a similar
impression. 'That copper had no right to arrest me; I was
just walking home.'

'Just walking home at three a.m. makes a man look
suspicious and beat officers are allowed, even encouraged, to
act upon suspicion.' Brunnie relaxed in his seat. 'Because it
is the case that if something doesn't look right, it invariably
isn't. So he stopped you, you gave a name . . . Malcolm
Christopher Raysin, and he phoned his control to check if you
were wanted and lo and behold, you're wanted for questioning
in connection with a murder. He had every right to have you
huckled. So, Milkie, how are you going to help yourself, I
wonder?'

'I'm not grassing anybody up, and no, I don't want to go
into witness protection.' 'Milkie' Raysin sat with his arms
firmly folded, his head permanently turned to his left. 'I like

the East End of London . . . it's my home. I belong in the East End; they're my streets, my back alleys. So I'll do time, I'll take what's coming to me, but eventually I'll be released, and when I'm released I'll be able to walk down any old street in London, you name it . . . any old frog and toad . . . with my head held high, and I won't be frightened of meeting anybody, and I mean anybody. I'll be able to walk into any battle cruiser, and I mean any battle cruiser, and folk will say that geezer is Milkie Raysin. He did time and he never grassed up a soul – that geezer is all right. You get street cred for that . . . real street cred . . . and that's worth some porridge. There'll be work for me when I get out. Some big man will want a gofer who can keep his north and south well shut. It's all about keeping your north and south zipped up nice and tight and me, mine's as tight as they come.' Raysin paused. 'But grassing up another geezer, giving evidence from inside the witness box . . . I don't care what you say, no one is safe in witness protection, no one. If the big man can't get at you he'll get your family . . . and I have relatives. OK, some I haven't seen for years, but they're still family.'

'You're looking at five years, Milkie,' Brunnie advised. 'That's more than you've done before and you haven't been inside for a long time. And you're quite a small guy – small guys need to watch their backs all the time on account of big guys who live with a sense of injustice and need victims.'

'Dare say that you could go into the Vulnerable Prisoners Unit,' Swannell suggested. 'You'll have some safety in there.'

'I'm not a beast,' Raysin replied with clear indignation. 'You won't get me among all those kiddie molesters, having to check my porridge for ground glass each morning. That copper took a right liberty stopping me, a right liberty.'

'You're still likely to be charged with conspiracy to murder,' Swannell continued. 'You approached "Chinese Geordie Davy" Danby when you were in the Scrubs together about renting two lock-ups in his name, for a drink each month. One lock-up was used to store firearms; the other was an execution chamber. Five years. Minimum. It could even get you ten. You're not a young man anymore, Milkie, and you're clearly not a fit man.

You might not live to be released, unless it's to be released to hospital for terminal care.'

'You won't be walking into any battle cruiser at all.' Brunnie spoke softly. 'And you won't have no street to have any cred in.'

'I can't see no road round it,' Raysin answered equally softly as he wheezed for breath. 'I'm not a grass . . . I never was . . . I never will be.'

'Well, supposing we help you?' Swannell suggested.

'How?' Raysin turned his head and looked at Swannell. 'How can you help me?'

'There are ways,' Brunnie added. 'There are a number of ways – quite a few, in fact.'

'How?' A glimmer of hope flashed across Raysin's tired-looking eyes. 'How can you help old Milkie?'

'What we're . . . who we are interested in is the man who "Chinese Geordie Davy" Danby rented the lock-ups for, the guy who used them. You and Danby are co-conspirators. Somebody must have approached you to ask you to find a gofer who was not known to be a crim to use to rent the lock-ups,' Swannell pressed. 'You were the intermediary, the go-between, between the gunsmith, the snuff man and Danby. Who did you feed Danby's name to?'

Raysin remained silent.

'Look, Milkie.' Brunnie sat forward in his chair. 'We keep all the evidence relating to unsolved crimes, and right now our firearms experts are test firing all the shooters we found in the lock-up in Stratford, and if one can be matched to a bullet taken from a crime scene where shooters were used or someone was murdered . . . then . . . that is ten years for you, Milkie. The clock's ticking. You know Danby made the same sort of noises as you about not being a grass and all the rest of it, but now he's accepted witness protection.'

'He has?' Raysin wheezed.

'Yes, he has,' Swannell added. 'You might do well to take a leaf out of his book.'

'He hasn't any family,' Raysin protested. 'I have, so no witness protection for me, even if I die in the slammer. I'm not doing it.'

'So how about giving us a name on the QT? If you do that, and we get a result, we won't charge you. We'll let you walk and nobody will even know you've been in the police station. But we'll need as much information as you can let us have,' Swannell explained. 'The more you scratch our back then the more we'll scratch yours.'

'I get the idea.' Raysin took a shallow breath and the action caused him clear discomfort. 'You're right; I'm too old for the slammer. Old Milkie is on the downward slope . . . well on.'

'So do you warm to the idea?' Swannell asked.

'Well . . .' Raysin took another difficult breath. 'Let's say I don't get cold; old Milkie don't feel cold to the idea.'

'So who do we need to look for?' Brunnie pressed. 'Name a name.'

'A geezer called Zolton.' Raysin turned to his left. 'I've just grassed someone up . . . I can't believe I've just done that.'

'You're kidding . . . come on, Milkie, get serious . . . he sounds like some character from a science-fiction comic . . . "Zolton the evil" from planet whatever,' Brunnie growled. 'Here we are making you a good deal and you play games.'

'No games,' Raysin wheezed. 'Straight up, governor, that's his name. It's a Polish name, I believe . . . I heard it was Polish.'

'First name or surname?' Swannell wrote on his pad.

'First, I think. He answers to it, so it's likely to be a given first name. But he's got a London accent. He's a serious guy; no one calls him Mr Zolton, so I reckon it's his Christian name. I mean, he snuffs people and you don't call a man like that by his surname – not unless you want to be snuffed.' Raysin took another difficult breath. 'Not unless you're tired of life.'

'Fair enough.' Swannell nodded. 'So where do we find him?'

'Can't help you there, governor, sorry. He's very private like that,' Raysin replied. 'He just comes and does the business . . . offs people with his point twenty-two. He always uses the same point twenty-two. If you find his house, you'll find the gun.' Raysin raised his index finger. 'And *that* you will be able to match but only if you find the body, and that's

very unlikely.' Raysin paused. 'Except maybe one body. One
girl he didn't have chopped into little pieces.'
    'You were there?' Brunnie asked with growing interest.
    'Yes, there were a few of us,' Raysin replied.
    'We know Danby was there . . . and his helper "Big Andy"
Cragg.'
    'And another guy,' Raysin advised. 'He was scared. He was
being shown a snuffing out . . . to make him behave for some
big man I should think . . . I shouldn't wonder.'
    'What do you know about the victim that wasn't chopped
up?' Brunnie asked.
    'Not a lot,' Raysin wheezed. 'He's good at his job . . . no
messing about, just comes out of the shadows, puts the point
twenty-two right up against the mark and pulls the trigger . . .
cuts down the noise. If you put the end of the barrel up to
the skin and pull the trigger it's like the gun has a silencer
– it don't make hardly any noise. But there was something
else about that girl; not only was she not cut up, he wore a
mask when he shot her . . . a pig's face mask, like he didn't
want her to know who was offing her. She was something
to him.'
    'That,' Brunnie turned to Swannell, 'is very interesting.'
    'How were the victims brought to the lock-up?' Swannell
asked.
    'They were delivered.' Raysin put his hand to his mouth
and coughed deeply. 'They probably still are if he's still in
business. They are left on the floor of the lock-up, then Zolton
arrives. Does the business then the mark is left there. He calls
it "curing" . . .'
    'Delivered,' Swannell repeated, 'by who?'
    'He has a small team of heavies on his payroll. Ex-soldiers.
He tells them who the mark is then leaves his heavies to work
out the how and the when.' Raysin again coughed deeply and
was clearly in some discomfort. 'They're not present when
the business is done, that's the deal I was told . . . it'll help
their defence if they get arrested. They didn't know why they
grabbed the mark and were not part of the murder.'
    'And you wouldn't know their names?' Brunnie suggested.
    ''Course not . . .' Raysin forced a smile. 'Besides, they

move on. Zolton might have been icing people for top firms for twenty years but the boys on his payroll . . . they're always coming and going.' Raysin paused again.

'Then when the mark has "cured" after a few days the butcher comes in . . . with a box saw . . . like those saws a gardener or woodsman uses: huge blade, cuts through tree branches like a hot knife through butter. Sometimes Zolton does it, sometimes he supervises it being done . . . sometimes a "butcher" is left alone with the job, but at the end of it the body is in about ten pieces: head, upper arms, forearms, thighs, lower legs . . . and the body.' Raysin patted his stomach. 'The stomach is always punctured to let the gases escape. The bits are wrapped up, put in bags and taken out and disposed of. I heard it's into the Old Father, but I've never seen that done – that bit is done by the "clear-up team", people like "Chinese Geordie Davy" and his helper, Andy Cragg, but you're right.' Raysin took a breath as if to fight a coughing fit. 'That girl wasn't cut up; she seemed special but the other girl was cut up.'

'There were two girls shot that night!' Swannell raised his voice.

'No . . .' Raysin managed to contain another wheezing episode. 'Just one. Then two nights later the other was delivered and shot. Possibly they were three nights apart but more or less at the same time, and looked about the same age. I thought they might have some connection. Most of the people who end up on the floor at the lock-up have "villain" written all the way through them like a stick of Margate rock but not those two . . . they were not hard street-workers either. They lay there trussed up like normal but not looking like normal marks.'

'Trussed up?' Brunnie repeated. 'How?'

'Wrists tied together behind their backs,' Raysin explained. 'One or both feet pushed under the rope. You can't escape from that. It's the way the ex-soldiers do it. Anyway, both girls were shot, close up, in the head, but only one girl saw Zolton's face and she was cut up . . . the other girl was shot by a geezer in a mask, taken out all in one piece and buried someplace.'

Swannell ran his fingers through his hair. 'All right, Milkie, this is good – this is something we didn't know. We didn't know about another girl being murdered at the same time – more or less the same time – and the way you describe it, it does sound like they had some connection. So what can you tell us about the other girl?'

'This will make the prosecution go away for Old Milkie Raysin?' Raysin asked.

'Possibly,' Brunnie growled. 'Maybe even probably, but no promises. But you're doing yourself a favour . . . so, carry on. What can you tell us about the other girl? Did you know her name?'

'No.' Raysin shook his head. 'She was just another job.'

'Can you describe her?' Swannell asked.

'Yes, a bit, from what I remember.' Raysin coughed and wheezed. 'She was a tall girl, really tall, possibly six feet . . . Very long legs . . . Body seemed normal but she had legs like a stork – they gave her height. Long black hair, and she had this odd birthmark on the inside of her left thigh . . . curved, it was . . . like a banana or a crescent moon.'

'So, tall girl, long black hair, crescent-shaped birthmark.' Swannell glanced at Brunnie. 'She'll be a missing person . . . same age as Victoria Keynes . . . a woman in her twenties. We'll flag up Zolton as a name of interest.'

'But that's all I can tell you,' Raysin insisted. 'That's all I'm going to say. I can tell you that Danby knows Zolton, so if Danby's going into witness protection, get him to sign a statement naming Zolton. Milkie Raysin is signing nothing.'

'We might just do that,' Brunnie said. 'We'll have another chat with him; see if he can tell us about Zolton.'

'So what happens to old Milkie now?' Raysin asked. 'You'll be letting me walk?'

'We'll be taking you home.' Swannell stood.

'That's kind, sir, I appreciate it.' 'Milkie' Raysin grinned. 'Very kind.'

'No kindness involved, Milkie.' Brunnie also stood. 'We just need to know where you live in case we want another chat.'

'I can give you my address,' Raysin protested. 'I can let you have it. No problem.'

'You can give us any old address,' Swannell opened the

door of the interview room, 'but we need your real address, and we only get that by taking you there and watching you unlock the door. Come on . . . on your feet.'

'That,' Brendan Escritt skimmed the black-and-white photographs across the table, 'is what McLaverty looks like now. And he's calling himself Woodhuyse . . . H-U-Y-S-E.'

'Woodhuyse,' Chief Inspector Meadows repeated. 'Fancy spelling for a common enough name, but that's McLaverty. How did you obtain this?' Meadows looked at the print which showed Woodhuyse by the side of his car outside his house.

'From information provided for us by the Murder and Serious Crime Squad,' Escritt explained, 'who are also interested in him, and by the sheer good fortune that a house is empty on the same street as his, opposite side of the road and just a couple of doors down. We had a word with the estate agents and they have let us use the house to mount a surveillance operation. Houses on that street sell very slowly; it'll be weeks before someone is interested enough to want to be shown round the property.'

'He looks like he's washing his car,' Meadows commented. 'People with his sort of money always use the carwash, have it done for them.'

'Yes, sir, but it means that he doesn't know he's under surveillance, and he thinks the police are only interested in him in respect of the murder of his wife, for which he apparently has a cast-iron alibi. We have a real chance of arresting him now, sir. With Ritchie's evidence we can put him away for a long time.' Escritt handed Meadows another photograph, also in black and white. It showed Woodhuyse leaning into the interior of an Audi. 'No telling who he was talking to, sir,' Escritt commented. 'It might have been some geezer asking directions, but we checked the number plate anyway. It belongs to a bloke called Zolton Lis, address in Pinner. Dare say a guy with an Audi would live in Pinner, but he's not known. The reason I really wanted to see you though is to pass on Chief Inspector Vicary's request to interview Larry Ritchie about McLaverty . . . whom they know as Woodhuyse. We owe them a real favour so I said I'd arrange it . . . if that's all right?'

'Yes . . . yes.' Meadows nodded. 'Will you be sitting in on the interview?'

'If I can,' Escritt replied. 'I'll make arrangements now. I'll be able to bring him down tomorrow.'

It was Tuesday, 12.35 p.m.

Wednesday, 11.45 a.m.

'I hide in one of the old houses.' Larry Ritchie revealed himself to be a nervous, fidgety, small, finely built man with quick darting eyes, one brown and the other green, as if he was constantly looking for both prey and danger and was seeking both at the same time. 'The protected persons' people put me up in a bungalow on the coast near the cliff top but right on the cliff top there is a row of empty houses. They're about to fall into the sea – the sea has worn the cliffs away. When they were built the cliff edge was a hundred yards from the back door, but now if you step out of the back door you take three paces and you're over the cliff edge. Those houses can be bought for a pound each, but they're not even worth that to buy to dismantle them. It's cheaper to buy new tiles and timber, you see.'

'So why go there?' Vicary asked.

'I feel safer there, that's why . . . safer than in the bungalow, even though only my police contact knows where I am.' Ritchie scratched his ribcage. 'But when you're dealing with McLaverty . . . They say he can find anyone anywhere. If he can't find them then he turns on your family. One old geezer he couldn't find so he traced this geezer's old mum and dad to their retirement bungalow, shoots them, shoots their dogs and torches their house. Not him personally – he contracts that business out. But that's McLaverty.'

'And you are giving evidence against him?' Vicary asked. 'You're not afraid?'

'I'm helping the Old Bill as much as I can . . . Don't get me wrong, governor, I am not a reformed character. I haven't got religious all of a sudden but I got the word that McLaverty was looking for me and that means only one thing . . .' Ritchie drew his finger across his throat. 'So I ran into the first police station I could find. It was the only place I was safe, otherwise it was the end of little me. All right, so I never amounted to much in life, but I don't want to meet my maker before I have to. If I grass on McLaverty I won't be safe anywhere but I'm safer in the little bungalow and even safer in the empty house on the cliff top. I leave the bungalow before dawn . . . I return after dusk, eat some food and then sleep. Just one meal a day but it's all I need.'

'You know McLaverty as a money launderer?' Vicary asked.

'I know him as many things, but yes, he is a money launderer and I can tell you that he is washing the money from the Southampton wages snatch . . . sixty million quid. He won't wash that sort of money in a hurry but he has his methods. He learned the tricks from a geezer called Dominic Hughes.'

'Yes, we know about Dominic Hughes's methods,' Vicary explained. 'Mr Escritt told us.'

'Where did Hughes vanish to?' Escritt asked. 'I've been meaning to ask.'

'There's no evidence, but the rumour is he retired,' Ritchie explained. 'He is said to be living in Malta with a couple of ex-dancers and enough money to see himself out. He lost a lot when he was arrested but kept enough hidden to see himself out. That's the rumour.'

'Interesting,' Escritt commented. 'We did wonder where he went.'

'McLaverty wants to do the same,' Ritchie advised. 'One last big job, then retire to the sun, but where he is and what he calls himself now I can't tell you. I was just a gofer, but gofers get to know things they shouldn't and we little gofers are more dangerous . . . we have nothing to lose, see . . .'

'So we have heard,' Vicary commented.

'It's true, though – a big man's lieutenants have investment in the firm; it's in their interest to keep schtum but a gofer can talk to the police and help himself if he needs to.'

'Well, we know where he is,' Escritt said, 'and we know what he calls himself now and has been calling himself for the last ten years. We'll be arresting him soon once the Murder and Serious Crime squad have finished their inquiries. And you don't know where he put the sixty million or where he is breaking up the sequences?'

'No.' Ritchie shook his head. 'But I can tell you the names of his gofers. Once you have rounded them up and told them the big man is going to topple, they'll start talking. One bit of information will lead to another and you'll find his "factory" and his warehouse. I can give evidence about a serious assault that will put him away for five years but you'll need more than that . . . and I've got more.'

'The five years will be useful,' Escritt replied. 'If he has a conviction we'll get a court order to allow the forensic accountants to look at his finances, but anything else, Larry . . . as much as you can tell us about McLaverty.'

'I can tell you about Zolton,' Ritchie said quietly.

Vicary sat up. 'That name has been flagged up by my officers,' he exclaimed. 'We need to find him. We don't know where he lives.'

'He lives in Pinner,' Escritt advised.

'You know him!' Vicary turned to Escritt.

'No . . . and we are not yet aware that his name has been flagged up, but a car pulled up outside McLaverty's yesterday. He and the car driver had a brief chat. We thought it might just be a member of the public asking directions but we took a note of the registration number of the car . . . turns out it belongs to one Zolton Lis . . . address in Pinner.'

'You're watching him?' Vicary gasped. 'We had an agreement. Murder takes precedence over economics crime.'

'And we are keeping to the agreement, Mr Vicary. I assure you we are being very discreet and we are good at our job. We are not moving against him.'

'Still, you should have told us. I'll be talking to your boss, Mr Meadows. I am not a happy man about this. Not happy at all. The ECU could have blown the whole operation.'

'Yes, sir,' Escritt replied. 'I am sorry.'

'It's essential the left hand must know what the right hand is doing.' Vicary spoke calmly but coldly.

'Yes, sir,' Escritt replied, sounding uncomfortable.

'So.' Vicary turned to Ritchie. 'What can you tell us about Zolton Lis?'

'He's a hitman. He's not on anybody's payroll. Gangland contacts him . . . and McLaverty uses him. When I first went to work for McLaverty I was told to wait on a street corner – I was told I'd be picked up. I was picked up by two guys. This was ten years ago. I was taken to a lock-up in the East End. There was a girl on the floor, tied up . . .'

'A girl?' Vicary repeated.

'A young woman, tied up so she couldn't move . . . she was about mid-twenties, long hair, long, long legs . . . A few other geezers were standing around and then this really small guy, Zolton Lis, comes out of the shadows, like from nowhere, walks up to this girl, puts a point twenty-two to her head and shoots her twice then once in the chest. Then he turns to me and says, "That's what Mr McLaverty wanted you to see if you're going to work for him. That's what happens to people who talk to the police." So I said, "OK . . . OK, but why did Mr McLaverty want her dead? She didn't look like she was a villain?" So Zolton, he says, "He didn't. I can tell you that was nothing to do with McLaverty, but she and another girl were going to the police about another geezer, a geezer I know well. They would have destroyed his life and his marriage; he thought it best if both girls disappeared. So I helped him out." But I didn't ask any questions. It's just that Mr McLaverty likes all his new men to see an "event" so they know that he's the man. McLaverty had told me a day or two earlier that I was a new man and there was an "event" planned, a "double event" in fact, but McLaverty said no need to see both, I just needed to see one. So I saw one and I got to know the triggerman over the years as being Zolton Lis.'

'Will you give evidence to that effect?' Vicary asked.

'Yes.' Ritchie nodded. 'If I am spilling beans I may as well spill as many as I can. McLaverty uses Zolton Lis now and then. If someone needs to be chilled, McLaverty will contact Lis. If you can tie McLaverty and Lis together, you'll bring McLaverty down and put him away for a lot longer than five years. An awful lot longer.'

'Sounds like something we need to do,' Vicary replied, 'but tell me . . . you've worked for the man you know as McLaverty for ten years but you don't know where he lives or where his business premises are?'

'I don't. Other gofers might. I can let you have a few names.' Ritchie scratched his ribs again vigorously.

'So how does he contact you?' Vicary asked.

'By phone,' Ritchie explained. 'I have to wait in at home until midday each day, every day . . . and I mean every day. If there's a job for me McLaverty will phone me but he's cagey, he always uses a public telephone and always a different phone. After the call I used to press 1471 to get the caller's number. I am called from a different number each time. Sometimes there's background noise . . . a road with a lot of traffic, a pub, a railway station. After a while I stopped phoning 1471. There was no point. If I am not phoned by midday the rest of the day is mine . . . or was mine – that was the arrangement. I'm not working for him no more. My money arrived each week – hard cash in the post. That's how McLaverty works . . . or whatever his name is now.'

'Woodhuyse,' Vicary said. 'No reason why you shouldn't be told that, but it's not spelled how you think it's spelled.' He paused. 'So, tell us, did you see Zolton shoot anyone else?'

'Couple of times.' Ritchie once again scratched his ribcage. 'When McLaverty contracted Zolton Lis to off a geezer he always wanted a witness so he'd send a gofer, and sometimes I was the gofer who was sent. I don't know how he brought the mark to his lock-up and I don't know where he put the bodies.'

'It's all right.' Vicary raised his hand. 'We know all that.'

'But I was there at three other "events" after I saw the girl killed.'

'You're going to be more useful than we thought.' Escritt smiled. 'Thanks, Larry.'

'Do I get to choose my new name?' Ritchie asked.

'Up to a point,' Vicary explained. 'You'll be given a list of names to choose from . . . but yes, this has been good. Very good indeed.'

'It would explain the pig mask.' Vicary surveyed his team as they sat alert and listening in front of his desk. 'You think but you're not certain, Penny?'

'Yes, sir, I think Mr Keynes said his brother's name was Zolton but I am not certain. It registered because it was an unusual name but I didn't take a note of it because at the time the name of Victoria Keynes's paternal uncle did not seem relevant.'

'Fair enough,' Vicary murmured. 'But as I said, it would explain the pig's face mask – he didn't want his niece to know that it was he who was going to shoot her . . . that look in her eyes realizing she had been betrayed would have stayed with him; even an ice-cold killing machine like Zolton Lis must have a soul deep down inside, and it explains why she, of all his countless victims, was not cut up and her body parts thrown in the river. She was family, so she stayed whole.'

'Quite some coincidence though, sir,' Brunnie commented.

'Yes, yes it is, but coincidences happen.' Vicary addressed Brunnie. 'As witness, Olivia Jessop, the lady who survived the sinking of the *Titanic* and then a few years later survived the sinking of the *Britannic*. Just ponder that for a moment: two sister ships both sank because they struck free-floating objects, an iceberg and a sea mine respectively. Olivia Jessop was on both when they sank and survived both sinkings. Also as witness, the man who was visiting Hiroshima and who survived the bomb and then returned home to Nagasaki and survived the second bomb. He lived to enjoy longevity. Both were lucky or unlucky, depending on which way you look at it, but the point is that coincidence does happen. And just as a second can be a very long time in certain circumstances, then in certain circumstances the world can be a very small place indeed. So it seems that Victoria Keynes was going to report her father for some misdeeds which are only hinted at, her father turned to his brother . . . and the brother, Victoria's uncle, unknown to Victoria, was a hitman contracted now and again to do some rubbing out for McLaverty, whom she knew as Woodhuyse, her husband. It is not impossible. So Penny and Tom, stay together. Visit Mrs Keynes and confirm if you can that her brother-in-law is called Zolton and that he lives in Pinner. Then follow the link to the other girl who was murdered at the same time. What was her name?'

'Short,' Penny Yewdall replied. 'Can't remember her

Christian name, sir, but I remember her surname because of the irony. Short, yet she was about six feet tall.'

'All right . . . Frankie and Victor . . .'

'Sir?'

'Hold yourselves in readiness for the arrest of Elliot Woodhuyse, aka Leonard McLaverty and his hitman, Zolton Lis,' Vicary said.

'Yes, sir,' Swannell replied.

'Meanwhile . . .' Vicary took out a sheet of paper from his desk drawer and smiled as he did so, '. . . we have just received notification of a murder you may all be interested in. The body of a large and powerfully built Afro-Caribbean man who appears to be in his mid-thirties and is distinguished by diamond studs in his teeth has been found at the edge of Romney Marsh. Shot twice in the head.'

Tom Ainsclough gasped. 'The geezer who sent me for a pint . . . him?'

'That's what I thought, Tom.' Vicary nodded. 'There'll be other bodies near where he was found – one gang getting rid of the opposition, I should not be surprised. We'll visit that flat in Notting Hill when we can, but that is one case to be closed and another opened.' Vicary paused. 'All right, so we all know what we're doing?'

Gillian Keynes stepped back from the threshold of her house. 'Won't you come in?'

'No . . . no.' Penny Yewdall smiled. 'We've just called to tell you that we have made a little progress but are still a long way from an arrest. We thought we'd reassure you and your husband that we have been busy and the file is not gathering dust.'

'Oh, that's very kind of you.' Gillian Keynes smiled broadly. 'I will tell my husband when he returns – he's visiting his brother.'

'Oh . . . yes, that is the gentleman with the strange name.' Penny Yewdall also smiled a relaxed smile. 'Zoldan?'

'Zolton.' Gillian Keynes corrected Penny Yewdall, 'Zolton with a "t" for tango. It tends to sound strange but it's a common Polish name and I have got quite used to it now.'

'Zolton,' Penny Yewdall repeated.

'Yes, he lives in Pinner. I never really know what he does; he seems a Mr Ten Per Cent, as though he has fingers in many pies. I don't even think my husband fully knows what he does for a living, but that is typical of the Lis family, I have found – they can be very private individuals.' Gillian Keynes glanced at the ground. 'A bit secretive. In fact, they can be very secretive. My husband even refused to tell me why he had resigned from his job. He wouldn't even become a supply teacher going from school to school standing in for teachers who are unwell. Supply teaching pays well but he wouldn't do it. So I have brought home the bacon over the years and he has kept up the house, that's been the way of it . . . but I will certainly let him know that you called and that we have not been forgotten.'

'While we are here,' Yewdall said, 'can you tell us if you ever knew a girl called Audrey Short? She possibly had some link with Victoria, your daughter.'

'Audrey?' Gillian Keynes nodded her head. 'They were good friends from Girl Guides. Audrey would call on Victoria on Guide night and they would walk to the Guide hut together in their uniforms. Victoria so short, and Audrey so tall, but they were very good friends. Why, is there some connection with Audrey?' Mrs Keynes asked with a worried tone in her voice.

'Possibly.' Penny Yewdall turned to go. 'But nothing definite.'

'I see . . . Well.' Mrs Keynes began to close her door, looking concerned as she did so. 'I will tell my husband you called. Thank you again for visiting.'

'She was indeed a friend of Victoria Keynes.' Mrs Short was a grey-haired lady who would, thought Yewdall, probably consider herself to be overweight, but she had also reached that age in life when she had stopped caring and stopped being figure conscious. She now chose clothes that were comfortable rather than because they were fashionable. Her home was a modest, three-bedroomed interwar house in Cornwall Road, overlooking Wanstead Park in Croydon. A framed photograph of a young woman in her twenties stood on the mantelpiece. 'So, there is some news at last?' she asked. 'It's been a long ten years. That's Audrey . . .' Mrs Short pointed to the photograph.

'Well, yes and no.' Yewdall shifted uncomfortably in the chair in which she sat. Beside her Tom Ainsclough took his notebook from his jacket pocket.

'And what does that mean?' Mrs Short asked in an inquisitorial tone.

'It means,' Penny Yewdall explained, 'that we have definite proof that Victoria Keynes was murdered.'

'Yes, so I read in the newspaper.' Mrs Short sat back in her chair. 'You know, I thought that Audrey might also have had some involvement, in the sense of also being a victim. They disappeared at about the same time, within a few days of each other. I felt there must have been a connection.'

'Yes, we think so too.' Penny Yewdall felt uncomfortable. 'I am afraid we have not one but two witnesses who claim to have witnessed the murder of a young woman at the same location where we know Victoria Keynes was murdered. That further strengthens the link between the two disappearances. The description is in keeping with the description of her in the missing persons report . . . long hair, tall, with a distinctive birthmark.'

'Yes, she was very self-conscious about that birthmark when she was a girl but eventually it didn't bother her. It wasn't as if it was a raised lesion, it was just a patch of skin which had a fawn colour about it . . . a bit like a banana . . .' Mrs Short's voice faltered. 'Oh . . . oh . . .'

'Yes?' Penny Yewdall asked. 'You've remembered something?'

'No, I have realized something . . . The birthmark was on the inside of her thigh, near the top of her leg. She always wore jeans or long skirts or dresses. The witnesses you spoke of could only have seen it . . . if it was exposed. What had happened to her that her birthmark was exposed? What state of undress was she in? What have you come to tell me?' Mrs Short's head slumped forward.

The officers remained silent.

Eventually Mrs Short raised her head. 'How was she murdered?'

'She was shot in the head,' Tom Ainsclough advised.

'Shot,' Mrs Short repeated. 'So her end was quick?'

'Yes, we can say that,' Yewdall remarked.

'It can't be easy for you,' Mrs Short forced a smile, 'bringing news like this to people's door.'

'It isn't . . . We do get some training . . . but it's never easy,' Yewdall replied.

'My husband passed away two years ago,' Mrs Short explained. 'He pined for Audrey, just pined himself away.'

'Is there anyone I can ask to come and sit with you – a neighbour perhaps?' Penny Yewdall asked. 'Or a friend or relative who lives close by?'

'No, I keep myself to myself.' Mrs Short stared straight ahead of her. 'I have a sister in Sutton. I'll phone her then drive over there. I'll stay with her for a couple of nights.'

'If you're sure?' Penny Yewdall spoke softly.

'I'm sure.' Mrs Short forced another smile.

'Did you know Victoria Keynes well?' Penny Yewdall asked.

'Not very well and only as a Girl Guide friend of my daughter's, but once, near the time of their disappearance, Victoria contacted me totally and completely out of the blue. She wanted to make contact with Audrey. I wouldn't tell her where Audrey was living, of course, but I did say I would contact Audrey and tell her that Victoria was looking to make contact if she . . . Victoria, would let me have her contact phone number. Victoria provided me with her phone number and I gave it to Audrey just a few minutes later, but I do not know if Audrey contacted Victoria.'

'Where was your daughter living at the time?' Penny Yewdall asked.

'With her boyfriend. It was a stable relationship, heading towards marriage, but I was still the next of kin so my name was on the missing persons report – not his, a man by the name of Davenport . . . Tony Davenport. I think Audrey quite liked the idea of becoming Audrey Davenport; it sounded a bit more classy than being Audrey Short.'

'We'll have to call on him,' Tom Ainsclough advised.

'I can let you have his address as it was ten years ago . . . he may have moved on but you'll be able to find him all right. He's a police officer,' Mrs Short forced a smile, 'with the

London Transport Police, keeping our underground safe for us. I'll just get my address book.'

'Yes . . . yes, it was a very distressing time.' Tony Davenport reclined in his leather-bound chair in his house on Somerton Drive in Cricklewood. He was a tall, broadly built man, as befitted a police officer, but off duty he wore faded blue jeans and a T-shirt which showed a faded print of the Golden Gate Bridge; a gift from a friend or a souvenir from a visit he had made to the 'Sunshine State'. He had warmly welcomed other police officers, pressed huge mugs of tea upon them and provided a generous plate of toasted teacakes, inviting Yewdall and Ainsclough to help themselves. 'She was just not the sort of person to walk away. She would always let her parents or me know where she was going or where she was. She was like that at all times. She was just that sort of girl. She had a responsible, thoughtful attitude to other people, especially towards her father, whom she described as a "worrier".'

'She was a friend of Victoria Keynes?' Yewdall asked. 'Or so we were lead to believe.'

'Yes, they were friends in the Girl Guide days . . . early teenage years . . . they seemed to drift apart and then seemed to rekindle their relationship,' Davenport explained. 'That happened just before Audrey disappeared. By just before, I mean the sort of period most conveniently measured in weeks, so about five or six weeks after Victoria made contact she disappeared. I now know that Victoria disappeared at the same time, but I didn't know that then, otherwise I would have alerted the Metropolitan Police. The simultaneous disappearance of two friends could only be deeply suspicious and would have merited an investigation.'

'Yes.' Ainsclough nodded in agreement.

'But at the time neither I nor her parents knew anything of Victoria Keynes also disappearing, and there was no reason for the police to link their disappearances because the association between them was not known.'

'Of course.' Yewdall reached forward and picked up a toasted teacake. She glanced round the room and relaxed as she saw Davenport's house was just as a sergeant in the London

Transport Police's house should be – all income appropriate, clean and neatly kept. The house, a modest interwar terraced development, was also just the sort of house a man of Davenport's position would live in.

'I heard that Victoria Keynes's remains had been found . . .' Davenport then asked, 'Has anything of Audrey been found?'

'No, I'm afraid not,' Yewdall replied, 'and frankly, there won't be. I . . . we . . . can't tell you too much at this stage.'

'Fully understand.' Davenport nodded.

'Do you know why Victoria looked up Audrey? Why their friendship was rekindled?'

'Not in any detail, but after she and Victoria went out for a coffee together, Audrey returned looking very confused and wouldn't talk about what they had discussed. But the two women began to meet up quite frequently and still she wouldn't talk about it to me. Then she insisted on sleeping in the spare room. She assured me that our relationship was still solid but she said she required "space". At the same time Victoria had left her husband and was lodging with a friend. Eventually she did say that Victoria had been "remembering things" and that when Victoria had told her that she had also started to remember things. She said Victoria wanted to go to the police but if she did then it would "destroy her mother". Audrey said that it was some issue with Victoria's father but it had been worse, much worse for Victoria than it had been for her.'

'That,' Yewdall commented, 'is very interesting.'

'Audrey told me that Victoria had decided to confront her father about "it", whatever "it" was. Then she would decide what to do. She said Victoria had decided that her sanity depended upon bringing "it" all out into the open. It was then, about then, that Audrey disappeared, and Victoria too. But, like I said, it was only latterly, these last few days, that I found out Victoria had vanished more or less at the same time as Audrey.'

It was Wednesday, 16.50 hours.

EPILOGUE

Three weeks later, Harry and Kathleen Vicary strolled arm in arm on a path beside a stand of trees on Hampstead Heath with the sweep of London laid out before and beneath them.

'He was right.' Vicary spoke quietly. 'It really was like watching the man's face fall off. We called on Woodhuyse and asked him to come to Scotland Yard with us to answer questions about his wife's murder, and so he came quite willingly. Me and Frankie Brunnie went over all the old ground and then we told him that we were now quite satisfied that he had no involvement in her murder. He smiled quite smugly really and began to stand up, and then DCI Meadows, who was also there, said, "Just a moment, please." It seemed to me that DS Escritt had done all the work for the Economic Crime Unit but Meadows pulled rank and made sure he was in at the kill. Anyway, Meadows said, "Just one or two other points, Mr Woodhuyse . . . or should I call you Mr McLaverty?" I kid you not, it really seemed like the man's face just slid downwards off his head . . . There he was, rumbled, in a police station . . . unable to escape to activate his getaway plan – to use his alternative identity and his cash hidden in numbered accounts. He went white . . . then he went green with fear.'

'And Zolton Lis?' Kathleen Vicary's eye was caught by a squirrel running in an undulating manner across the grass; she then cast an aesthetically appreciative eye upon a young male jogger in his twenties as he ran across their path some distance ahead. 'What happened to him?'

'He was arrested on the same day,' Harry Vicary replied, 'as was his brother, Eric, Victoria Keynes's father. Zolton Lis was charged with the murder of Victoria Keynes and Eric Keynes was charged with conspiracy to murder her. The charges were based on witness testimony from Andrew Cragg and David "Chinese Geordie Davy" Danby, and also on the results of the test firing of the point twenty-two we found when we searched Zolton Lis's house. Striations on the control bullet matched the striations found on the bullets which Doctor Shaftoe extracted from Victoria Keynes's body. Once he realized the game was up he gave all sorts of information about the jobs he'd done for Woodhuyse, aka McLaverty, but we'll still have difficulty proving he ordered the deaths of the men Lis claims he ordered.'

'No bodies?' Kathleen Vicary clarified.

'Yes . . . exactly; it matters not what is claimed, it is the fact that no bodies have been recovered which will make the Crown Prosecution Service reluctant to act on Lis's claims, but Woodhuyse doesn't know that, so he'll sweat for a while.'

'But Lis won't be able to apply for protected persons' status as a means of getting away with it?' Kathleen Vicary's voice contained a note of urgency.

'No . . . not a chance . . . no way.' Harry Vicary shook his head vigorously. 'Zolton Lis and his brother Eric will both collect two life sentences for the murders of Victoria Keynes and Audrey Short, but their cooperation, particularly Zolton Lis's cooperation, means that they might, just might, avoid a whole life sentence, which means they'll serve less than twenty-five years each . . . that, though, remains to be seen. It depends on the judge.'

'Woodhuyse's team?' Kathleen Vicary asked.

'Scattered to the four winds from his lieutenants down to his gofers . . . All gone, all saving their tails. The Economic Crime Unit boys will probably never find all of them – maybe in the future they'll be arrested in connection with some other felony, but not in connection with Woodhuyse's money-washing operation.' Harry Vicary glanced up at the clear blue, cloudless sky. 'But the good news is that the ECU found the weight of the sixty million pounds stolen in Southampton. As soon as Woodhuyse's arrest was made public a haulage contractor came forward. He told the police that they'd found all the loot in an old derelict bus he had in the corner of his yard. It was apparently the case that Woodhuyse had threatened him and his family with serious harm if he didn't cooperate, and he also threatened to torch the man's fleet of lorries into the bargain . . . all thirty-eight of them. It would have put him out of business. The ECU accepted his story and he won't be charged with any crime.'

'And the minor players . . .' Kathleen Vicary squeezed her husband's arm. 'What happened to them?'

'Well, Cragg and Danby slithered down the protected persons' mole hole. They'll give evidence against him and start a new life somewhere north of the River Trent. "Milkie" Raysin . . . well, he'll wheeze out his last days in his beloved East End. He is of no more interest to the CPS; he's a dying man and too peripheral to the case.'

'Mrs Keynes?' Kathleen Vicary glanced at her husband.

'Oh . . .' Harry Vicary groaned. 'Poor, wretched woman . . . she really is the third victim of the brothers Lis. Penny Yewdall went alone to see her to break the news that for the last twenty years she had been sharing a bed with a man who had fully sexually exploited their daughter from the age of about thirteen, and had also sexually exploited, though to a lesser extent, her daughter's friend in the Girl Guides – and who knows how many other girls? When Victoria confronted her father and told him she was going to the police, both brothers decided it would be better if Gillian Keynes knew nothing, and so both girls disappeared using Zolton Lis's specialism in that area. It transpired that Eric Keynes knew of his brother's service to gangland London, though he took no part in it . . . They rationalized it away like that. Woodhuyse didn't know that Lis had murdered his wife. We were obliged to tell him . . . He was speechless.'

'Meaning it was better for the brothers Lis if the girls disappeared?' Kathleen Vicary stared fixedly ahead as she walked. 'Even if it was his own daughter?'

'Exactly. They were not at all concerned about Gillian Keynes's feelings but fortunately, probably at the request of his brother, Zolton didn't cut up Victoria's body and it was eventually discovered when a drunken man told an undercover cop all about it.' Harry Vicary paused. 'But Gillian Keynes, when Penny broke the news as gently as she could . . . the poor woman went into a state of shock and Penny had to call an emergency ambulance. She was discharged from hospital a few days later and will probably be on anti-depressant medication for the rest of her life.'

'As you say,' Kathleen Vicary commented, 'she was the third victim.'

A crisp, dry, bronze-coloured leaf fell to the ground immediately in front of the Vicarys. Both noticed it, but neither commented.